CAGE OF SECRETS

Cage of Glass Series Book II

GENEVIEVE CROWNSON

Dreamspire Publishing

Dreamspire Publishing

www.genevievecrownson.com

Publisher's Note: This is a work of fiction. Names, characters, places, and incidents are a product of the author's imagination. Locales and public names are sometimes used for atmospheric purposes. Any resemblance to actual people, living or dead, or to businesses, companies, events, institutions, or locales is completely coincidental.

Cover Art by Rebecca Frank

Cage of Secrets/ Genevieve Crownson—1st edition

ISBN: 978-1736171110

For more information on this novel or Genevieve Crownson's other books please visit www.genevievecrownson.com

For Lailah, my constant companion, who kept me company while writing this book.

CHAPTER 1

LUNA

The blackness disintegrated around me. Arcs of white light flashed in circles above my head like strobes causing the pounding in my head to turn into a full-blown orchestra of pain.

And one thing kept going around in my mind, again and again.

I should have stayed.

My breath caught in my throat in the stifling air, and my body dripped with sweat as I came out of the shadowy gloom. For a moment, I was convinced I was careening down from the top of a roller coaster. Then, with no warning, the ride stopped and I had no idea where I was.

I peeled back my eyelids, but everything blurred before me. I blinked a few times in an effort to clear the white cloudy haze. As the world came into better focus, my heart lurched.

I was trapped in a cage.

Panicked, I attempted to lift my hands to push against what appeared to be a glass coffin, only to find them clamped down at my sides. My arms tingled with the movement like they'd been immobile for ages; my small attempt left them tired and weak. My inner elbow throbbed, and when I looked down, I noticed a golf ball-sized welt where my vein had been punctured. A million wires lay listlessly beside me in my prison, indicating I'd been on some kind of drip. But somebody had taken it out—and recently.

I lifted my head and the world spun. I realized my body was encased in a sleeveless wet suit of sorts, nearly the same color as my skin. It pinched me, too tight. I wiggled my toes to see if my feet were free. Pins and needles shot down my feet, answering that question.

Great. I was surrounded by four walls of glass with no way out.

My memories of what happened returned in a flood. Zander and I had been in an alternate universe, P8, and we'd jumped into a void we'd discovered to escape. We should be free. Somewhere else.

But we had simply traded one prison for another.

Zander.

Where was he? When we jumped, we'd been clutching each other's hands for dear life. I turned my head to peer through the glass, but struggled to focus on anything outside this bubble I seemed to be trapped in. I willed Zander to appear—but my efforts were fruitless. I lay back for a moment trying to gather my strength. This was not how this was supposed to go. When my mother sold me back to the government so she could live a better life, I didn't think it could get much worse.

But it had.

Ending up on P8 with Zander had been a gift and a curse. They hadn't wanted us to remember, but we couldn't forget. So we'd fought our way out. But where did we end up?

I sighed.

Just thinking about Zander resurrected all my confused feelings. And my bone-chilling weariness wouldn't allow me to sort through it all now.

A noise on the other side of the room startled me, and I jerked my head up, sending me into a dizzy spiral. I closed my eyes. *Stay calm, Luna, don't freak.* I took a deep breath, but it didn't work, the thin air suffocating me. I needed to free myself soon before I passed out.

"Damn it!"

My eyes shot open. Who said that? A figure with a slim silhouette hovered over another identical cage on the other side of the room. Something pointed was clutched in their hand.

A sudden stab of anxiety slammed into my gut. It was a syringe full of some type of red liquid. Whoever lay in that cage was about to get a big dose of it. That couldn't be good.

My pulse pounded in my ears, and my nails dug into my palms. I pulled on my restraints again but barely moved. My arms and legs felt like jelly. I would bet good money, I'd been drugged.

Had Zander tricked me—was this a trap? But then again— what if it was him in the coffin?

I strained every muscle, edging just a hairsbreadth closer to the glass wall, allowing me to see that the mysterious figure was a boy, about the same age as me, a lanky beanstalk with long red hair that brushed his hunched shoulders. Nothing distinct stood out about him unless you counted his god awful silver one-piece jumpsuit. He would have blended in seamlessly, but he botched the job with his gawdy gold chain bracelet peeking out from under his sleeve with some kind of charm dangling from it. Amateur. Clearly.

Why was he here? To spy? To finish the job? Or did some-body send him? The questions whirled inside my mind like a tornado. I hardly dared breathe, fearful any noise would make him turn this way.

The boy's fingers fumbled on his com, cursing. He stared at it. "Answer," he whispered. "Come on."

Licking my dry lips, I ignored the pain in my extremities and bore down on my restraints, never taking my eyes off the boy with the flaming red hair.

I stopped mid-struggle as the coffin took on a life of its own, opening silently, exposing the person within.

I gasped, blinking twice.

Zander. I tried to scream but all that came out was a weak croak as the boy plunged the syringe into his neck. In a cascade effect, the tubing attached to Zander untethered, freeing his arm.

I tried to yell again with all the energy I could muster. I was louder this time, but it appeared this guy couldn't hear me. Was this some kind of strange, one-way, soundproof glass or something? Because I could certainly hear him.

After a moment, he seemed to sense my frantic pleas and looked up sharply. He placed a finger to his lips and shook his head as if imploring me to stop.

Before I could react, footsteps echoed in the hallway beyond the room. The boy hastily closed Zander's coffin, but not before Zander began to move—first his hands, then his head, swiveling from side to side, like he was having a bad dream.

The redhead sprinted over to me, almost tripping en route. Definitely not a smooth operator.

"Be still. They're coming. Please," he begged.

Without another word he pocketed his empty syringe and grabbed the mop he must have left propped up by the door. He moved it back and forth along the sterile white tiles until he made his way to the door, disappearing before anyone suspected anything.

The voices drew nearer. My first instinct was to yell for help, but I stopped myself. These people most likely put me in here. No one could be trusted. Besides if my theory was correct about the soundproof glass what good would it do? They would never hear me. A sliver of light cast a shadow on the floor as the door opened. I gritted my teeth and forced my body back into position. My eyes snapped shut.

"I'm surprised they're not awake yet. It's a bit unusual. Did you check the monitor, Dr. Maia?" someone asked in a deep baritone.

"Nah, I figured the longer they're out, the less problem

they'll be for us. Their brains are recalibrating back to real time."

"Good thinking. I still can't believe they jumped—damn kids. I was looking forward to the night off when I got called in."

"Tell me about it," Dr. Maia said. "I missed dinner for this. I'm starving." She paused considering. "At least we aren't these two. You couldn't pay me enough to trade places."

The male voice echoed an agreement.

"According to this data, it appears doubtful that participant thirty-three will recover her memories. However, participant forty appears to be trending toward a full recovery. The higher ups will want us to keep a close eye on that. It will cause a problem if he does remember."

"He'll definitely have a lot of explaining to do."

"Yeah, I don't envy that kid. He'll be attacked at both ends. Luna is no pushover."

They both laughed a little, and my stomach soured.

"Let's finish our card game. I'm feeling lucky tonight—you better be worried."

She snorted. "Please. You always say that."

"Let's go find out then, shall we?"

"You're on, Dr. Neiren."

As their footsteps moved away, I opened my eyes and took a quick glance at the man and woman exiting the room. They wore white lab coats, hairnets, and underneath, the same silver jumpsuit as the kid that had messed with Zander.

I swallowed dryly. What did Zander need to explain to me? There had to be a mistake. I knew everything about my life. Didn't I?

I would find a way out of this cell and discover what cocktail that boy had plunged into Zander's bloodstream. And then I would do whatever was necessary to find out the truth.

Because there was one thing those scientists were right about.

I was no pushover.

And they had no idea what they were up against.

CHAPTER 2

ZANDER

The sound of voices pulled me out of my sleepy cocoon. Disoriented, I struggled to comprehend where I was.

Then I remembered. Gradually, like pieces of a jigsaw glimpses of my past came in shadowy and mysterious, slowly coming together. My heart leapt as I remembered.

Luna. P8. The void.

My eyes flew open, tears streaming out, my world out of focus. I blinked against crusty lids, my retinas burning. I went to rub my eyes, but realized my arms were shackled.

What was going on? I raised my head, determined to find Luna. Was she okay? The world spun and exhaustion wept into my veins like someone poured concrete into my body. I pushed back against the head rest and bit my lip in frustration.

Come on Zander, focus. Eyes first. Then you can figure out the rest. I lay there a moment, willing my vision to clear. Finally, after an agonizing moment I could see.

I realized I lay in a coffin of sorts, completely tied down. Had the authorities in P8 caught us as we took the leap? Surely, I would have remembered if they had. I shook my head trying to free the tangled mess of confusion from my mind, but instead the world tilted on its axis and my stomach roiled. I pushed back the nausea and forced myself to sit up as much as I was able with the shackles.

I peered through my glass prison frantically scanning the room and my heart stopped. Memories of this place overwhelmed me. I had been here before. Memory after memory piled on top of one another like dominoes, almost in a painful succession, my brain charging into overdrive. Pain lanced through my skull and I winced. Determined, I gritted my teeth searching for Luna. Everything appeared the same. Luna and I were still being held at the original energy outpost, isolated from the others. I spotted her glass cell across the expanse but couldn't see her. Ours were the only ones in the room. A small consolation—making for an easier escape. I inhaled deeply, turning inward and tried to sense her energy, but came up empty. It was disconcerting to me I hadn't been able to sense her, but I really shouldn't have expected much different. During my time in P8 some psychic abilities had appeared. I didn't fully understand my gifts, but one thing I knew for certain—they weren't reliable. That was certainly clear now. Visions had shown up more recently, but my control over those were about zero. Whether more skills were yet to appear, I didn't know.

As I let my gaze wander the area, I realized that I must have memorized the grid of this place ages ago, trusting it would come in handy when the opportunity came to bust out of here with Luna. A new posting would have killed any chance of freedom. I knew I'd been missing pieces. This grid knowledge confirmed at least that much for me.

Out of the corner of my eye, I noticed the tubes in my arms lay unused beside me. My heart leapt in hope. Had someone from the resistance already been here? I couldn't imagine why the doctor's in charge of this operation would wake me up... unless they planned on taking me away from here...and soon. I swallowed hard against the lump in my throat. No. That couldn't be it. I had to focus. Stay positive. But if the resistors, specifically the protectors division designed to help us had been here where were they now?

The voices faded before I could catch any of the conversation, followed by the sound of a door slamming shut. The subsequent hush left only the eerie bleeping of machines, echoing in the cold, sterile room.

Perhaps the government doctors assigned to our case came to check on our progress. That would explain the half-botched break out. Still, if the searing throb on the right side of my neck was any indication, I'd been recently stabbed with a substantial needle. If I went along with my theory that the resistors had been here, they must have had enough time to dose me.

That explained why I was awake and functioning. Without the revival drug, I wouldn't be able to move after being trapped so long in this hydraulic chamber.

Yet something must have gone terribly wrong.

Someone on the outside should have hacked the system, disarmed the coffin sensors, and popped this God-forsaken prison wide open.

I wondered if one of the resistors was caught trying to free me. The evidence gave all the indicators of an abandoned mission. The protectors never left a job half done.

Not good news.

Luna must be freaking out. I couldn't imagine what this looked like to her. Unless...they failed to reach her in time.

Beads of perspiration formed on my forehead as it dawned on me Luna would have to be told everything. What would she say when she found out how much I'd known this whole time?

I took some deep breaths in an attempt to subdue my mind. I needed a plan. It wouldn't be long until the doctors returned. When they read the monitor by my bed, they would discover I was awake. Especially if the protectors didn't take my health stats offline.

I shuddered. If they uncovered the truth in my data, what would they do to me?

None of this had gone according to plan. But plans had a way of doing that—taking a sharp curve without permission. I learned that the hard way over these last few months. I hummed under my breath, letting the familiar notes of my favorite song wash over me. I didn't have any memory of where the tune originated, but as far back as I could remember it had always calmed me down.

I would find a way out of this for us.

I glanced over at Luna's cage. My vision, still a little fuzzy, could have been playing tricks on me. But I almost swore I saw a blur of movement in her closed cage.

Luna was awake.

I wiggled around in the cramped confines of my glass coffin, trying to gain some traction to loosen the metal at my wrists and ankles—but as I suspected, they wouldn't budge.

I gritted my teeth and tried one more time, the pain searing through my body like a hot knife. Nothing happened.

That's when I understood I had to use the clock key. There was no other way.

Luna and I had come too far to give up. I wouldn't let those government thugs take her—she meant too much to me—and we were too valuable to them. My mouth soured at the thought of what they would do to us if we didn't escape.

I stretched my hand out reaching under the lining of the coffin, searching for the object hidden so long ago. "Please be there." I muttered.

I hit pay dirt when my fingers grasped the small, hard-grooved circular device.

The Clock Key was still there.

I waited a beat, listening for footsteps—relieved when the room stayed silent. I quickly placed the brass medallion up to the glass, contorting my hand against my bindings, to allow the heat from my palm to ignite the biochip within. My energy, weak from being siphoned for fuel for God knows how long, was slow to react, but I willed myself to sense the familiar hum of the device under my skin.

As the warmth built, the power flowed through my palms onto the glass, using me as a conduit, entering through the surface of the cage, down the seams and into the restraints. With a small, glowing light everything burst apart. The manacles on my ankles popped first, next my wrists, freeing them from their contorted agony. Finally, the best sound of all hit my ears as the coffin released. My shoulders relaxed, so far so good.

My arms shaking with effort, I cracked open the lid of the cage, and forced one leg, then the other, over the side. I landed hard on the tiles. Every nerve howled in protest as I forced myself up from the cold floor. But I continued to focus on the task at hand.

"Work, revival. Do what you're supposed to," I groaned. The worst part was over. The initial pain indicated the drug had reached my heart and would be pumping into my extremities within minutes. Only then could I move freely. The only problem—I would have a killer headache later. A horrible side effect, yet to be fixed.

Painstakingly, I placed one foot forward and fell again. "Damn it, *come on*."

A muffled thud distracted me and I looked up, concerned they had caught me before I had even gone anywhere.

The sound came again, and I realized it originated from Luna's coffin. Her face looked blurred, but her hand pressed against the surface, created a foggy imprint against the clear glass.

"I'm coming Luna," I whispered, even though she most likely couldn't hear me. With stiff determination, I picked myself up and staggered over to her, my lungs burning with every ragged gasp. I managed to press the clock key up to the glass, willing the activation to start. Sweat poured down my forehead, and I swiped it away with my free hand.

The brass color of the disk glinted between my fingers as I

attempted to release what little energy remained inside me. Just when I was about to give up hope—the quiet whisper of the cell disengaging filled the air. I leaned against it, catching my breath in relief.

With shaking hands, I pushed open the lid.

"Hey there," I joked. "Fancy meeting you here. Do you come here often?" It was meant to be a joke, to break the ice between us, but with the raw croak in my unused voice, I sounded like a weirdo.

Cool, Zander. Way to win the girl over.

Luna didn't say a word, her big green eyes staring blankly at me.

Her semi-catatonic state sent alarm bells through me, and I clenched my fists in an effect to stop any stupid knee-jerk reactions. I almost laughed; here I stood almost wishing for her wrath. Anything would be better than this comatose version of Luna. I comforted myself with the knowledge that a small amount of the sleeping agent must still be in her bloodstream. She'd soon be her old self.

Her matted hair clung to her scalp, her face white as a sheet. I reached out and picked up her hand squeezing it tight. She had been through so much, and I couldn't help wondering if I could have prevented some of it from happening. I rubbed my thumb over her pale skin, and noticed the moon-shaped scar on her hand had returned. The familiarity of it brought me an odd comfort. My Luna. I took a deep breath to collect myself. Now wasn't the time to be getting lost in memories.

We had to get out of here fast. I would carry her if necessary. But it would be better for both of us if she could do it on her own. I hoped the resistors had administered the revival shot on her first. "Can you move, Luna?" I struggled to control my voice, not wanting her to notice my fear.

Pain flashed across her face as she slowly eased her leaden body up. I resisted the urge to kiss her. She could move. That meant she'd been given the resistor's pharmaceutical cocktail.

Thank God for that.

I gently put a hand on her arm, whispering. "Your body is going to remain sluggish for a few minutes. It has been out of use for quite some time."

I expected her to yell at me, pelting me with a million different questions, but instead her brows just furrowed in confusion as she gaped at me. She shook her head in an attempt to clear it, but immediately stopped, her face wincing in pain.

I bet that had cost her. "Sorry, I should have warned you. No sudden movements. That must have felt like a bullet train going through your skull. Take it slow." The drug was working to deactivate the sleeping agent, an agonizing process, but explaining that to her now would be a lost cause.

"Luna, you'll want to scream bloody murder when you try to stand. But it will pass. You must fight the urge to yell. I hate to rush you, but we don't know when the doctors might return."

She nodded to tell me she understood, as she simultaneously grabbed her right leg. I leaned over to help, but not before looking back at the door to make sure no one was coming.

"Come on, Luna, you can do it," I grunted as I grasped her heavy limb. She gritted her teeth, her expression tortured, as we hoisted both extremities over the side. She gripped the edge with her hands and rolled herself out, practically falling to the ground in a heap.

I caught her around the waist before she splatted flat on the floor. I righted her gently, steadying her until she found her own feet. The agony in her eyes was apparent as her nerve endings came alive. But to her credit, she said nothing. She had other things on her mind.

"What is this place?" she rasped.

As delighted as I felt to hear her speak, I also realized time was ticking down.

"There's no time to explain. Let's go!" I grabbed her hips and looped one arm around my neck, lifting her a little so her feet barely touched the floor. God, sometimes I forgot how tiny she was. She was affected more by the tranquilizers than I was due to her small size. She would have to fight even harder to get movement back, even with the revival in her veins.

Luna's face took on a determined look. "Let's go, I'm ready."

The relief on my face must have showed, as I hastily lurched forward. Luna sucked in a breath as the pain hit her full on. Her fingers gripped the back of my neck, her fingernails digging painfully into my flesh. Fortunately, at that moment, the revival kicked in full throttle. Adrenaline rushed through my veins hard and fast. I felt like I could fly.

"The discomfort will pass, I promise. Just hold on to me."

"You better not let me down Barringer, I'm trusting you to get us out of this mess."

My heart lurched a little. She had finally decided to trust me, against all the odds, but she didn't even know the half of it yet.

Would I lose her forever when she discovered the full truth? The thought followed me like a shadow as we stepped out of the room that had been our prison.

CHAPTER 3

LUNA

I couldn't go on, every step I took caused my whole body to ache. As for my brain, it was obviously filled to capacity with cotton balls.

It would be so easy to succumb to the weariness that threatened to overtake me. I allowed my eyelids to droop just for a second.

"Keep moving your legs, Luna," Zander said, jolting me back. "The blood is returning to your extremities."

I wanted to scream at him. *What's the point?*

I'd run out of steam. Tired of all the deception, I didn't have the strength for any more drama.

Then I remembered Trinity. What if she needed me? I had to find my sister.

And what if Dara was still alive?

I clenched my free hand into a fist so hard, my knuckles cracked. I inched forward, one lumbering foot in front of the other in unadulterated agony. My fingernails dug deep into Zander's shoulder as I attempted to hold myself up. It annoyed the heck out of me that I still needed him as a crutch.

"Ouch, let up on the claws," he complained as he led us into the corridor. It was pitch black, save for a small light casting a diagonal line across the floor. A door stood ajar—only steps away from us. Laughing voices filled the air and echoed down the passageway. The acrid stench of antiseptic burned my nostrils and my stomach recoiled.

It had to be those scientists, no doubt playing their stupid card game.

I licked my dry lips and willed my heart to stop galloping. Zander had been out cold when they'd come to check on us. Should I warn him?

No. We were so close to the techs, I could smell the sweet tang of their fruit drinks. Speaking now might blow our cover entirely.

As much as I hated to admit it, I needed him, if I wanted to survive at all.

Zander motioned me in the opposite direction. We hugged the wall as much as possible, trying to stay under the radar, as we inched our way towards freedom.

At least I hoped that's where we were going.

But instead of aiming straight for the glowing red exit sign ahead, we stopped outside a thick wooden door labeled Lab Room #6. I opened my mouth to say something then thought better of it. The scientists still weren't that far away.

Zander turned the knob. I stood behind him, waiting with bated breath. The stabbing pain in my extremities disappeared, replaced with an adrenaline rush of mammoth proportions. I felt ready to rip this door right off its hinges.

Focus, keep your eye on Zander, I told myself. It had been a bad idea to trust him. We should have taken that exit at the end of the passage. Unsure if my thoughts came from being scared out of my mind or pure gut instinct, I pushed back on my heels and began rocking back and forth, counting the rhythm of my feet on the cold tile in an attempt to settle my agitation.

One, two, three, four...

I stopped when Zander peered through the crack in the door. Seeing the coast was clear, he pushed it open and entered.

He turned back to look at me. Eyes questioning.

I crossed my arms and stared him down, unsure what to do.

Zander decided for me and seized my arm, yanking me inside.

"Watch it," I admonished as he shut the door behind us.

"The stakes are too high for games, Luna."

I resisted the urge to slap him. Games? I bit back a retort. Once we got out of here, I would give him a piece of my mind.

Zander either didn't notice my hostility or he chose to ignore it. He'd already crossed to a cabinet located on the far side of the room. He pulled out some gauze, tweezers wrapped in plastic, a tiny blade, and some kind of clear liquid solution.

My eyes narrowed at his back and suddenly I was sure of one thing. Zander was acting way too confident.

The depth of Zander's lies hit me like a brick, and I gasped for breath.

Hearing my sharp intake of air, Zander spun around in a panic. When he saw I was alone, his shoulders sagged in relief, and he turned back to the job at hand. Gathering his materials, he came back over and motioned for me to sit on one of the metal stools standing near the wall.

"Sit down, Luna. Hurry."

I scowled at him. "You know where we are, don't you? You've been here before. You're a liar, Zander Barringer." I hissed under my breath. "Otherwise, how would you know how to escape?"

He frowned frustrated. "I'm not a liar, Luna. I just left some things out. And for good reason. Please trust me."

I let out a low, guttural laugh. "You expect me to trust you? Now? After all this? Why should I?"

Zander placed the medical supplies on the counter and slowly turned to me, face solemn. "Because if you don't, you might end up as good as dead."

My mouth must have dropped open because Zander gently shut it with his finger.

"I don't mean to scare you, but if you get caught by them, they'll put you back in that glass cage. Is that what you want?"

The large lump forming in my throat prevented me from speaking, so I simply shook my head.

But it didn't mean I trusted him one bit.

"Please sit, Luna. I have to remove your tracker. Otherwise, no matter where we go, they'll find us."

"Tracker?"

"Yes. We both have one." He sighed. "It's a long story, one I don't have time to explain. But I will if we ever get out of here safely. There's probably only about five minutes left, if we're lucky, before our glass cell alarms go off. If they go back in the holding room before that..." his voice trailed off as if he didn't want to think about the possibility.

"Where's the tracker?" I asked.

Zander lifted a slightly shaking hand and tenderly rubbed at the soft spot behind my left ear. His electric touch set my heart racing a hundred miles a minute.

I clenched my fists together, annoyed at my body's betrayal.

I pushed him away and traced the line behind my ear. Sure enough, something hard and tiny lay just beneath the skin.

I whipped my arm down and sat stonily on the stool—knowing one thing for certain.

I wanted it out.

I schooled my features and turned to Zander. "Okay, do it. But hurry up before I change my mind."

"Pay attention to what I do," Zander said. "You'll have to do mine next. And with your body full of revival it will be harder for you to concentrate. But try your best."

"Revival?" I asked almost not wanting the answer.

"A drug used to counteract the sleeping agent. Without it, it would take you weeks, if not months to be up to full function again after lying immobile so long."

I recoiled, getting off the chair.

"That doesn't make sense. We've only just arrived here."

Zander pushed a hand through his matted brown hair, leaving it in complete disarray. "Time is not what it seems, Luna. I promise I will explain everything later. But first, we need these trackers out, so we can get the hell out of here. Please, no matter how mad you are at me, you don't want them to find out where you are. Please," he pleaded again, reaching out his hand to me.

"Fine. But don't cross me, Zander. You will live to regret it."

"I wouldn't dare."

I ignored his offered hand and sat back down. Zander wasted no time getting back to work.

He grabbed some cleansing agent that had been left out and sprayed the black slab counter in front of us. "Step one is keep everything sterile. We don't want to risk an infection. Especially once we're out there." He nodded toward the back.

I let my gaze wander in the direction he'd indicated. Weak sunlight filtered through some small windows but the tiny square openings didn't offer any clues as to what lay beyond the dirty panes. Maybe that was the point. What awaited us outside this building obviously concerned Zander a great deal. I gulped.

"Luna? Are you ready?"

I glanced back at Zander, then shifted my attention to the table where he had prepared the tools. The odd looking tweezer things were now unwrapped and ready for use. The sharp blade next to it, glistened under the artificial lights.

"Ready," I said trying to sound casual. I could do this. A little knife wouldn't hurt that bad. I'd experienced worse.

He nodded and spritzed his hands with another bottle from the lab bench.

"What's that?"

"A hand coater. It completely seals my hands, so they remain sterile. It also stops me from leaving any fingerprints. Cool huh?" He gave a slight smile, but seeing he failed to impress me, he turned and plucked an alcohol wipe from his stash.

"The first thing I'm going to do is locate your tracker and clean it with this," he held up the wipe. "Then I'll make a cut over the top of it. These things are microscopic so there's no need for a large incision. You aren't squeamish, are you?"

"No. I patched up my siblings all the time. Blood never bothered me." The memory of them brought tears to my eyes. Were they safe? I didn't know.

"Okay. Let's get started."

He showed me the steps quickly and efficiently, missing no detail.

A sharp sting made me flinch, then the tiny tracker came free. "There. All the evidence is gone. No one will suspect a thing. Are you ready to take mine out?"

"Sure, why not?" I said sarcastically.

Zander gave me a pained expression. But I didn't care. He deserved way more than a snarky comment.

I stood and motioned to the stool I vacated. "Well, aren't you going to sit down?"

He regarded me sheepishly and gave a lopsided grin. "Yeah, I guess that would help."

"Is it always behind the left ear?" I asked. "Or is there another spot?"

"Yes. Usually, it's the same for everyone."

I wanted to ask more, like who else had the trackers? Why behind the ear? But I didn't. I pressed my lips together and got to work. I followed Zander's instructions carefully and only needed a little coaxing from him when it came time to make the cut—pulling out his tracker with a swift efficiency I was proud of, especially considering how much my hands shook.

I stepped back admiring my handiwork. "I think you'll live."

Zander grinned. "Thanks, doctor."

I scowled. "Don't be cute. You're still in a lot of hot water with me."

Zander lifted his hands in surrender. "Sorry. I—"

He suddenly stopped talking and turned pale. "Did you hear that?"

I strained to listen. Sure enough, footsteps echoed in the corridor, headed in our direction.

I turned to Zander, wide-eyed. "Now what?" I whispered back.

"We run."

In seconds, Zander had swiped the counter clean and placed everything down a weird contraption that silently incinerated it. He then grabbed my hand and together we sped to the door at the back, labeled closet.

We pulled the door shut behind us just as someone entered the lab.

I took a quick look around; there had to be a way out of this. The sterile space held nothing but boxes of extra equipment and supplies neatly stacked against the wall and a few lab coats hanging from hooks. Another door led to what I assumed was a duplicate laboratory. This place appeared to be a labyrinth of doors. How many were labs or chambers? I shivered, turning cold at the thought.

Zander placed a hand to the small of my back, sensing my unease.

We stood still, not daring to move a muscle.

"They're not in here. Let's try the next lab. And call security. We're never going to find them on our own. They must not escape. The boss will have our necks."

I gulped hard and closed my eyes. I recognized that voice. The scientists. Please let them forget to check the closet.

"Security? Yeah, this is Dr. Maia. We need a unit up here stat. We have a couple of missing batteries... It doesn't matter how, just do your job...over and out."

I heard a click as she cut off the communication.

"You didn't tell them who it was?" Asked Dr. Neiren.

"No way. We'd have the whole goddamned fleet up here. Then we really would be fired. Let's keep it as low key as possible."

"Good idea."

I bit my lip. What was going on here? Would they be in danger if we got away? The desperation in the man's voice spoke of way more than job security.

What could be so important about us?

Their footsteps came closer. But nobody opened the closet door.

Zander gripped my hand, but I yanked it away.

I didn't trust him. Even if he had plucked a tracker out of me. That just meant he wanted to save his own skin.

The voices faded away and the door closed. I released a long breath. I circled around, checking for anything that might help us escape.

Think, Luna. Think.

My eyes landed on the lab coats.

"Perfect," I murmured.

I left Zander's side and went to the hanging coats. They looked big.

I shrugged one on. The long sleeves covered half my hand, but would do the job of disguising my figure. Next, I turned to the supplies.

I knelt in front of a couple of boxes labeled hair nets and face masks. I ripped the tape off and pulled out a hair net and mask. The cap, solid blue, covered up my dark hair, while the mask obscured most of my face, leaving only my eyes exposed.

Zander inspected my ensemble dubiously. "I'm not sure that's going to work, Luna. Not many scientists are working at this hour."

I glared at him. "Any other great ideas, Sherlock? I would love to hear them."

Zander hesitated. "I planned to make a run for it. I know the layout of this place. I think we have a good shot."

I tried not to dwell on the words *'I know the layout of this place.'* I would kill him later. Right now I needed to focus. "Thinking you can get us out of here is not the same as doing.

Here. Wear these." I shoved a cap and mask at him, and he meekly took them.

"Don't just stare at them," I hissed. "Put them on. I know what I'm doing."

While Zander did as I asked, I grabbed a lab coat I thought might fit. As he shrugged it on, I opened the door a crack just to see what lay on the other side.

Just as I suspected. Another lab.

My heart leapt in my throat at the sight of the two doctors scouring the room for us. I hastily shut the door, plastering myself against it.

"They're heading this way. Hide!"

I grabbed Zander's coat sleeve and pushed him behind the row of boxes, just in the nick of time. The door opened and someone flicked on the light switch.

"Why are we looking in the closet?" Dr. Maia asked.

"We can't leave any stone unturned," Dr. Neiren replied.

"Well the trackers show them still in the building. That better be accurate for both our sakes."

The lights dimmed as they closed the door. I collapsed against Zander in momentary relief, and he gently wrapped his arms around me, pulling me closer.

I swiftly backed away. What was I doing? Zander and I were not friends or anything else for that matter. Not anymore.

My heart leaped at the thought, and I quickly redirected my focus to the task at hand.

I awkwardly stood up, ignoring his hand and returned to the door. "The doctors are gone," I said abruptly.

"Let me lead. Please?"

I scowled, but moved aside.

We hugged the wall tight until we reached the exit. He signaled that the coast was clear, and motioned for me to follow him. We made it all the way to the end of the hall before we heard pounding footsteps behind us. I dared a glance back and spotted some security guards turning the corner.

One of them spotted us, and my mouth went dry.

My panic, however, was short lived when I realized they didn't recognize us. I beamed under my mask. Looks like I hadn't lost my touch.

I murmured to Zander in a low tone so the guards couldn't hear. "Keep it casual. Walk slow, pretend you are talking to me about a case or something."

"Tell me about you case study, Doctor. I would be interested in combining it with my own findings." Zander said as the guards walked by.

When they were out of earshot, I replied. "Nicely played."

He shrugged. "I do what I can. Now come on we have to get out of here."

"No kidding," I muttered.

We continued down the long corridor until Zander took a sharp right turn. A guard came from the other direction. We continued as if nothing was amiss—but my blood froze in my veins as I saw the doctors assigned to our cases right behind him.

They slowed when they got near. Dr. Neiren spoke first. "Excuse me, hold up there. We need to check everyone's credentials; we have a potential security breach. You know how it is, protocols must be followed. Would you mind scanning your wrists for us?"

"Sorry, we're in a hurry," Zander supplied.

"It won't take a moment," the officer, a big man of at least six feet, said stepping forward.

"We have an emergency back at the lab. We can come right back. In say five minutes?" I offered.

Dr. Maia narrowed her eyes. "Wait a minute."

Zander grabbed my hand. "Run!"

We took off at lightning speed, taking our friends by surprise and giving us precious seconds to get ahead.

"Stop!" The officer shouted as they sprinted after us.

"This way!" Zander said grabbing my hand and sprinting toward another corridor.

CHAPTER 4
ZANDER

The guards were closing in on us. Cold struck my gut like a slap as the reality of our situation became clear.

Then I saw Crane.

I grinned, never so happy to see anyone in my life.

He came casually around the corner with a bucket and mop in hand—he stepped between us and the guards. I didn't stop, but heard, "get out of the way," followed by a big commotion—giving us just enough time to escape. Crane's apologetic voice wafted down the hall. "I'm so sooorrry," he spluttered. "I...I..."

"Stupid boy!" the officer barked.

I hung a right and shoved Luna into an elevator. The doors instantly closed, and I smashed the button for the first floor.

"What are you doing?" she demanded. "They'll meet us in the lobby and grab us! You've trapped us both, you idiot!"

I clenched my teeth frustrated as hell. "I'm buying us some time. Look."

I pointed to the back of the elevator where a small panel was cleverly hidden by the call button box.

Crouching down, I ran my finger against the cracked lining, looking for the sweet spot in the wall. I pressed my thumb into the telltale exterior ridge and the panel popped open. Luna gasped.

As I pulled it away, a rushing wind whooshed through the gap, tugging at my hair cap.

"We have to go. Now. Don't fight me on this if you want to live." My words were harsh—but I wanted her to understand the gravity of our situation. I was tired of her questioning my decisions at every turn.

She swallowed hard, fighting back her own inner demons, before she finally responded, "What choice do I have? But if you're double-crossing me Zander B—"

Before she finished her sentence, I grabbed her hand, not needing any more encouragement. I glanced back to check our floor level and groaned...20, 19, 18...it would only be moments before the elevator door opened again.

I knelt down in front of the opening and pulled Luna down with me. "See the little platform that juts out, extending beyond the elevator? I need you to step out onto it and climb to the roof. Hold on to the center cable until I get there."

Doubt crossed her face as she peered at the paneled hole. The so-called platform was little more than a piece of metal support beam. Despite the skepticism in her eyes, she lifted her chin in defiance and glared me. She knew we were running out of time; the only other option being to face a slew of security guards at the other end.

"Okay. I get it. But what about you?" Her eyes narrowed. "Why am I going first?"

I pulled down my mask, letting it hang around my neck. "I have to go last, so I'll be able to smash the panel back into place before shimmying up behind you."

She nodded reluctantly, seeming to believe me, and without another word, gripped the ridge of the shaft, placing her feet on the tiny joist to haul herself toward the top of the elevator box. Her hairnet blew off as we sped downward, and she pushed down her own mask in the hot, cramped space.

Her arms shook as she clawed her way up the metal contraption. Her feet scrambled to make purchase, and I reached out as far as I dared, half hanging into the elevator shaft to propel her forward.

"You can do it, Luna. Hurry!" I encouraged.

She managed to swing her legs over on top of the elevator. I dared to look up and make sure Luna was all right. Rather than clinging to the wire, she must have taken a calculated risk and scurried to the edge. She gripped the ledge so hard her knuckles turned white.

I immediately followed, clutching the panel in my left hand. I grunted as my feet slipped, and I fell out of the narrow opening. At the last second, I lurched forward and caught the lip of the elevator with my fingers, dangling by a literal thread.

"Zander!" Luna screamed.

I didn't dare respond. Every muscle in my arm roared at me to let go. With strength I didn't realize I possessed—probably thanks to the revival—I used my upper body strength to propel forward, slamming the door panel onto the compartment floor. With my hand free, I hauled myself to the safety of the steel ledge.

The elevator slowed.

We were out of time.

With my heart in my throat, I lifted the divide back into place just as the elevator stopped.

Shouts and bangs reverberated from the other side of the door and a stab of anxiety pierced my gut. I bit back a curse and edged up the cold metal wire like a cat, even as the hard steel tore at my flesh. My grip loosened, as my palms became slick with blood.

Luna reached out for me, and for the briefest of moments, I wondered if she would use this opportunity to shove me down the shaft. But instead, she yanked me up, and together we tumbled over the top.

I jumped to my feet, ignoring the wire burns. "Come on. We need to get away from here before it moves again!"

I pulled her up, and we made the small leap from the elevator to one of the many ladder rungs that surrounded us in the long narrow column. I began climbing, Luna at my heels. When we got about halfway, the cable squealed as the lift churned into action, moving towards us at frightening speed.

"Zander," Luna shouted over the din, "we're going to be crushed!"

"Keep going, Luna!"

I pushed harder, my calves screaming. The sound of Luna's heavy breathing was overtaken by the racket of the motorized mechanism, and the force of the wind wouldn't allow me to turn and look for her. I cursed myself for not letting her go first as I moved faster, finally making the last rung before I threw my body under the eaves of the roofing.

I crawled on my belly back to edge. A cold fist closed over my heart. Luna was too far back. The distance between her and the elevator was horrifyingly small, and she still had several bars to climb. Seconds remained before it would come lurching towards her, crushing her into a million pieces.

"Whatever you do, don't look down," I yelled over the din.

I gritted my teeth. No way in hell would I let Luna die now. Not after all this.

I reached down and latched my foot to the corner of the rail to steady myself. Then I grabbed hold of the lapels on Luna's lab coat, pulling her to safety.

Seconds later, the elevator whizzed by.

She landed with a thud on top of me. Both of us lay there for a moment, stunned by how close we had come to death.

When my pounding heart finally calmed down, I realized I was squeezing her tight, my arms wrapped protectively around her. I buried my face in her hair. "Thank God," I murmured. I allowed the warmth from her body to envelope me. In that moment it didn't matter if she ever remembered us. She was alive.

Luna lifted her head to look at me.

"Close call," I rasped, my lungs filled with dirt and dust from the shaft.

"Yeah."

I raised a shaking hand to her lips, tracing them with my fingertip. I wanted to kiss her, but wasn't sure I dared.

My body, however, had a mind of its own, and in a brave move, I braced my hands on her hips and slid them slowly up her torso. She brought her head toward me, linking her arms around my neck. I needed no other invitation.

Her mouth felt soft against mine, I cradled her neck, as I deepened the kiss. I didn't want to let go—but Luna pulled away, a hitch in her breath, shattering the moment. The cool air, a vast ocean between us.

"No, Zander. You lied to me. You're still lying." She quivered. Almost unsure of her own words. The truth just out of reach under the surface.

I sighed and sat up, shaking the dust from my hair. My hair net long since gone, lost somewhere in that dark pit.

The mistrust had returned to Luna's eyes and pain stabbed through my heart.

"I told you, Luna, I never lied, only omitted some things. Besides, it's not like you would have believed me anyway. You barely trusted me."

She crossed her arms glaring at me. "You didn't even try."

I grimaced, glad of the shadow's protection. She always used to cross her arms when she felt betrayed or wanted to protect herself. But it never had been directed at me before.

Once upon a time, I had been her anchor in the storm. I sighed. No point in attempting to recreate the past now.

"Yes, well, can we discuss my shortcomings later, and focus on the issue at hand?"

She considered. Her features molding into the tough as nails image she hid behind when she was scared. She knew I was right. But would never admit it. My stubborn Luna.

"So, where to next?" she asked.

My shoulders relaxed. At least for now, we would remain a team. "We can reach the rooftop from here. Come on, I'll show you."

We crawled over to the other side of the roof's eaves, and I grinned when I saw the oddly shaped rudimentary door cut out of the wall. This was one of many escape hatches the resistors had implemented around the capital. I thanked my lucky stars I'd memorized the resistor map of this place when I had the chance.

Luna remained silent, even though there must have been a million questions floating inside that head of hers.

I pushed open the hatch and light flooded into the small space, almost blinding me. After being in the dark so long, it took some adjusting to. I looked around. We were on a fully designed green roof made from plant particles that produced much-needed oxygen to the air. I hauled myself free and turned to help Luna. As soon as we were out, Luna brushed off all the dust and debris that had accumulated on her coat. I noticed the blood on her hands.

"Hey, let me take a look." I opened her palms gently. Small cuts crisscrossed the surface, but the blood had already dried.

She jumped back and immediately shoved them in her coat pocket. "They're fine. You have blood on your hands too, in case you hadn't noticed."

I glanced down and sure enough, mine replicated hers.

"Are you sure you're okay?" I said.

She rolled her eyes. "You are such a worrywart." And with that, she looked away, dismissing the conversation, her gaze turning to rest on the city before us.

It must have seemed so strange to her, building after building crammed in like sardines. A very different landscape from the one we'd been in these last months.

The Washington Monument and National Mall were mere shadows of their former glory. The beautiful green that once led from the monument had been replaced long ago with washed out stone, thanks to the meteor of 2053 that rained down on the earth, causing devastation all along the east coast. Even the White House wasn't immune. Half its infrastructure gone and the forbidding white columns replaced with grey, reinforced metal. To Luna, the capital probably looked more like a bomb shelter surrounded by a few small trees.

And I suppose it was.

Luna turned back to me. "What is this place," she murmured.

I gave a sheepish smile and shrugged. "Welcome to Washington D.C."

She frowned. "But—"

I cut her off. "We have to get off this roof, in case they initiate the robot drones." I scanned the sky above for any sign of activity.

"Robot drones?" she echoed.

"Yeah, don't ask. Come on. I have an idea." I grabbed her hand and started running toward the edge of the building. In the back corner of the roof, one of the glass dome emergency hangers was suspended from the outside of the facade.

Half our height and built for one, I wasn't sure how two people would fit. But fortunately, Luna's petite stature worked in our favor. We could make this work. We had to.

"Are you kidding me?" Luna said pulling her hand back. "I am not going in that thing. It looks like it was built for a cat."

"The technical term is emergency escape hatch; there's one on every level. The designers of this building, and most of the others in this city, said anything bigger would look ugly, and they didn't believe the required number of hatches were necessary."

"Sounds like the Titanic, when they didn't carry enough boats," she grumbled.

I gazed at her quizzically. "Luna, do you ever wonder how

you know about the Titanic?"

She looked at me blankly. "Don't be dumb, Zander. Everyone knows about that piece of history."

I sighed dropping the subject for now. "Sure. Fine. Forget I asked. Anyway, the reason we don't have enough hatches is because the higher-ups are cocky bastards. Now hurry. Try to fold up as much as possible, to maximize space."

She crossed her arms and raised her eyebrows at me. "We are going to fit in there together?"

"Yup. We don't have time to take separate trips. And I don't know what will be waiting for us at the bottom."

I pressed the latch that opened the glass box. A shiver ran up my spine at the thought of another enclosure. I'm sure Luna had the same sentiment.

I ignored my clammy palms and squeezed inside, adjusting my body, leaving the center empty for Luna. A difficult task due to the skin-tight clothing they made us wear in the coffins.

"Come on. Get in." I motioned for her to join me.

She sighed. "Fine. But only because I don't want to be stuck on this stupid rooftop forever."

I grinned. "That's my girl."

She frowned at me. "I am not your girl, Zander Barringer. Take that back."

I looked at her sadly. "But it's the truth."

She raised her eyebrows at me. I knew that look. She wasn't going anywhere unless I retracted my statement.

I held up my hands. "Fine. I take it back, okay. Can we go?"

Seemingly satisfied, she sized up the situation, then tentatively stepped inside, crouching in the center of the space, placing her head on her knees to fold into the smallest ball. A little squished would be an understatement, but as cheesy as it sounded, I liked being this close to her.

"Well, are we going or what? This isn't comfortable, in case you hadn't noticed."

"Okay, calm down, princess. We're going." I froze. I'd used

my pet name for her. Her back stiffened, but she said nothing. I had been so careful on P8 never to use it, but with exhaustion filling every pore, my guard was down, my revival high crashing down around me.

In the awkward silence that followed, I forced myself to act normally, focusing on the task before me. I pulled down the door and hit the small green button above Luna's head. Within seconds, we were hurtling towards ground level at a dizzying speed.

Luna chewed her bottom lip and instinctively reached out to take hold of my wrist.

The touch of her hand ignited a dull ache inside. I missed the part of her that understood everything and how we used to be. What I wouldn't give to share my memories with her. But I couldn't think of that now. I glanced out the pod to look, but the world flew by in a blur, and before I knew it, we suddenly came to a crashing halt.

A little jarred, Luna attempted to rise on her already wobbly legs and instead keeled over into the side of the glass enclosure.

"Ouch."

"Here, let me help you." I leaned over to undo the latch, pausing an extra second longer than necessary, to inhale her familiar scent.

"Come on, Zander. What's the holdup?"

"Uh, sorry, had a cramp," I lied.

Popping the lever, she leapt from our cramped quarters like a shot.

I scrambled out after her, scanning our location, searching for any signs we'd been followed. We were back on pavement level, a few passersby, mostly in suit and ties, eyed us warily, probably wondering why we rode the escape pod when there was no sign of a fire. On second thought, these hideous skin-colored leotards might be enough to make anyone look twice. I pulled the lab coat closer around me. Then gave up trying to look inconspicuous when I realized there was blood on it.

Satisfied our only concern were gawkers, I reached over and pressed the release button on the roof of the escape unit. The door closed, and I watched as it whizzed up and over our heads.

"I have a contact on the outside that can help us. The greater the distance we make from this place the better."

"What do you mean on the outside? I don't like this, Zander."

I raked a hand through my hair in frustration. "I need you to trust me a little while longer, okay? We're going to ride the monorail to the last stop. Are you with me?"

She looked up to where I pointed. The air tram looped around us in a circle hovering above the city, whizzing by carrying people to all different locations around the capital.

Luna wouldn't remember riding the rail, W1 and P8 were her only memories. She didn't recall any glass fire escapes in her past either. A day for firsts.

"Fine." she conceded. "But—"

Before she could elaborate, I grabbed her hand again. We raced down the national mall, over the bridge, where a river used to flow, but had dried up and was now home to large volumes of pedestrian traffic.

"Keep your head down. We can't take any chances," I whispered as we battled our way down the crowded streets. Occasionally, a random car passed by, but they were few and far between. Not much had changed. The ultra-rich could afford cars. Even for them, though, it was a luxury only permitted above ground. The underground city didn't permit them.

Finally, we made it to the air tram terminal, and I bee-lined for the take-off zone. A sign read, *5 credits for the full loop, 2.50 credits for a half loop. Star Line Red Loop to the right. Star Line Blue Loop to the left.*

I made a hard left and followed the stairs marked with blue tape. A robot at the top of the stairs stood like a statue, reminding me of one of the Queen's long-past guards that at one time protected Buckingham palace. I swiped my wrist twice at the turnstile, to cover the cost for both of us, and pushed my way through.

Luna hissed in my ear behind me. "Can't they track you through your credits?"

I grabbed one of the silver poles that lined the length of the train, pulled her closer and murmured, "I have it under control. They can't trace my footprint through my chip."

I motioned for her to sit down in one of the plush patterned chairs and did the same. A woman wearing an enormous diamond necklace around her neck sat down across from us, leaving a waft of gardenia in her wake. People riding this transport had money. Loads of it. And the impeccably clean car reflected that. Bankroll talked here. I just hoped everyone was so wrapped up in themselves they didn't notice our skin-tight spacesuits or our bloody, scratched up hands. Thank goodness Luna had suggested the coats. That helped some. I gave a little smile. She always did have a great mind for subterfuge.

The air tram took off and Luna stared fascinated out the window. I resisted the urge to touch her hair, glowing in the artificial sun like a shiny black diamond—and instead turned my eyes toward the landscape. From above, the city shone sparkling clean, with different sized skyscrapers lining the faux skyline. Trees appeared like dots of green in the otherwise beige panorama, as grass had always been hard to grow here.

Luna said nothing, taking in the view that whipped past. Her leg twitched nervously as we neared our destination. I surmised Luna was in full count mode, numbers tumbling around inside her head like dominoes, something she always did to calm herself. The city soon disappeared from sight as we entered the outskirts of the capitol. I stood as the train slowed, wondering if any help had been dispatched from the resistors camp.

Had Crane made it out? Or had they suspected him when he created a distraction back at the lab? Let's hope they just assumed he was a bumbling fool.

There were only two people left on the train besides us, but neither moved to disembark.

"Come on. This is our stop." Luna cast one last glance out the window, then turned to me brow furrowed. "Where is everyone? The place is a ghost town."

"Exactly."

Despite her reservations, she rose from her seat and followed me, quickly hopping down onto the platform. We made our way back down to street level.

The lone store for miles, Capitol Quick Stop, still had a rusty sign that dangled precariously by one hinge off the dilapidated porch. Luna read it aloud. "Grab your last minute items here— before leaving the convenience of the Capital Dome. Capital Dome?" Luna asked questioningly.

"Yeah. The entire city lies under a dome, you can't tell because they've done such a good job of camouflaging it."

"Why did they put it under a dome?" Luna asked.

We were interrupted by a man exiting the store, the old wooden boards creaking under his weight as his worn cowboy boots veered in our direction. His grizzly gray beard almost reached his plaid shirt, which was missing a few buttons— revealing a protruding beer belly scattered with more gray hair. I grabbed Luna's hand, pulling her away from the train stop and the old man's prying eyes.

When we were alone, I continued, "The poor air quality outside the dome is nearly unsurvivable—at least for long periods of time. The earth is dying, and the atmospheric conditions are a reflection of that."

Before she could reply, I placed a finger to her lips and listened. The only sound was that of our breathing. I let her go but remained close, explaining. "A camera is on the left quadrant of the building, but I think it's disabled. At least I hope to God it is because I know a way to get us the hell out of the dome. It's not going to be easy and..." I hesitated for a beat. "It will require some sacrifice."

"Sacrifice?" she asked doubtfully. "Wouldn't it make sense to stay in a place we can actually breathe?"

I shook my head. "No. Trust me you don't want to stay here or we'll end up back where we started. We won't be out there for long. There's an underground city called New Earth beyond these walls that's much safer. You'll see."

Luna sighed. "Underground city?" She waved her hands in the air in defeat. "You know what I don't even care at this point. Anything has to be better than going back. But you have some serious explaining to do when we get out of here."

I grinned at her and Luna scowled back at me. "You can wipe that smug smile off your face. You haven't won this. Now tell me about this sacrifice or whatever."

I sobered and took another quick look around before returning my gaze to her. "Under the store, there's a hidden chamber."

"Chamber? God Zander, you're turning me into some kind of repetitive monkey drone. Can you just say what you mean for crying out loud? I'm sick of sounding like an idiot."

"Nah, you're not an idiot," I teased tucking a strand of her hair behind her ears.

She swatted my hand away. "Answer the question, Barringer."

"Wow. Last name status. Burn."

Luna gritted her teeth, eyes flashing. She had a look like she wanted to punch me. "You're still speaking in riddles, Zander. I changed my mind. I'm not going anywhere with you or promising anything until you spill. A chamber sounds just as bad as a glass cage."

She frowned at me, and I turned away for a minute, briefly closing my eyes and taking a deep breath. It was harder here. Being home and not having her remember anything. On P8, it had been manageable, stranded in a strange place together. The reality was a much bigger pill to swallow.

"You don't understand, Luna," I said voice strained. "You were a part of all this, too."

"So, you're saying I just happened to forget everything and I should know all about your schemes? And why we were in those glass coffins back there? What the hell, Zander." She grabbed my arm and spun me back around, her cheeks flaming red with anger. "I demand you tell me what's going on."

I took her hands. But she pulled away. I sighed. "Look—"

She held up her fists in frustration. "Don't even bother, I know what you are going to say. You're like a broken record. Let me guess. You promise to tell me everything. But later?" She pressed her lips into a thin white line, then in a controlled voice said. "Sorry, Zander. I'm not going anywhere with you."

"Damn it, Luna. Why are you being so stubborn?"

She didn't speak. The silence was palpable.

"Fine. I'll tell you. I just hope Beth and Scott understand. If they ask—tell them that some part of you already knew and you simply forgot." Warming up to the idea now, I started pacing, letting the pieces settle in my mind.

Luna looked at me, her eyes flashing with anger. "I'm really getting sick of you implying there are holes in my memory, Zander. Did you mess something up in that brain of yours on our jump out of P8 or something? I don't even know who Beth and Scott are. I think we'll be fine. Did you ever think maybe you are the delusional one?"

"I'm not delusional, Luna, I promise you. I can get us out of here. For now, the rest of it—who remembers what—is inconsequential if we both end up caged again. Let me help you."

I grabbed her hand again and this time didn't let her pull away. I was going all in. Well sort of. Baby steps. First, I had to break the news to her that the only way out of here...could possibly shorten her life.

Should be no problem. I took a deep breath and blurted it out.

"They've discovered a way for humans to demolecularize. And that's our ticket out of here."

CHAPTER 5

LUNA

His deep, azure eyes swirled with emotion as he pleaded with me to understand, to believe him. A truth I couldn't ignore hid behind his gaze—but it was his truth—not mine. Zander had been acting weird ever since we got out of those pods.

"Demolecularize? Doesn't that mean we will turn to nothing?"

"No. Well sort of. We will transform into small particles so we can travel through the dome and materialize on the other side. But we need the chamber to do it."

I pulled my hands back and jammed them into the pockets of my lab coat. "It sounds crazy."

Zander's voice grew solemn. "There's no other option, Luna. They're coming for us. And what they have planned is worse than any demolecularization."

My temper flared, and heat burned my cheeks. "I can make up my own mind, Zander Barringer. Besides, what do you mean? What will it do?"

Zander shook his head, face pinched. "Well, all the testing is complete, but the process still carries some repercussions."

I sighed. "And that would be? God, Zander, you might make this a little easier."

Zander shuffled his feet and stared at the ground. "You may not be the same—it could shorten your life."

I let out a hollow laugh. "Oh well, no big deal then, I guess."

Zander met my gaze. "The latest specs show a possible life reduction of as much as ten percent. So be sure, Luna. The way I figure it? Losing ten percent is better than one hundred percent and living a zombie's life."

What was I supposed to do? The thought of returning to the glass cage made my stomach churn. I couldn't go back; that wasn't an option. I stared out beyond the barren wasteland, attempting to make out the edge of the dome. We had to be close; this was the borderlands, after all. I prayed for a sign.

When nothing moved, I sighed, frustrated. So much for a sign. I closed my eyes, trying to make sense of everything that had happened since I jumped into that vortex. There had to be something redeeming about Zander, despite the betrayal. I thought back to some of our moments together back on P8. Not all of it could be a lie. Could it? I had trusted him to take us this far.

But that didn't mean this was over. If we made it out—he was toast.

"Luna, I hate to rush you, but security detail comes to search the perimeter at nightfall."

"Fine. How could it get any worse? Suicide mission sounds perfect."

"Seriously? You're going to come?"

Before I could respond, he grabbed me, twirling me around. "Thank you, Luna," he said, his voice muffled in my ear.

"Set me down, you Neanderthal, before I change my mind," I said through gritted teeth. I ignored the race of my heart at his mere touch. I fumed at my body. *Traitor.*

"Sorry," Zander said, returning me to the ground. He pointed westward with a nod of his head. "The sun is setting. Once it's dusk, we can head behind the store. We'll find a hidden door that will take us underground. The shop is closing in a few minutes if I'm reading the sun in the sky correctly."

"So, do we stand here like idiots till then?"

"No. Let's get out of sight," Zander said, ignoring my sarcasm. "We took the last air tram, but I don't want to take any chances of anyone seeing us. As it is, the storekeeper may be curious."

I snorted. "I doubt they pay him enough to care. Besides, I never had a problem stealing from them."

Zander grabbed my shoulders again. "Vigilance is key here, Luna. Remember that. We can't be complacent."

The fear I saw in his eyes ate away at my confidence.

I didn't say anything, but instead, let him lead me from our hiding spot, away from the air tram tracks and back toward the store. The clerk stepped out onto the front steps. He adjusted the tight collar on his shirt, pulling it away from his red neck, and leaned against the post. He stared at us, and I was sure we'd be busted. Had a warning gone out to everyone to be on the lookout?

Perhaps there would be no choice after all.

⚜

As it turned out, the only thing on the shopkeeper's mind was closing up and going home. He left with no ulterior motives right as the sun set over the horizon. Not that it appeared normal—it had an artificial quality about it, neon yellow, rather than the natural red, orange, and pink hues of a regular evening sky.

"What's with the sunset? It looks like a highlighter exploded up in the sky."

He smiled. "We're under the dome, remember? The actual sun has been shrouded in a cloud of pollution for years. Sunrises and sunsets are pretty much non-existent past these walls." He nodded his head towards the clouds. "That sunset is almost entirely artificial."

I swallowed hard. No sunrise or sunsets? What else was broken in this godforsaken place? Did I really want to leave the dome? It sounded barbaric out there. A twinge of remorse flooded through me. Perhaps the better choice would have been to stay in P8 and accept whatever fate life dealt. At least there, I had oxygen to breathe. What had the humans of this universe done to their planet? Were they so stupid as to not take care of their home?

"Come on. He's gone," Zander said, pulling me out of my morose thoughts. He steered me around to the back of the store and placed his hand on the brick wall of the shop. An electronic keypad appeared out of nowhere between the bricks, and I gaped in astonishment. He typed something into it and the door popped open, silent as a mouse, revealing a series of dark stairs that led down into inky blackness.

"Watch your step. I don't have a flashlight. I'll go first, twenty steps straight down."

Without waiting for my agreement, he took the first two steps. Not knowing what else to do, I followed him into the creepy pit. Zander patted his shoulder. "Here, hold on to me and shut the door behind you. Be careful and go slow."

I took Zander's shoulder and did as he asked, pitching into the cramped void. I gripped Zander tighter than I wanted to admit and painstakingly made my way down the steep narrow steps, rough with old cement gravel, counting as I went.

After what seemed an eternity, we reached the bottom.

"We should be good now," Zander said. "The door's straight ahead." A pink light pierced the darkness, and I realized Zander had placed his palm on the wall next to the door. Another keypad appeared and Zander punched in another code.

"You certainly run a tight ship around here, don't you?" I muttered, tired and a little sick of these theatrics.

I wasn't sure if he'd heard me or chose to not respond, but Zander kept moving, feeling along the wall.

"Bingo," he said under his breath. I heard the squeak of a knob, and the door swung open. His so-called underground chamber looked more like a glorified basement to me. A windowless space, cluttered with complex machinery that flashed red, green and yellow with a large dashboard situated near the center of the room. I walked in behind him and turned to the rear of the enclosure. I gasped.

"Zander. Someone's down here!" I yelled, instinctively reaching in my boot for my knife, but came up empty, realizing I no longer had either my boots or knife. Only these damn flimsy ballet shoes someone had obviously placed on my feet while in the cage.

Zander spun on his heels; his face ashen under the artificial lights. He put a hand over his heart in relief, when he saw where I pointed. "Luna, that isn't a man, it's a robot. He isn't even turned on." He went over to it and tapped on his head as if to prove a point, smirking at me.

Bastard.

My face flamed with embarrassment. I walked over and inspected him more closely. Sure enough, the telltale signs of a droid were evident—blank eyes stared back at me, and his rough, hardened skin was clearly not mortal. Still, it was the best robot I'd ever encountered. He would easily pass for a middle-aged man.

"What's he doing down here?" I hissed.

"Somebody has to run the machine. It's a hell of a lot easier than trying to smuggle people down here to operate that thing." He pointed to the complex motherboard. "This robot is designed to understand every nuance of the demolecularization procedure. Once we're on the other side of the wall, he's the one that will press the button that will reform all our atoms back into existence. Without him, we're kind of stuck."

Zander noted my wide-eyed expression of horror and shrugged sheepishly. "Did I forget to mention that part?"

I crossed my arms and glared at him. "Yes. You did."

Zander turned to the droid, searching for something on the back. "I'll show you how rad Burt is."

"Burt? You seriously expect me to put my life in the hands of a robot named Burt?"

"Hey, Burt's a great name. Give him a chance," Zander said his voice muffled as his fingers probed across Burt's anatomy. "Got it!"

The next thing I knew, whirring white circles lit up Burt's eyes as his program became activated. He blinked a few times, his stiff neck swiveling in each direction before landing on me. He tilted his head slightly, as if computing, and then flashed me an insane, white-toothed grin. I was officially creeped out.

"Mistress Luna. Master Zander. So good to see you both again. I haven't seen you in precisely sixteen months, four days, seven minutes, and three seconds. Welcome home."

I backed away. "How does he know my name? Why is he saying welcome home?"

Zander sighed. "You've been here before. Do you remember how I asked you about the Titanic back there? You have some subconscious memories of history from this place Luna. Why would you have that if you weren't from this world? Burt is programmed to record everything including time. He remembers you. He scans your eyes and receives the impression of your identity."

I closed my eyes for a moment, trying to collect myself. Thinking of Wı Nova. My real home. Did eye scans happen here too, to determine life status? Could it really be true? Had I forgotten an entire lifetime? I didn't want to believe it. How could a life I didn't remember be my real identity? I wanted to yell at Zander and tell him to prove it. But I couldn't bring myself to do it. The truth could be a real pain in the ass some-times, and I had enough to deal with.

Zander laughed. "You can open your eyes, Luna, you're too late, he's already figured out who you are."

I opened them, scowling at him and Burt.

"Well, Burt don't you have a job to do?" I asked crossly.

"I don't understand, Master Luna. I don't recall receiving instructions. Let me verify this in my database." The droid made a whirring noise, firing off some command for his computer system, but before he finished, Zander interrupted. "Burt, please initiate sequence 434, and prepare for DM Transfer. Luna Redwood and Zander Barringer for transport."

"Order understood. Preparing for transfer."

Burt strode over to the dashboard and at a dizzying speed began punching in codes and plugging in wires. His movements, smooth and precise, were far from robotic.

Zander spoke softly in my ear. "Burt is a state-of-the-art model, designed by some of the founders of New Earth for solely this purpose. Once he has finished the initial sequencing, we will be good to go. It should only take a few minutes. Are you sure you're ready?"

"Ready as I'll ever be," I muttered.

"Good." Zander gripped my hand tightly, making no comment about my sweaty palms. To be fair, his weren't exactly bone dry, which I found strangely comforting. A part of me wanted to pull away and pretend I didn't care about what lay ahead—a potential suicide for us both. However, the human contact steadied me, and I hated to admit it, but without Zander I felt lost at sea. He had the ability to anchor me like no one else.

Without turning around Burt said, "Command sequence 434 is initiated. Please proceed to the hyper chamber pod for final transfer."

"Hyper chamber pod?" I squeaked. "I don't want to go into any more coffins, Zander."

"It's more like an elevator," he explained.

I raised my eyebrows and snickered. "Yeah, because we didn't

have a terrifying experience in an elevator less than an hour ago."
I blew my hair out of my face in frustration. Zander didn't
speak, waiting me out. Finally, I threw my hands up in the air.
"Fine, I'll bite. Where is it?"

Zander pointed to a shadowed corner of the room, where a
rectangular glass enclosure, the size of an old-fashioned phone
booth stood, lit up with a thousand lights. The transparent glass
made up of triangular prisms projected dazzling repetitive rainbows against the walls.

"Initiating door. Please stand clear," Burt said in his
monotone voice.

Sure enough, a small hatch opened at the front, barely wide
enough for one person to get through.

"Why don't you go in first, it will be safer if we go
separately."

"What? No way. We go in together or no deal."

"I had a feeling you would say that," he muttered under his
breath.

"What was that?" I asked innocently pretending I hadn't
heard him.

"We will go together," he said sounding defeated.

I cast a glance at Zander, and he nodded encouragingly.
"Come on then. Let's go." Without batting an eye, he led me
over to the glass contraption. "Step over the piece at the bottom;
don't worry about hitting your head. Since you're tiny, you'll
clear it no problem."

I glared at him. "Tiny?"

He grinned, holding up his hands in surrender. "You know
what I mean. No offense, I promise."

I sneered at him but stepped inside, ignoring his offer of
assistance. The nerve. I might be small in stature, but I was
quite capable of doing anything he could do—including de-mole-
cularizing.

Zander stepped in beside me, wiggling around so we faced
each other. The cramped space had us practically standing nose

to nose. Well, okay fine, nose to chest if I was being completely honest. Zander towered over me, clearly his fault, not mine.

"I'm going to hold tight to both your hands during the transfer. Whatever you do, don't let go, otherwise, we might end up separated. Burt can give us a general location window, but in reality, we only have a correctional capacity of one mile from the chosen area. They might have improved the accuracy since I was last home, but I don't want to take any chances."

He gripped my hands. "Ready?"

I nodded without saying a word. I didn't want him to hear the tremble in my voice.

Never let them see your weakness. Never. My mother's voice rose in my head like a broken record. To distract myself, I began to count the tiny triangles that made up the wall.

"Burt, initiate sequence 800. We're ready."

"Initiating sequence. Happy transfer."

The door eased shut with a sucking sound and the pod began to shake. The air became thinner. "Normal breaths, Luna. You may experience some light-headedness. It will only last a minute," Zander said, squeezing my hand.

I stared up at him and watched in horror as a piece of his face started to disappear. Before I could react, pain erupted in my skull and the world spun away, my body sucked straight into a vacuum—then total blackness.

I came to, coughing and spluttering, my nose and mouth filled with dirt. Someone was patting my face.

"Luna? Are you okay? You hit your head. Beth and Scott need to work on the landing," he teased as he brushed my hair back from my forehead.

Too stunned to speak, I simply stared into Zander's face, also covered in dirt. A thin cut left an angry line along his cheekbone. Without thinking, I lifted a shaking hand, wiping the trail of blood that slid down to his lip.

He blushed sheepishly. "I guess I hit something, too. Say something Luna, anything, you're making me nervous."

My lungs burned and my entire body ached. I tried to take a deep breath, but ended up coughing again. "I'm fine. Really," I wheezed, lying through my teeth. He would not catch me complaining. I could handle this. The last thing I needed was to appear weak.

"Take it easy, Luna. The air out here is not your friend." He pulled up the mask that had been hanging under my chin and adjusted it so it covered my mouth and nose, then extracted his own from his pocket. "These will help with the dust."

The mask didn't do much, but now that I had my coughing under control, I sat up on my elbows, taking in my surroundings. It took a minute for my eyes to focus—when they did, I stared horrified at the barren land, devoid of any kind of vegetation. Trees stretched out as far as the eye could see, like hollow scarecrows. The dry air and scarred acreage left evidence of a massive fire that must have burned through here at some point in history.

"What is this place?" I whispered, struggling to force enough breath into my lungs to speak.

"People call it the in-between. From what I've been told, it used to be a beautiful park in the middle of Washington D.C, full of fountains and trees. But the pollution we created destroyed that a long time ago."

"What happened?" I asked.

"Fires. Floods. You name it. And that's true all across the Americas."

"The Americas?"

"Yeah. Welcome to America, or what's left of it anyway. Come on. We better get out of this air. We're about a ten-minute walk from the entrance, and we are going to need all the strength we can get. A contact I have will help us once we get there."

He offered me a hand up. Zander mentioned this so-called contact before. I opened my mouth to ask him how in the world that was possible, but as soon as he pulled me to my feet, a sharp pain pierced my temple and I fell to my knees.

An image flashed before my eyes—a man with slick gray hair and a deep tan stood beside a woman of about the same age, her hair in a tight bun, her suit immaculate. They oozed money, judging from the expensive earrings at the woman's lobes and the flashy gold ring on the man's pinky finger. They both stared at a small disk lying in the guy's palm before giving each other a meaningful look. Whatever was on this disk was important to them.

Familiar, yet all together mysterious, I searched for any clue that might link them to my past. I shivered, and goosebumps covered my arms as I realized that somehow I knew that it was important to me too.

As the image faded to dust, my mouth went dry, and I suddenly became aware of one thing. These people were my parents. But not Mama. And not my P8 parents. My heart thudded in my chest.

"Luna? Are you okay?" a familiar voice asked sounding far away, and I realized Zander had been talking to me. Probably for quite some time.

"I'm fine. I must have hit my head harder than I thought. The pain's gone now," I stood up and to prove my point, began brushing the dirt from my clothes.

"God, Luna, you scared me. You went deathly white. I thought—"

I cut him off. "I'm fine. See? Standing and everything!" I said, gesturing to my upright form. "Didn't you say we had to get going?"

Zander hesitated for a beat before conceding. "You're right. Follow me. The underground network isn't far."

I had a gazillion questions, but I bit my tongue. The exertion of simply talking exhausted me in this air. Walking was going to take everything I had and then some.

We kept a slow pace, heading deeper into the barren wasteland. A sudden blur of movement caught my eye. In an instant, Zander tackled me to the ground and rolled me sideways. All the air whooshed out of my lungs, leaving me breathless.

What the hell?

"Sorry! I really blew it, didn't I?" A high-pitched voice chirped.

Zander groaned as he stood, simultaneously plucking a dead leaf from his unkempt hair. I jumped to my feet, fists raised, ready to combat the owner of the somewhat familiar voice. Where had I heard it before?

"What the devil are you playing at, Crane?" Zander exclaimed. "You scared me half to death. You didn't have to spring on us like that."

Crane? I looked over at the stranger. And froze.

Zander must have noticed my stricken expression because he placed a comforting hand on my arm. "Luna, this is the contact I told you about."

"You can't be serious," I said pointing at the tall, gangly teenager. "This is the jerk that stuck a syringe full of creepy red stuff into you while you were still unconscious, he—"

Crane interrupted. "Aw, I missed you too, Luna. Thanks for the lovely sentiment."

I frowned at him. This Crane certainly had a lot of nerve.

"Hey don't look at me like that. You know I was just following orders, doing my job and trying to save your scrawny necks. I'm one of your protectors." He beamed at us proudly like he deserved a medal.

"Protectors?" I started to laugh. "Yeah right like we need protection from you."

"Hey, I may not be a muscly dude, but I do my job." His face fell.

"Luna, Crane injected us with revival. We would still be in a

49

sleeping coma without it. He helped us get out of there. Didn't you see him get between us and the guards?"

I regarded Crane doubtfully. In all honesty I hadn't had time to look at the person that got in the guards way back at the capital. But he didn't give off a threatening vibe. And if Crane had delivered a lethal injection, I'm sure Zander would be dead by now. A bit of guilt crept in, but then I shrugged it off. I scrutinized the overgrown fellow. Without the glass coffin between us, I got a much better look at him. His green eyes were the color of a ripe forest, accentuated by subtle eyeliner under his lids. A tiny gold earring I hadn't noticed before glittered from his left ear. The guy clearly liked his accessories.

"Whatever," I snorted, fed up. "Can we go? My lungs are about to break."

Crane burst into a broad grin, his momentary hurt forgotten. "Absolutely, my lady. I'm sorry about the mix-up. The original plan was to move you to another energy outpost before I busted you free, but I ran into some technical difficulties—basically, you two are too smart for your own good—and I had to break you out from headquarters. Madeline said it couldn't be done. But I knew that if you guys hacked yourself out of the game without Madeline's help, I could do the impossible on this end, too. Madeline was the one who disabled your coffin. Well, part of it. Some of your shackles were still intact, and you were still asleep, which meant you must have been dosed with the sleeping agent last night when it should have been shut off. But it—"

Zander cut him off. "Crane. For the love of all that is holy, stop talking," he said, irritated. "You're freaking Luna out. She doesn't have her memories. So she doesn't remember anything."

Crane's words pierced through my addled brain. I came to an abrupt halt. Hacked out of a game?

I whirled on Zander. "What does he mean, we hacked ourselves out of the game? What's he talking about? And stop telling him I have no memories. I definitely remember my lives. Mama, Dara, my parents on P8, all of it."

Crane stepped between us. "Guys, you can hash this out later. I have word on the com that drones were initiated back at the capital."

I pushed Crane aside, annoyed.

"We have to get to the underground, Luna. Please. I will explain as soon as we're safe."

I glared, too infuriated to speak. Sick of all their damn subterfuge and excuses. I breathed heavily adjusting my askew mask as I wracked my brain for a solution. If things weren't so dire, I might've tried to escape from these two clearly delusional characters.

But God help us if those scientists caught us.

I didn't want to think about what they would do.

"Let's go," I muttered under my breath, already regretting every syllable as we ran towards New Earth.

And then I heard the drones.

CHAPTER 6

ZANDER

The sound of the drones heading our way intensified.

I pumped my legs harder, lungs burning, as stars clouded my vision. I looked to Luna, who's lips had turned blue, her face ashen.

She had to remain conscious if we wanted to survive. We both did.

"Stay with me, Luna," I rasped, using precious oxygen. The world wavered in front of me for a minute, but I pressed on. "The underground entrance that leads to New Earth is just ahead. Only a few more steps."

In the lead, Crane waved his long arms at us, indicating he'd opened the hatch leading to the secret entry into the city. Few knew of it—it's only landmark was an old sign of the map tunnels from the long-gone metro system. The two main entrances, well-known to all citizens, involved an ID scan and decontamination procedures, which we had no time for.

Thank God Scott and Beth had thought of every contingency.

I pushed myself to the point I thought my heart might burst and slid to a halt at the opening. Crane had brushed off the dirt and twigs revealing the open escape hatch in all its glory. He motioned for me to go in.

"Hurry up, Zander. Get inside!" Crane ordered.

I shook my head. "No. Luna goes first."

She drew up beside me and bent over, putting both hands on her knees as she inhaled great gulping breaths. Sweat beading at her forehead dripped down her face. Her eyes were glassy and unfocused. I took her elbow and rushed her to the entryway, as Crane tapped his foot impatiently.

"Try not to pass out, Luna. Just a little further and then we can take it a bit easier. "

"You guys..." Crane said nervously, his eyes darting towards the sky. "Look."

I followed his gaze and saw the faint outline of metal piercing through the murky gray as a drone swooped and swerved heading in our direction—it would be upon us any minute. No way could they miss us, we were like sitting ducks out here in the open.

"Go!" I shouted to Crane. He jumped into the darkness, and I grabbed Luna's hand and pushed her through, not giving her a chance to protest. I leapt down after her and Crane yanked the door closed, just as the drones roared past.

All of us panted heavily, and feeling more than a little dizzy, we waited a beat. It was hot and stuffy down here, not to mention dark. And we still had to traverse a mile down—at least a fifteen-minute trek—through the linear tunnel system to reach the sealed hatch at the end.

A headache started to pound at the back of my skull, wrapping around my brain in a vice grip—the side effects of revival kicking in. Between running and the less-than ideal-atmospheric conditions, the symptoms appeared way faster than normal.

Luna, from what I could ascertain by the dim track light of the door, looked a little disoriented and her rapid breathing concerned me.

"Hey Luna? You okay? We've got about another fifteen minutes until we reach some good air. Can you walk?"

She nodded, strangely compliant to my suggestion. Very un-Luna like.

I staggered forward and held out my hand to help her up. She took hold of it and somehow managed to pull herself upright. But a second later she stumbled, tripping over her own feet. Low blood oxygen levels were taking their toll.

"It can be a pretty harrowing hike down to the city," Crane said in a bad British accent. "But lucky for you, I always carry my trusty pocket torch with me." With a flourish, he whipped a mini pen light from his pocket and switched it on. A tiny stream of light pierced the cramped space as we cautiously started to move down the sloped tunnel, deeper into the earth.

"Actually, I know what you're thinking—*that's not going to help Crane, it's pitch black in this pit*—but look, I've been tinkering, and if I do say so myself, I've created a brilliant masterpiece." He beamed broadly as he pressed another button. The two sides popped apart, instantly casting the cave into a warm halo of light.

Luna, obviously unimpressed with his inventor talents, started to slump. I caught hold of her waist just in time, propping her up against me. At least she was still walking somewhat. I tried to remain positive, anything to keep our minds off the interminable trek before us. "Great trick with the pen light, Crane. But what's with the fake British accent?"

He loped towards us like a skinny giraffe, closing the few steps between us in seconds. I caught his grin. "Personally, I thought it made me sound a bit posh—since I'm a protector for you guys and all. I wanted to up my game. Been practicing loads. Are you impressed?"

I shook my head, wincing, as pain sliced through my skull. "Impressed isn't really how I'd describe it," I said.

Crane looked to Luna, "I'm sure Luna was impressed," he said.

She didn't even look up at him, too busy trying to stay upright. Ignoring this important detail Crane continued on, "In fact Luna I bet you've been asking yourself; *how come he's not suffering from lack of oxygen like us?* I know. I know. the air quality down here stinks, not much better than outside. But I have a secret weapon."

Crane winked then skipped ahead of me, light dancing off the dirt walls. "Okay, okay, if you're going to drag it out of me. I'll tell you. I'm a swimmer—I've the lung capacity of a whale." He frowned. "No wait, do whales have good lung capacity? I'm not certain, never had the pleasure of course, since they've been extinct for ages, but..."

I let Crane rattle on, concentrating on putting one foot in front of the other, hauling Luna along with me with each stride. A green tint shadowed her face, a warning sign she was close to fainting.

The sooner we got to New Earth, the better.

⊰⊱

Fifteen minutes later, we faced a sealed metal door especially designed for any eventuality. Even nuclear war. If something happened up above, New Earth would be a safe haven.

"I'm not sure if my ID chip still works on this door, Crane. Do I still have clearance?"

Crane bobbed his head up and down vigorously. "Absolutely. But allow me. Your hands are full," he said, nodding to the barely conscious Luna draped over my right shoulder.

Between exiting the coffin and running like a banshee breathing the polluted air, it was a miracle I was still standing, let alone supporting Luna. Thank God for the trickle of adrenaline still circulating in my system.

Crane flashed his hand over the wall adjacent the door. A pad appeared and he scanned his wrist chip. The door hissed open like a jagged pair of jaws, exposing a whole team of medics.

I turned in surprise to look at Crane. He shrugged sheepishly. "I called ahead," he said.

I slumped, relieved.

Several hours later, after multiple breathing treatments and a deep cleanse to remove environmental pollutants from my skin, I began to feel almost human again. My headache had lowered to a dull throb, and I was able to think clearly for the first time since leaving the dome. Luna and I had been separated when one of the medics had carried her off to an oxygen chamber. Now refreshed, I was eager to find her. Coming here may have triggered memories. At least that's what I hoped.

I glanced in the mirror. I'd donned some fresh clothes, jeans and a blue button-down shirt borrowed from Crane. The pants were a tad long, but not bad. A vast improvement over the skin tight flesh colored tracksuit of the institute, and my bare feet. Turns out running in government issued ballet flats is less than ideal.

I closed my eyes for a minute, tuning into the energy of my surroundings—directing my heartbeat and breath to slow, until they moved in perfect tandem together. I attempted to tap into my psychic abilities again to see if I could detect Luna—but came up empty. I had learned over time that if I remained calm, my chance of tapping into them increased.

But in this moment, I couldn't even manage to tune into a cockroach. Too many distracting thoughts swirled around my brain, beasts that I couldn't seem to tame. I sighed in frustration and turned from the mirror. I would just have to do this the old-fashioned way.

I left my room, and headed toward the main dining hall. The medics had transferred us to a low rise on the far side of the city —a smaller facility, only about three stories below ground. One of the many headquarters for the core resistance team that were scattered all around New Earth. The area was familiar, as we both had been here before for meetings. Stark white hallways reflected a bright glare against my eyes, and my borrowed sneakers made a loud squeaking noise on the newly polished tile. A few pictures hung on the wall, depicting sunrises, sunsets, and animals long since extinct. A reminder for resistors to remember what we were fighting for.

I reached the elevator, not meeting anyone on my travels. No doubt people were still in late-night debriefings. Many resistors had day jobs, plus it was safer this way.

Registering my arrival, the elevator opened and I swiped my wrist on the palm pad as I entered. I shrugged off the rising sense of doom that churned in my stomach as I recalled the harrowing escape from the dome elevator shaft only hours earlier.

"Zander Barringer. ID 1397. Please indicate level number," a robotic voice said reverberating through the speakers.

"Level three."

"Thank you."

The elevator whizzed down and within seconds a bell chimed. "Level three."

I stepped out into another long white corridor, identical in every way to the previous one. I paused for a second to get my bearings, remembering the dining room was in the left wing. My stomach growled in protest. My body could no longer maintain itself solely on that liquid nutrient crap provided in the glass cages—I needed food. But first I had to make sure Luna was okay. I made a beeline for the mess hall, betting good money Crane would be there with feelers already nosing out her where- abouts. If by some off chance he didn't have her mapped, I could always ask one of the droids on duty in the med wing.

I found the dining room easily; the architecture of the place was quite impressive, with its domed ceiling, and contemporary faux limestone floor. The main hall displayed white arched columns that led to private rooms beyond. The custom-made steel tables and chairs in the common area held only a few patrons—most of the commotion seemed to be coming from a room just out of sight. I maneuvered my way around the dining seats and headed towards the source of the noise. Crane's loud voice floated above the din. Without waiting for an invitation, I barreled through the door.

Crane's scrawny form was sprawled in a wooden chair before a polished black table. Some familiar faces joined him—Zee, Cat, and Jay. A fire blazed in the small stone hearth behind them warming the damp earthen walls of the room.

Crane immediately jumped to his feet, coming over and clapping me on the back. "Hey, Zander! Feeling better?"

"Much, thanks, buddy."

The rest of the crew looked up from their meal of mung bean eggs, tofu sausage meat, and baked beans. Things like eggs and real meat were impossible to come by. If any even existed, they never left the capital.

"It's so good to see you," Cat squealed, pushing back her chair and bounding towards me. Her violet, poppy-themed, hippy skirt embraced us both like a parachute as she hugged me tight. "We heard you were back." Her bracelets jangled as she clapped her hands in glee. She emitted a warm welcoming energy that washed over me like a balm immediately cheering me. Her teased hair sprang wildly around her ebony-toned face and her brown eyes shone with pleasure as she greeted me.

"Good to see you too, Cat."

Jay remained seated, giving me a chin up gesture. "How's it goin', bro?" he asked. "Didn't think you'd ever get out of Dodge." He tucked his fair, shoulder length waves behind his ears and continued to make short work of his meal, not waiting for a response.

"You and me both," I muttered.

Zee sat at the head of the table, decked in a full piece suit, as usual, complete with pencil skirt and hat. Her silken hair smoothed tight against her scalp in a tight bun. She ignored me and continued to type furiously into her com.

I grinned. Looked like Zee hadn't changed either. Forever studying trajectories and objectives for the team, ready to present to Scott and Beth, the founders of New Earth, at a moment's notice.

I turned to Crane, already back at the table, inhaling his food.

"Where's Luna?" I asked, trying to sound casual.

Crane stopped mid-bite, a baked bean stuck to his chin. He swallowed hard, and I couldn't help laughing.

"You've got a little something on your chin, Crane."

"Right. Sorry." He gave his face a quick swipe, and the loose bean landed back on his plate. "Luna is still above deck. I gave the bot instructions to bring her down when she's ready."

I nodded.

"How's she doing?" Cat asked.

I scrubbed a hand over my cheek, every inch tired. "She doesn't remember much. Only her interactions on W1 and P8 remain intact."

"It's so unfair," Crane complained. "She thought I was the enemy, can you believe it? Little old me?"

Jay snorted. "There's nothing little about you, buddy. I think you have giant cred."

Crane sat up straighter. "Hey, I take offense to that."

Zee held up her hands. "Stop being so childish, Jay. Leave Crane be. What we should all be worrying about is not the fact she thinks we're the enemy, but the implications her memory loss holds for us. We can't trust her loyalty now. She's standing smack in the middle of our secrets, all the Intel we shrouded from the capital. We could be sitting ducks letting her in."

I leaned forward angrily, my hands pressing into the table. "Luna's been through a nightmare, Zee. But that doesn't mean she would do anything stupid."

"Oh really? Right now, she doesn't even remember her real parents. Without that kind of motivation, she probably wouldn't have joined the resistors in the first place."

"What the hell is she talking about, Zander?"

I whirled around. Luna stood in the doorway, her pale face pinched in anger, hands clenched into fists at her sides.

Oh great, how much had she overheard?

I went over to give her a hug, but she stayed rigid, pushing me away. "Get off me, Zander, and please tell me what's going on."

I gestured toward the table. "Come in and have some late-night breakfast—a little tradition of ours. We can talk while we eat. You must be starving."

I noted with some dismay that she still wore the capital's skin-colored suit and filthy lab coat. At least someone had given her some decent shoes. Why not clothes? I made a mental note to find her something to wear as soon as we'd finished eating.

Luna warred with herself—but finally curiosity triumphed, and if I knew Luna, her insatiable hunger won out. I pulled out a chair for her, and she sat down. I piled mung bean eggs and sausage onto a plate and passed it to her, before making one for myself. She didn't comment on the weird-looking eggs but accepted the strange-looking food without question. Luna's time on W1 had left their scars, leaving her grateful for anything she received.

"The food isn't top-notch, but it fills the void," Jay said. "I would kill for a burger. But none of that fake crap."

"Luna, I would like you to meet everyone. This is Jay," I said pointing across the table. "And Cat, and Zee. They are old friends of ours. And you've already met Crane."

Crane gave her a cheery smile, bits of sausage caught in his teeth.

Luna snorted and picked up her fork. "Supposed friends."

Cat leaned across the table and patted her hand. "Don't worry, Luna. Things will get better. It's always confusing at first."

Luna yanked her hand away. "You don't know anything about me."

Cat looked to me, as if to say, *now what?*

I sucked in a deep breath and took the plunge, "Okay, Luna,

do you recall what I told you back at the store just before we left the dome? I explained to you that you were a part of everything? Well that's because in real life you are a part of all this," I spread my arms wide to encompass everyone. "Right here, right now is your true reality. The life you remember—well that was a virtual world imposed upon you."

I could tell Luna still wasn't completely sold on the idea she had a life she had completely forgotten about, but she was wavering. Her eyes were filled with doubt. Finally, as if to deflect, she said, "So what is this place?"

"It's called New Earth," Cat said hopping in to help. "Scott McMillan and Beth Nigels, who you will get to know soon enough, are the brain child behind it. And this," she said with a wave of her hand, "is one of the safe houses."

"Safe house?" Luna echoed.

I interjected. "Quite a few resistors live down here, along with many others. And there are safe houses scattered across the city for our protection. You were kept in a mental prison for months—subjected to playing out their virtual reality game scenarios. The government placed you in W1 first, then P8. The entire time you were trapped inside a glass coffin. That's why your limbs were so wobbly when you first tried to walk. They'd been immobile for months."

Luna's fork shook in her hand, confusion flashing across her face as she absorbed what I told her. The room stilled as we waited for her reaction. She pressed her other hand to her forehead.

"It seemed so real. How is that possible?" she whispered. "Mama? Dara? My sister Trinity?"

The words died on her lips as if she couldn't bear the answer.

I pried the fork from her fingers, setting in down gently. "They are real people, Luna. But they aren't who you think they are. They had a role to play in the game just like you did."

She looked at me. "If that's true, why don't I remember anything? You do."

"Before you enter the game, they wipe your memories and give you new, detailed memories for the virtual scenario. But obviously that didn't quite work out in your case as you could recall what happened to you on W1 after being transferred to P8."

"But...I don't get it, why would they do that to us?" Her voice shook.

Zee piped in with her usual, politically-correct clipped tone. "Greed from the higher-ups. They needed energy. And they saw an opportunity."

Luna glanced over at Zee. "Energy?"

Jay leaned back, swinging his feet encased in hot pink high tops onto the table. "Hate to say it girlfriend, but these sexy bodies of ours are considered a power source. Cue energy outposts."

"They theorized that the human body could become a 'renewable' source of energy, given the right conditions," I explained.

Luna looked curious now. She leaned forward. "So how does it work?"

Zee chimed in again. Pushing her glasses up her snubbed nose with authority. "You are essentially wired into virtual reality, and your energy is siphoned off." She shuddered. "It's barbaric, if you ask me. The sooner Scott and Beth figure out an alternative to the use of people, the better. The person inside the coffin is plugged in, while the body is maintained. These centers where the cages are placed are called energy outposts. And they are all over the country."

Luna sprang up from her chair and paced the room, raking a shaking hand through her tangled hair. "How are you so calm about all this? And how is this even allowed? You can't just use people like that, it's inhuman. All of this sounds way over the top. You actually expect me to believe all of this?" She stopped and whirled on all of us.

"Yeah, we do," Zee said. "You did wake up in a cage, did you not? And what reason would we have to tell you a falsehood? We have no time for games here, Luna."

Luna turned her big green eyes on me. "If what you're saying is true. And this is my real life. I want more proof. I heard Zee mention my parents, Zander. I want to meet them."

CHAPTER 7

LUNA

The entire room went silent.

Zander cast his gaze downward, not wanting to look me in the eye. "I don't think that's a good idea."

"What is that supposed to mean?" I demanded.

Before Zander could respond, the room exploded into furious beeping. Zee jumped out of her seat, her hand gripping her com so hard her knuckles turned white.

"Oh my God. An emergency meeting is happening in five across the street. Threat level seven has been issued. We're being tracked. Everybody move!"

Zee shoved her com into her pocket and picked up her tablet from the table. Zander took my hand, about to follow the others, when Zee put a hand on his chest.

"Do you really think it's a good idea to bring her? Considering everything?"

I dislodged her hand and moved closer putting my body in front of Zander's—so I was almost eye to eye with Zee. "Is this the big secret you don't want to be leaked?"

"All right, enough, you two." Zander stepped between us. "Zee you're being ridiculous; Luna is a member of this team and is coming with us."

She scowled disapprovingly at me for a moment, then saw the time on her watch. "I'm going to be late!"

"Well, that would be a first," Zander muttered under his breath. "Come on, Luna, let's go. We don't want her to shut us out."

He took hold of my hand again, and led me into the immaculate hallway, towards the elevator where the drone had dropped me earlier.

The elevator doors slid open and Zander swiped his palm on the ID pad. "Main floor," he said. The robotic doors squeezed together, and shuttled us to the lobby. It looked like any ordinary reception area—deceptive probably for safety reasons, after all, they wouldn't want anyone to discover what really went on in this place. They had even laid a nice welcome mat at the entrance.

We exited the gateway, and I took in my first glimpse of the city. I stopped mid stride surprised at its unusual character. Lantern lights illuminated very familiar-looking streets, casting deep shadows on the emerald-colored pavement. I stared at the odd buildings—rather than high rises, they spiraled downward, coring into the earth in an intricate maze.

"Follow me," Zander said. He cut across an expanse of green grass—identical to the other lawns that encircled all the inverted structures—and hopped on one of the clear skyways that led us to an elaborate entry guarded by old stone columns. A robot stood on duty, but said nothing to us as we walked past. It didn't seem like very good security measures were kept here.

As if Zander read my mind he said, "He has face recognition technology. Only those scanned into the system have access." He went through the rotating door, pulling me from behind.

Zander saw Zee and yelled at her to hold the elevator. She smirked at him and let it close.

"Damn it," Zander complained, slamming his hand on the now closed door.

"There's one free over here," I said. "Come on."

Zander followed me down the hall and into the empty elevator car. He pushed a button on the panel, and we began our descent.

I didn't say anything as we rode down, still annoyed with him about vetoing my idea to meet with my parents. I nearly asked him what his problem was—but the elevator had already arrived at ground level. On the way out, I glimpsed a diagram of the building—and realized this complex descended into a pyramid shape, and we were at the point. This floor opened straight out into a spacious room, filled with about twenty people, all of whom turned to stare at us as we entered. I didn't recognize anybody, save for the small group I met earlier.

Zander nodded his head in greeting and then eased quietly into a backseat by the wall. I followed suit.

"As I was saying, we need to discover how they are tracking us. If we don't, we risk being exposed," said a tall woman addressing the gathering. She wore army camo and black boots that screamed old school military. Her pink hair, cut pixie style, spiked out in all directions giving the impression she had run her fingers through it a few times instead of using a comb. I noted she had mismatched eyes. One blue, one brown. I wondered what W1 would think of that.

I swallowed hard when I remembered Zander's words. W1 was fake, a stupid game. Yet this life—this crazy new one—was real.

My stomach pitched, bile threatening to rise in my throat. I put a shaking hand to my neck, as if that could calm my pounding heart. My palm came upon something small and hard in my collar. I tried to pull at it but it seemed buried in the stretchy fabric. I worked my fingers over the object trying to figure out what it was. Finally, I just yanked at it, and ripped it away from the neckline. Curious, I pulled it out and examined the small contraption, little more than the size of a button. I turned it over, face up, and the interface blinked, casting a red glow against my palm.

Whatever the purpose of the strange object, it couldn't be good. What if there was more than one tracker? I nudged Zander.

He briefly glanced over at me, his attention focused mainly on the lady still rambling at the front of the weird triangle room.

"What is this?" I hissed, giving him another prod and shoving the device under his nose. "I found it sewn into my neckline."

Zander finally looked down and stiffened, visibly turning pale as he registered what I held in my outstretched hand. Even before he said anything, I knew.

It was a tracker.

He grabbed it from me, stood up and began to shout to the crowd. "The tracking device is here."

Zander threw the gadget to the carpet and smashed it with his foot. "Everyone disperse now! If the government cronies catch this many of us together, we're done for."

A loud murmur broke out amongst the crowd.

The camo clad woman who seemed to be in charge raised her hands for quiet. "Where did the tracker come from Zander?"

My cheeks flamed with embarrassment. I wanted to retch. This was my fault; we were going to have to run, because of me.

Like a stubborn idiot, I had refused to take off my clothing and put on fresh attire in front of that damned robot. What was her name? Wendy? Wanda? Some crap like that. It had given me the heebie-jeebies the way those shifting grey eyes followed my every move.

Now, look at the mess I had gotten us into.

"It's not important where it came from, Cassandra. What matters most is it's been destroyed. And for the safety of the resistors, I suggest we separate into our respective groups and immediately head to our secure houses." Zander said, covering for me.

A female voice I didn't recognize piped in shrilly from somewhere in the middle of the group. "Obviously, it was Luna. We can't trust her. I think she—."

"Enough, Madeline. We will discuss this later. Scott and Beth are well aware of Luna and Zander's circumstances, so we will take our cues from them. I will debrief them on the events of this meeting. But for now, I urge everyone to take this breach of security seriously. Depart in groups of three or four and please spread out, go to your assigned emergency safe house. Over and out."

The voices, only a murmur a moment ago, now erupted into a loud crescendo. Everyone in the room turned and cast a suspicious eye on me, then looked away, gossiping about their theories as soon as they thought I was out of earshot.

Crane popped up out of nowhere in front of me, reminding me of Tigger from Trinity's Winnie the Pooh book. I'd stolen it from a rich kid while hustling for food on the streets. I figured she could easily get another. And I'd have done it again—it had made Trinity happy for months.

"How exciting was that?" Crane whooped. "You acted like a frickin' superhero when you destroyed that tracker." He clapped Zander on the back. "I totally feel bad though, I should've spoken up for Luna," he said regretfully. "I'm her protector, after all. It just happened so fast I was stunned—"

Zander placed a hand on Crane's skinny arm. "Crane. Calm down. No sense in worrying. Besides we have a bigger problem, like where we're going to stay. Do you have a safe house for us? We need a place to sleep tonight."

He beamed. "Yup. Sorted it all out. Did you want to grab your stuff first? He asked dubiously regarding my hideous leotard.

I stood taller and smoothed down my coat, trying to hide my humiliation.

"We don't own anything Crane, remember? Everything we possessed would be at the capital—and that was probably destroyed ages ago. We only ever visited New Earth before, so there isn't much here for us."

"Did my parents keep my things?" I asked hopefully.

Crane let out a low whistle. "If they did, I wouldn't want to retrieve them, protector or not. I'd rather lose all my teeth."

"Crane..." Zander said, exasperated.

He looked sheepish. "Okay. Okay. I get it. I'll butt out. Let's move. Cassandra is shooting the stink eye at me—and it's the brown one. I don't like that. Her blue eye is kinder, you know?" Laughing, Zander shook his head and pushed him toward the door.

Crane led the way, talking nonstop until we reached street level, then Zander interrupted his chatter and turned to me.

"Sorry I didn't warn you about the tracker. You took me by surprise. And as soon as I registered what you were holding in your hand, my gut instinct told me to destroy the thing. I didn't mean to embarrass you like that."

I ignored his platitudes. I didn't need to be reminded of my humiliation—or the fact I may have unwittingly brought the government to the compound. So, instead I changed the subject.

"Why are you so against me seeing my parents? I mean they could help, right? If nothing else, it would be somewhere to crash."

I didn't mention my vision—but I knew they had to be the parents Zander referred to earlier.

"You can't live with them, Luna. We ran away. We're going to have to jump around safe houses for a bit until the coast is clear. Besides..." he trailed off.

I scowled. "Let me guess. You can't tell me the real reason."

Zander stopped walking, turning to look me straight in the eye. "Luna, you can't see them because they're the ones who locked you up and threw away the key."

CHAPTER 8

ZANDER

"You were never more than an experiment to them, Luna."

Luna stepped back. "Experiment? I thought we were energy objects or whatever you call it."

I shifted uncomfortably. "Well in our case, both."

She crossed her arms. "Oh really. Do tell," she said sarcastically.

"Look, we have to catch up with Crane. We can talk and walk." I took her arm and propelled her forward.

"The bottom line is your parents weren't the nicest folks in the world. Why do you want to find them so much anyway, knowing what they did to you? I don't get it."

"I have my reasons. Let's just leave it at that," she said mysteriously.

I eyed her suspiciously. "Is there something you're not telling me, Luna?"

She rolled her eyes. "I think you have bigger problems than worrying about me. Your friend Crane is trying to get your attention."

I squinted, peering into the dark; Crane had halted about six feet in front of us, waiting. The bright neon yellow jacket he wore shone like a beacon in the blackness—not exactly covert—

and to top it off, he was waving his arms at us like he was flagging down a cab in old New York.

"He enjoys the protector gig. Besides, he's your friend too."

She stopped short again. I groaned. "Luna, what part of, 'you had a tracker on you,' did you not understand? Keep walking."

"Not until you explain to me why in the hell we need a protector. Also, what possible reason would there be for someone to choose us for an experiment?"

"Keep moving and I'll tell you."

She raised a sardonic eyebrow.

"Scout's honor," I said holding up three fingers.

She scowled but started walking again. I looked ahead and noticed Crane was still waving to get my attention. I gave him a high signal in return.

He immediately lowered his arms and excitedly hightailed back to us. "We made it. Last house on the corner. Do you guys want me to—"

I cut him off. "Actually Crane, would you mind giving us a minute? We'll be right in. Thanks for leading the way and getting us here safely."

Crane puffed up his chest with pride. "It's my job to please." He gave a quick salute and grinned. "See you inside, Captain."

"Crane you don't have to call me—"

But he was already gone, enveloped by the darkness.

I breathed out heavily, wondering how to explain to Luna everything she needed to know. I sighed; it wouldn't be easy. She could be so pig-headed at times.

When we reached the house, I took a minute to look around. I hadn't visited this part of the city before. My meetings were usually confined to headquarters. It was difficult to tell in the dark, but my guess was we were in one of the poorer sections of town. A trash bin overflowed onto the sidewalk, and I caught a glimpse of the glowing gold eyes of a rat staring at me from an alleyway. No doubt annoyed we were impeding on his territory. I bet money he had friends close by. The hair on the back of my neck prickled in alert. I had a gut instinct that more than rat eyes were watching us. Clearly, we couldn't linger here too long; this whole area held a dangerous vibe.

Just spit out what you need to say and get inside, Zander.

"So, are you going to talk or what?" Luna demanded as we stopped in front of the weedy path leading up to the safe house.

She tapped her foot impatiently as she waited for me to answer.

I stuffed my hands in my pockets but looked her in the eye, hoping she understood I was shooting straight with her.

"Luna, we're both Elite. Does that ring any bells for you?"

Her brow furrowed, and she bit her lip. Almost as if willing herself to recall the name. Finally, she gave up and kicked at the dirt. "God, this is frustrating."

Pain flashed in her eyes. I couldn't imagine how strange this must seem to her.

I took a deep breath. "Elite 9 was a rare, now extinct, mineral that could bond to a host. When introduced to living test subjects, they discovered it conformed to the DNA, giving the host a unique ability—time travel. However, most don't survive the DNA transformation."

Luna shook her head. "I don't understand. What does this mineral have to do with us?"

"Tyrone Harrison and his group of cronies, known as the Black Mark or *Nigrum Markam*, figured out a way around that. They inserted the Elite 9 into an embryo. A human embryo in the beginning stages of DNA development. They found that the embryos survived at this level and eventually were even able to grow into healthy children."

Luna gasped. "Isn't that illegal? Did they do studies to identify the risks to the child?" She frowned.

"Luna, the Black Mark is in the government's back pocket for a very important reason. They're using the children as pawns for their own purposes. Once they reach maturity, they plan on sending them back through time to alter three key events in history that ultimately led to the planet's destruction. The only problem is they don't know if they can safely bring them back. It's like sending lambs to the slaughter."

Luna stepped closer, peering at my face. "So, we're supposed to stop them, right? Is that why we're so important in all this? Why we need protection?" Her voice was earnest, almost pleading.

But I think deep down, she knew the answer.

"No, Luna. You and I are two of those embryos. We're the Elite. The mineral lives inside us—and the government will go to any lengths to get us back. And I mean any. As for your parents? They're the ones that agreed to donate you. You're an experiment for the cause."

Luna looked at me, aghast, not able to believe the truth.

A memory flashed across my mind—the day we met. She'd been given up by her parents only hours before and had just been assigned to my group. Her face now held the same look of raw horror as it had then.

Soon after that day, we began plotting our escape.

But we failed. I had failed her.

And with every cell in my body, I wished I could change it.

As I watched her, something shifted in Luna's gaze. A steely gray flint flashed in those green eyes, and she lifted her chin in determination.

"I'm going to find my parents, Zander. Uncover the real truth."

Before I could stop her, she'd raced up the overgrown path and pushed open the door of the house and darted inside, slamming it shut behind her.

I stood in shocked silence.

This was not good news.

CHAPTER 9

LUNA

In my haste to escape Zander, I didn't look where I was going and ran smack into a solid body.

My heart caught in my throat.

An odd-smelling mixture of cherries and metal filled my nostrils, and I pulled back to see who or what I'd collided with.

My worries abated a little when I realized I'd run into a woman. But no ordinary woman. She was stunning, akin more to a Greek goddess than mere mortal. Her gleaming ebony hair hung in cascading waves down her back and her flawless olive complexion glowed. She loomed over me, and I instinctively shrank back, recoiling into myself like a diminutive snail. Her cold gaze made me squirm, making me feel like a freak of nature. I concluded that perhaps I was right—definitely a goddess.

Crane suddenly popped up between us, and I nearly jumped out of my skin. I put a hand to my chest. "Crane, you scared me half to death!" When I had a chance to recollect myself, I turned to him and whispered, "Who's the chick with legs for days?" Nodding at Miss Greek Goddess.

The unworldly violet eyes continued to stare blankly at me. With an awkward tug, I pulled my filthy lab coat around myself.

Crane handed me a tissue, ignoring my question. "Want to talk about those tears?"

Embarrassed, I snatched the tissue out of his hand and wiped away the tears. I didn't realize I'd been crying. "Of course not. What are you, a therapist as well?" I snapped.

He opened his arms wide. "I can be anything you want me to be, oh wise one."

"You're such a smart ass."

He beamed at me.

"So, are you going to tell me who or what this stunner is? A friend of yours?" I asked, pointing at fantasy Barbie.

Crane puffed out his chest. "Might be."

I circled her, examining every detail. "Spill, oh wise one," I said sarcastically, throwing his words back at him.

"Her name is Ariel 5, the best cyborg in New Earth," Crane said.

"She's exquisite. If she hadn't eyeballed me so intensely, I might never have noticed she was an automaton. Where did she come from? She's the most beautiful droid I've ever come across. Even better than Burt," I said.

"I prefer the term robotic companion," Ariel 5 said with a purr. "It's more politically correct."

I raised my eyebrows at Crane, he helplessly held up his hands. "Okay, okay, I may have set the voice to sexy kitten. But look at her. She's magnificent, and I am a man, after all."

I shook my head but couldn't withhold a burst of laughter. "Okay, Mr. Macho," I teased.

"But why don't you call her sexy kitten then?"

Crane's cheeks flamed. "Well...um..."

"I'm kidding, Crane."

"Right, of course you are." He pushed his unruly red mop away from his face and pointed to Ariel 5. "Ariel here is going to escort you upstairs, show you where you can clean up a bit, and also get a change of clothes. Not that the leotard isn't...I mean..."

"I think the word you are looking for is sexy," Ariel 5 interjected.

Crane chuckled loudly, waving Ariel 5 away. "She's a robot, she sometimes repeats stuff she overhears. One of Beth's cast-offs she donated to the cause. Ariel probably needs a few kinks worked out."

"I can run a diagnostic," Ariel purred.

I grinned. "I think she likes you, Crane."

Crane tugged at the neck of his t-shirt. "Anyhoo," he said, side-stepping my snide remark. "Take the first set of stairs to your right. Your room is the third one down. There's some clothes in the dresser-drawer you can pick from; you should be able to find something that fits."

"Thanks," I said, biting my lip trying to stifle a giggle. "I'm sure Ariel and I will be fine."

"Yes. I am ready for my assignment, Crane. Unless you need anything else."

"Uh. no. Please, you ladies enjoy yourselves." He spun on his heels and disappeared into the kitchen.

I turned to Ariel 5. "Is he always like that?" I asked.

"One moment. Let me check. I heard a slight clicking as if her entire brain had to activate to figure it out. Then she said, "Historical data from past interactions indicate, Crane Sky, is showing typical behavior patterns."

I grinned at her. "Good to know."

"If there are no further questions, please allow me to show you to your room," she replied.

"Of course. After you."

"I'm sorry, I don't compute."

"It means you can walk ahead of me."

"Certainly."

Ariel 5 glided up the stairs, a faint whir emanating from the pistons in her hips. I trailed behind, fascinated. She moved smoothly, ascending each wooden stair effortlessly until she reached the landing. Quite a few people passed us, and I wondered how many of us were staying at this safe house. Nobody seemed to take any notice of Ariel or me for that matter. She led me to a small room, simple but tidy. A single bed hugged the corner wall, and a chipped dresser stood beside it. A Navajo patterned rug covered the linoleum floor, bringing a touch of color to the drab beige decor.

Ariel glided across the room and opened one of the drawers. "According to my calculations, these pants I found in my inventory will fit you perfectly. She pulled out a pair of worn blue jeans, one knee a little ripped, but otherwise serviceable. I wanted to ask who they belonged to, but Ariel appeared engrossed in her mission to find me a suitable outfit. She took out a purple sweatshirt and some undergarments.

"The sweater is one size too big, but based on your dimensions it will be comfortable. The underwear is new. I understand this is important to the human population."

"Right. Well, thanks," I said lamely.

"No thanks is required," she purred. "Now come this way." I sighed. Crane definitely needed to fix her voice setting—she sounded like a hooker.

I followed her out of the bedroom, through a connecting door, and into an old-fashioned bathroom. The tan toilet matched the mottled walls. A standalone shower completed the space.

Ariel bustled to the vanity and pulled open the cabinet below. She gathered up a small towel and placed it on a rusty crooked rack hanging near the stall. "You can bathe here, then rest." She went to the shower, indicating a button on the wall. "Use this to turn the water on and off. Quick showers are encouraged. Water is a precious commodity."

She motioned for me to follow her back out into the main room. "I have instructions to procure you a travel bag for the duration, since all your personal effects seem to be lost."

"I'm not sure I had any to begin with," I muttered.

Ariel's face crinkled into an unnatural frown. "I'm sorry, I don't compute."

"It's nothing. Forget I said anything."

"Of course, Luna. Consider it forgotten."

It was so weird to hear my name spoken in that sexy kitten vibration. Hell, I might rewire Ariel myself, right here on the spot, if it meant I didn't have to listen to her x-rated operator's tone anymore. However, I managed to restrain myself and returned my concentration to her instructions.

"I will collect all the items required and leave them in the chair by the door. Do you need any food refreshment before I go?"

"No, that's okay," I said rubbing my belly. "I don't think I could eat anything." My queasy stomach had twisted itself into knots. "Do you have any bottled water?"

Ariel tilted her head as if confused for a minute. "Ah yes. Bottled water. An outdated model for water containment. I'm sorry due to the environmental act of 2060, the use of plastics in any form for food or beverage is completely forbidden. However, there is a glass on the sink, you may fill that with water from the tap. It is a standard water quality."

"Okay," I mumbled. Had I just received a lecture on plastic from a robot?

She bowed then. "Signing off. Ariel 5 for Luna Redwood." She abruptly turned and left, clicking the open door shut behind her.

I looked around, alone for the first time since waking up in that ghastly cage. I sat down on the edge of the bed and rubbed my face. My whole body ached, and my head pounded. I should have asked her for something for the pain. Probably best I didn't. I might have risked a serious talk from her on drug usage.

Maybe I'd find some painkillers in the bathroom. I crossed to the small vanity mirror above the sink and pulled at the front corner. Sure enough, it opened, but revealed nothing but empty rusted shelves.

I closed it dejectedly and caught a glimpse of my reflection, wincing. The neat ponytail I had put in earlier hung in a tangled mess around my face. As for the lab coat, it didn't even look like a lab coat anymore, it was so covered in grime. I quickly shrugged it off and inspected the skin-colored leotard underneath. The neckline sagged a little where I had torn away the hidden tracker revealing a small amount of blood where I must have caught my skin in my haste to get it out. I ripped the fabric further away and saw it was only a small scratch, nothing too bad. My skin crawled at the mere touch of the government issued one piece, and I quickly stripped it off.

I pushed the button on the shower and jumped in, gasping as the frigid water hit my skin. Apparently, hot water wasn't an option. Back on W1, I had plenty of cold baths, but here in this dimly lit bathroom, it all seemed a bit overwhelming. I leaned my forehead against the tiled wall.

I had to remember W1 wasn't real, not Mama, Trinity, or Dara. It was just a game. We'd all been pawns in some sick version of virtual reality. I pounded my fist against the tiles, Zander's words echoing in my mind.

You're Elite.

I didn't want to believe it.

Were we really that special?

I sank to my knees, allowing the icy water to wash over me, blending in with my salty tears. The sound of the cascading water muffled my sobs as I grieved for the only life I had ever known.

I recalled zero about this strange barren wasteland I found myself in.

And I had no clue how to act or be in this hostile environment. My only lifeline being a snapshot memory of my so-called parents. Zander must have thought I was a complete nut job for wanting to meet my parents so much, especially after what he told me about them. Let him think whatever the hell he wanted. That wasn't my problem. I had to find that disk.

Exhausted and emotionally spent, I let myself sob until no more tears came. I was pretty sure I'd used every ounce of water in the house. I didn't care. They could all rot in hell.

They lied to me.

And I would be damned before I let one more person boss me around.

Because I finally had a plan.

CHAPTER 10

ZANDER

I knocked quietly on Luna's door, filled with a mixture of longing and trepidation. The hallway, awash with morning sunlight, illuminated the dust bunnies floating like feathers in the air. I watched, still amazed at the ingenuity of the underground.

When engineers constructed New Earth they managed to configure in the remaining natural light, adding it to the artificial, then directing it below ground using a system of remote skylights based on parabolic reflectors and wireless optic fiber cables. From there, they utilized electronic coding to channel the light through a program that created the sense of sunrise and sunset. It kept the human body functioning at a healthy metabolic rhythm.

I shifted nervously back and forth on my feet as I waited. I left Luna alone last night, knowing she needed sleep. But now there was no putting it off. Her life was in danger.

"Luna?" I whispered softly through the door. "It's Zander. We need to talk."

I expected to be ignored—or at best she'd crack the door ajar, barely awake, forgetting how much she loathed the sight of me.

But instead, a fresh-faced Luna swung the door open, her hair brushed smoothly back into her signature ponytail. She looked incredible, already dressed in tight fitting jeans and an oversized purple sweatshirt. I swallowed hard, unable to stop staring.

"I've decided to find my parents Zander. And you're not going to stop me."

My thoughts came crashing back to reality. "Well, good morning to you, too."

She glared at me. "You dumped a lot of crap on me last night. And I don't have any way to discern fact from fiction. But one thing I'm sure about is I need to talk to Mom and Dad."

I bridged the gap between us and tried to take hold of her hands, but she backed off and went to sit on the bed.

I sighed and strode over to the window, the view only a brick wall from the adjacent building. "Look, Luna. I'm just trying to protect you. The last thing I want is for you to end up back in that glass cage. But if you find your parents, you may as well sign your life away." I turned to face her, almost begging her to see reason.

But her arms were crossed defiantly, her eyes lit with furious sparks. "What about your parents, Zander? Don't you want to see them?"

I looked down at my feet, embarrassed. "I don't have any."

Luna snorted. "Everyone has parents. Nice try."

I ran a hand through my hair. "No. I mean I don't know who they are. I'm an orphan."

She stood then, a light of compassion in her eyes. "I'm sorry about your parents, Zander, but you have to understand, I need to find mine. It's important. Please don't try to stop me."

"I went to her and pulled her back onto the bed. "I promise I would never deny you your parents. What kind of monster do you think I am? For God's sake, I'm just trying to protect you. Can't you understand that?"

She stared down at her hands, avoiding my gaze. Then after a beat, she lifted her chin. "You don't get to decide this for me. I do."

A pain suddenly pierced my skull, and Luna disappeared into a blur.

I recognized the signs. A vision. I hadn't had one in so long. My mouth went dry, as a familiar, ashen-grey face swam into view. The glassy eyes were vacant, devoid of life. I staggered to my feet, about to vomit.

Someone was dead—one of our own.

Before I could explain my odd behavior to Luna, Crane burst into the room breathless, his red hair flying out like a horse's mane behind him. "There's been a murder. We just found the body. We must evacuate to another safe house, one on the other side of the city. They're expecting us. Hurry, this place could be raided at any moment!"

He raced off to warn the others.

The nausea I'd experienced a few seconds ago vanished almost instantly, replaced by naked fear. How would I coax Luna to come?

I needn't have worried; she'd already snagged her backpack and headed for the door. She looked pale and her hands shook, but apart from that, you'd never know anything was amiss.

We didn't speak as we walked briskly down the stairs. The lower floor had erupted in noisy chaos as people jostled and scrambled for the exit.

I scanned the room, and my eyes landed on Sepha, who manned the front door. She placed two fingers to her lips, releasing a piercing wolf whistle. Everyone stilled. Sepha, one of the resistors' most experienced protectors, demanded respect. Luna and I were her assignments at the moment. She'd not changed since I last saw her, tall and slender but with the strength of a warrior. Her indigo streaked hair decorated with multicolored beads framed a high cheek-boned bronzed face. But her most arresting feature lay in her azure blue eyes, which right now commanded the room as she spoke.

"Resistors! Calm down. Protocol 1098 is in place for a reason. Stand down and create order. The two officers in charge today will remain and deal with the fallout."

The crowd immediately broke off into groups of two and filed systematically out the door. I grabbed my backpack from under the stairwell and guided Luna to the exit. As we passed Sepha, she clapped me on the shoulder. "Welcome back, Barringer. Redwood. Good to see you." She glanced at her tablet, then said, "Head to safe house ten and try not to get caught this' time."

Luna snorted as soon as we were out of earshot. "Who the hell was that? She was rude."

"Sepha. Another one of our protectors."

"No wonder we're screwed," Luna muttered under her breath. "How many protectors do we have, anyway?"

"Two. Crane and Sepha."

"Now keep your head low, and don't talk to anyone on the street. Pull your hoodie up."

Annoyance flashed across her features. I could see she wanted to argue, but decided against it. And without another word, we merged into the sea of people from the morning rush.

Whoever had killed that resistor had sent a clear message.

They wouldn't stop until we were found.

CHAPTER 11

LUNA

The new safe house turned out to be a mirrored fortress that perched on a hill overlooking the city. Despite being sandwiched between two other buildings, a clear view to the west gave a perfect lookout.

For the first time, I had an aerial vista of the underground city. No cars whizzed by in this metropolis, only battery-powered carts and horses—and instead of black asphalt, strange smooth green streets lined the avenues. Why all the antiquated technology? This place literally lived in the dark ages.

As we walked up the cement path to the inverted high rise, Zander explained, as if reading my thoughts. "We utilize a lot of reusable energies down here—thermogenic, hydro. They even use a few human batteries, but they are gradually weaning themselves off those, for obvious reasons. Cars are strictly prohibited, save for the produce trucks that head to the capital, and even those are scarce. The last thing we need is car pollutants destroying what we've tried so hard to build. We even reuse biodegradables and turn them into workable concrete that comes out this green color," he said pointing to the street. "The olive shade releases less heat into the false atmosphere than traditional black."

Zander opened the door and ushered me through. Crane was already there, standing at attention just inside the entrance, a big silly grin plastered across his face. The hot pink t-shirt he wore with its glitter lightning bolt and the word warrior emblazoned across the front, officially announced him as a complete knucklehead. He spread his arms wide. "Welcome home! Not too shabby, huh?" He gave us a wink.

Crane's voice faded into the background, as I gawked at the interior of the place—it was like we had stepped into an ice castle. What appeared to be swirling glass walls held up heavy wooden beams, though it was unlikely to be wood with no natural grain. Probably constructed out of some kind of biodegradable material —which made sense, since trees must be in short supply around here. I reached up a hand and touched the smooth surface, cool to the touch but much more malleable than I expected. I lifted my eyes skyward and could see now that the roof was composed of the same identical clear material, revealing the man-made sky above. Sure, the atmosphere wasn't quite as good as the real deal —the blue, a little too blue, and the clouds never moved—as if stuck in a painting—but it was still convincing.

Zander nudged me forward, jolting me from my musings. "Come on. You're hungry. I'll show you where you can drop your stuff, and then we can go down to the cafeteria. Crane said there's one on level six."

I whirled on him. "How did you guess I was hungry, are you a mind reader or something?" I demanded.

Zander gave a broad smile, and I hated that I found it comforting. He pointed to my belly. "Your stomach growled."

I blushed. "Fine. Maybe I'm a little hungry."

"Right this way my lady," Zander said giving me a sweeping bow. If he thought for one minute he could lighten my mood by being funny, he was dead wrong. I scowled at him.

"Tough crowd," Zander muttered, motioning me to follow him.

"Where did Crane go?" I asked ignoring the gesture.

Before I could hear Zander's response, another pain shot through my head, less intense this time—but enough that I knew I was getting another memory. This was one was brief, a flash like a photograph. Hazy images cleared to show my parents once more—but this time they weren't alone.

A man I didn't recognize towered over my parents—slender and well over six feet tall. His slick black hair neatly combed, gave him an air of authority. A tiny scar in what looked to be the shape of a star at the corner of his right eye stood out against his pale skin. All three of them watched someone I couldn't see, with a fierce intensity—and I realized, with sudden clarity, it had to be me.

I felt a hand on my arm, and I jumped startling back to reality.

Zander cocked an eyebrow at me. "Weren't you listening? He went ahead to grab something to eat. He'll meet up with us later."

"Right...of course...I forgot," I hedged, my mind still consumed by the mysterious man I'd seen with my parents. His forced smile and sharp blue eyes had given off a cruel demeanor not easily forgotten. I shook my head trying to rid myself of the stranger's face. I could try to figure out who he was later. First, I had to get my bearings.

Zander smirked. "You can admit it. You zoned Crane out. Don't worry we've all done it. He likes to talk." Zander placed a hand at my back. "Now, can we go?"

Reluctantly, I trailed behind Zander through the expansive mezzanine and downward into one of the glass tunnels that would carry us deeper into the building. We passed a couple of office floors and some rec rooms where people played table tennis, cards, and other games. Things I'd only read about in history books. Few watched television—not a popular pastime, apparently.

Finally, we reached the fourth floor. Zander left the walkway and exited onto an adjacent hallway. "Why don't you take the elevator?" I inquired curiously.

"The elevators are another drain on energy. Until we find a good source of power that doesn't come from human batteries, we cut corners wherever possible. We do have magnetic levitation systems in many buildings, but this one is still powered by electricity, so everyone in this safe house uses the walkways. We have rigged up the battery-powered footpaths to help you move a little quicker if you need to. But around here, using your good old-fashioned legs is considered the preferable and wisest option. And of course, big surprise, the capital refuses the new technology because they hate change and believe anything coming out of New Earth is likely inferior."

I didn't respond to that, still pondering this strange, new place. Zander entered a large room, that had about ten sets of bunk beds lined up against stark white walls. "This is where we'll sleep tonight. We never know how many beds will be filled each night. Depends on the workload. I recommend taking the closest available one to the door you can find, that way you get first dibs on the communal bathroom in the morning. At least that's what Crane says. But you can never be too sure with him," he grinned sheepishly. "Any bed without a pack is fair game. It's still early, most resistors haven't arrived yet, except for those that escaped with us from the last safe house. So, it's your lucky day, you get your pick of bunks."

He rambled on, nervously. He'd yet to mention the murder—maybe this was his way of coping. However, you could hardly call babbling on about bunk beds an emotional upheaval—especially for Zander. He was more in touch with his feelings that I was. Hell—I was freaked enough for both of us, but no way would I let him see that.

I paused a minute, thinking. Might this be some big conspiracy? I'd seen no evidence of a dead body, and Zander had whipped me away from the place pretty fast. What if everyone was in on it? Even Crane seemed to recover quickly from the shock.

But what would be the point?

I sank down on the nearest bunk bed and dropped my pack, closing my eyes for a minute, not giving a flip that Zander stood over me, staring like a hawk. I replayed again the memory of my parents. As I observed the scene, the same sensations returned —that gut instinct that told me the disk in their possession was very important to the cause. Well, at least to my cause. I didn't know enough about anybody here to trust them yet. But I would soon figure it out. The vision of my mother and father would remain a secret until that time came.

"Luna? Are you okay?" Zander crouched down in front of me in concern. "Do you feel sick?" He put a hand to my forehead.

I kept my eyes closed, enjoying the comfort of his touch. Zander lied too much for me to trust him, but sometimes the loneliness overwhelmed me. My heart skipped a beat as unwanted feelings bubbled to the surface. Worried they would be my undoing.

I needed to stop. Be strong. Emotions like this made you weak.

"Luna? Is there something wrong?" I felt the familiar tug of his fingers as he brushed back a strand of my wayward hair.

I jerked my eyes open and swatted his hand away. "I'm fine." I jumped to my feet and smoothed down the nonexistent wrinkles on my jeans. "A little light-headed is all. It's been a while since I ate."

Not a total lie. I had barely consumed a mouthful of food since I'd woken up in that god-forsaken coffin.

"Well let's go eat then," he said picking up his pack and hurling it onto the top bunk.

I swallowed hard. I could handle sleeping near Zander, this wouldn't be a problem. He meant nothing to me. I just had to remind myself of all the stuff he'd kept from me and it would be easy to believe.

Still, somehow that didn't stop me from letting Zander take my hand and lead me to the dining area.

⚶

The cafeteria, with its ornate fresco interior, looked like a cute cafe in Paris. Mosaic tiles covered the floor, and wicker chairs with glass-covered tables made for an inviting atmosphere. Chandeliers hung from the high ceiling, casting a warm light onto the shrubs and potted plants dotted around the atrium. Jazz music piped in through hidden speakers, created a faux bubble of tranquility.

Zander grabbed two trays from the stack next to the buffet table, handing one over to me. "Help yourself, the food is free to all resistors staying here. We lucked out, this is by far the nicest of the safe houses, and they have the best grub."

"This is the most food I've ever seen in my life," I whispered in awe, staring at the mounds of fruit, vegetables, desserts, and multiple covered dishes spread out across the gold leaf table.

"You won't find any animal products here, but they've come up with some really creative replacements," Zander said piling his plate high with some kind of pasta.

"I'm not picky. Anything is better than having a hollow belly-ache all the time."

Zander paused holding a tong full of green leafy salad. "How bad was it? On W1, I mean. The stories coming out of that place sound pretty gruesome. I was fortunate in a way, I only had to deal with P8."

"W1 is not reality, according to you, anyway. So, does it matter?"

Zander put the tongs down and turned to me, placing a hand on my shoulder. "Of course, it matters. VR is no joke. It feels very real. And the memories of those experiences haunt even the strongest of people."

I shrugged. "I got the short end of the stick. My eye scan placed me at the bottom of society. Hunger wasn't a foreign concept. But I managed okay." I busied myself by grabbing a plate—not wanting to meet his gaze. "Now what's good here?" I asked, changing the topic of conversation.

Zander took the hint. "Pretty much everything, honestly. The food here is great." He tried to appear cheerful—but his drooped shoulders and flat monotone voice gave him away.

I gritted my teeth. I didn't want anyone feeling sorry for me.

I picked up a miniature mock-chicken pot pie, French fries, some kind of chocolate mousse, and a salad filled with vegetables I'd never seen before. A little early for lunch, but I was starving.

We found a corner table and sat down. I looked around owlishly. "Shouldn't we be worried about being seen out in the open?"

Zander shook his head. "Don't worry, we're among friends. This is the resistors largest headquarters, with top of the line security. You can't enter without facial recognition. Trust me; no one around here wants to return us to those cages."

Zander took a bite of his pasta.

"Why is that?"

"They're on our side, Luna. In fact, we're not the only Elite that Scott and Beth have managed to recruit."

"You talk a lot about Scott and Beth."

"Well, they're the creators of New Earth and their goal is to save the planet. And us. They're important, Lun."

I took a few bites of my chocolate mousse, then decided I better start with the pie first—my P8 mother's voice rushing to mind, scolding me for having dessert first.

She isn't real, Luna. Get a grip.

Zander reached across the table and took my hand. "Hey, it's going to be okay. I promise."

I retracted my hand and refocused on the food. I didn't dare meet his gaze. It would be so easy to cave. "I'm not sure I have the blind faith you do."

He lifted my chin forcing me to look at him. "Well, you can borrow some of mine. Because I have faith in you."

I turned away, and Zander let go of my chin. I didn't want to have this conversation anymore.

I had just finished my pie and started in on the salad when Crane arrived, waltzing up to our table like he owned the place. He grinned at me, giving me the usual salute. "Reporting for duty, Miss Redwood."

I rolled my eyes. "Nobody asked you to be on duty, Crane," I said.

He dropped his hand, deflated. "Okay, fine. I was kidding. But I did come here for a reason."

Zander wiped his mouth with a cloth napkin. "What's up, Crane? Do we have a debriefing?"

"Not yet. Actually, Marshall's here, and he wants to speak with you."

Zander sighed. "I'd hoped to avoid him. Where is he?"

"Meeting room two, same level, down the hall."

"Was Marshall there when they found the body?" Zander asked lowering his voice. "I didn't see him, but I went straight to bed pretty much after we arrived."

Crane nodded. "Yeah, he was on duty before Sepha logged in. He's angry as a honey badger. Not that I'm well versed in honey badger life, I've only seen vids. But man, do they act like ferocious beasts. You don't remember Marshall, Luna. But don't worry, I'm sure all your memories will come together at some point. Believe me, I sometimes forget what I've eaten for breakfast—"

"Crane," Zander said sounding exasperated.

"Am I rambling again? Sorry about that. Are you coming?"

Zander stood and picked up his tray. "Yeah."

I went to follow suit, but Zander motioned for me to remain seated. "This will only take a few minutes. Finish your food. Marshall Raven isn't worth losing a meal over. He's a jerk."

I pointed to his half-eaten pasta. "What about you?"

"If I don't go, he'll come get me. And then we both lose. I'll be back in ten."

"I want to go and see for myself who this Marshall guy is. Maybe he'll jog a memory."

Crane cocked an eyebrow. "No offense, but the last thing you want to do is jog a Marshall memory. And besides, you don't need him to ruin a perfectly enjoyable early lunch." He whipped a French fry from my plate and winked at me before darting off. "Come on, Barringer!" he called.

Zander gave me an apologetic look. "Trust me, it's better this way," he said before scurrying after him.

I slammed down my fork. Who the heck did Zander think he was? I had as much right as anyone to meet this Marshall dude. I had a deep suspicion that there was much more to this meeting than they were telling me.

I smirked. I knew the exact room of their get together, didn't I? It's not my fault if I happened to walk by and take a listen.

I got up casually, grabbed the last few French fries on my plate, stuffing them in my mouth. I looked forlornly at my mousse before putting the tray up.

The mousse I could do without. The answers, not so much.

I spotted a girl reading at a small table under a pretty frond plant and stopped. "Can you tell me where meeting room two is?"

She smiled at me. "Sure. It's on the left, third door down."

"Thanks!" I said, already making my way down the hall. I didn't want to miss a thing.

As I approached the closed door, muffled voices drifted out into the hallway. I looked both ways and seeing no one, pressed my ear to the door.

"...you can't be serious. I realized she was a spy the moment I laid eyes on her. It's obvious she isn't one of us anymore. And why would she be? She doesn't remember *anything*." I bit my lip to contain myself. I knew that voice. Zee.

"Think about it, Zander. You two show up, and the next thing we know, a dead body appears in the closet of one of our airtight safe houses."

"Luna isn't like that, Marshall. She's one of us. After everything, she's been through how can you—"

Marshall cut him off. "Bottom line, Barringer, there is a spy in our midst, a dead body, and someone out there who could be giving away key information. The government sent a clear message—they want us back in our cages. And I am not going to take that warning lying down. Luna is on my radar."

Zander snorted. "You always were a jerk, Marshall. Luna is not the enemy here. She doesn't even have her memories Maybe it's you."

"You don't believe that do you?" Zee scoffed. "Don't you remember what happened to Sepha's old charge, Cosette? After she escaped the game? She chose the government over us, Zander. Luna wants to find her parents. Connect the dots. Besides who's to say she hasn't been lying to you? It wouldn't take much to get you to believe her. Think about it. She could remember everything and be pretending to work for us."

Marshall let out a hollow laugh. "Maybe we should blame Sepha. They have a mutual protector in common."

I gasped as a strong hand clamped down on my arm. I'd been so involved and angry at the conversation, I hadn't heard anyone come up. I whirled to discover Sepha beside me.

"You gonna let them talk about you like that, Redwood? I'm certainly not. I didn't hack you out of your glass cell for you to turn soft."

She opened the door, and I saw the three of them freeze.

"So which one of you assholes is using my name in vain?"

I stepped in behind Sepha, ready to fight. But everything suddenly went to hell, the words dying on my lips as a bright red light started flashing overhead.

An alarm signaled, piercing the air with a high-pitched wail, sending swarms of people into the hall.

Zee flew to her buzzing com. "There's a raid somewhere in the fourth quadrant of the city. We need to take cover. I bet my life they're looking for these two," she said, pointing at Zander and me.

Sepha ignored her and began barking orders. "Down to cellar level now. Lights off. Coms and devices stashed. We have about a ten-minute lead time. I'm going down to the control room to see what's going on and get a better read on the location. I'll voice com anything I find out to you, Marshall."

"Roger that, Sepha." He clapped his hands together. "Move, people, move. This is not a drill. I repeat this is not a drill."

The five of us moved out of the cramped room joining the throng of people now organized into long lines, angling down to the deepest level of the building.

As we pushed our way into a fast-moving line heading toward the moving steps, I asked, "What quadrant are we in?"

Zander pressed his lips together. "Three."

"So they're close."

"Very."

"What are these raids for? Are they just looking for us? Would someone really go to all that trouble?"

Zander's shoulders slumped a little as if the thought of what he was about to say was too much to bear. "Yes and no. Like I told you last night, we are very important to President Reznor and his cabinet."

"President Reznor?"

Zander nodded. "Yes, he is the current president of the Americas. Has been since 2088. When he rose to power, the first thing he did was dismantle the armies and send them to the outposts. He will gather energy at any cost. He promotes the so-called conveniences of the domed cities and how they are the safest place to be."

"Are they?" I asked, while inside I was screaming, *The presi-*

dent of the Americas knows who I am? I swallowed hard against the lump in my throat. This had to be a nightmare I would wake up from.

Zander guided me forward, leading me out of the main area before answering. "No. His goals are to amass power and prestige, and he doesn't care how he achieves them. He's also aware that he needs more people in the outposts because the ones he has in there are dying. Mostly of old age. Not many people are volunteering for the virtual reality life anymore. It used to be, when President Gates was in power, only prisoners were forced to become batteries. He told the American people that criminals received a large percentage of their rations, so it was only fair the incarcerated did their part to ensure the population of United States had what they needed. Suddenly, there was an increase in affordable energy. People could keep their lights on for extended periods, which led to longer working hours. Laborers' wages increased, and the economy improved. Periodically, the military would go through a town and round up troublemakers. And they would disappear, never to be seen again."

I gasped. "They disappeared?"

"Not in the same way as P8. When people mysteriously poofed there, they were simply being taken out of the game. But these troublemakers the government rounded up, disappeared into energy outposts. I swear Luna; I had no clue about any of that stuff until we were out. I didn't even remember we'd been placed in a game. I had memories of New Earth and the domed capital. Moments, snapshots of my life. That's why I told you I had memories too when we were back on P8. But it wasn't everything, not by a long shot. But I discerned enough over time to understand we were trapped. I didn't recall the full details until I woke up here."

He seemed earnest. But how could I be sure? We walked on in silence for a minute as we made our way down into the building. The lights were getting dimmer as we went deeper. Zander, figuring he'd given me enough time to absorb the last bit of information, continued. "A reporter uncovered what they were doing. But there wasn't much of a public outcry because the conveniences of TV, radio, computers and cell phones had been returned. They could cool and heat their homes easily, and it increased the safety in cities across the country. They didn't care how it happened; they were just pleased things were starting to return to normal."

"So why raid us now?"

Zander stepped down to the next lower level, leading to the cellars. He took my hand and helped me down. "My guess is they are looking for us and using the raid as an excuse. Losing us is a huge problem for them. But these raids happened even before our escape. They use them to collect whenever they need."

I felt sick. Would they find us? Turn us back to batteries as punishment? I speculated on my time in W1 and P8. Every memory of mine had been based on a stupid fake reality some gamers had dreamed up?

I shook my head. " It felt so real," I breathed.

Zander squeezed my hand, seeming to understand my train of thought. "I get that it's hard. I can't imagine how difficult this has all been for you, not being able to remember a thing. But what we had. That was real. We are real. We met here. And found a way back to each other within a game. Doesn't that count for something?"

I stopped walking and stared at him, not knowing how to respond.

"Get moving, you two. This is a raid. Not a goddamn show and tell," a harsh voice said. Someone shoved me from behind, causing me to lurch forward. Zander caught my elbow.

"Hey, calm down, buddy. We're going," he said to the big dude behind us.

"Which did we choose, Zander? Did we want to go into a virtual world? What happened to us?"

Zander's jaw clenched; his blue eyes sharp. "No. We didn't have a choice, we were placed there as prisoners."

It didn't seem too farfetched to think I might have broken the law. Heck, I'd done my share of stealing to survive in WI. But was that who they'd wanted me to be or was it my true character? I wasn't sure anymore. Zander hardly fit the credentials of lawbreaker.

"I doubt you're a criminal, Zander."

"Yeah well, some people have different definitions of the word."

"What does any of this have to do with the raids?" I asked, exasperated.

"There's a cost to everything, and people are starting to realize that. President Reznor changes laws around here as often as he changes clothes, and he has the full backing of the cabinet. He decided he would pull regular folk and their families into the outposts against their will. Especially when he noticed the death numbers for batteries were increasing and the forays into New Earth for recruits became less than fruitful."

Zander grabbed my hand and pushed forward against the throng, winding through a narrow part of the passage. When the hallway widened again, he continued. "So New Earth developed early detection systems to prevent the government from seizing our citizens. The warning that there's a raid close by is a critical element of the system. And why we're heading further underground.

"We've also negotiated a deal that states we'll send supplies from our agricultural hubs—that means the ultra-rich have access to fresh vegetables and grains that can't be sustained on the surface. In return, they are supposed to keep their raids to a minimum. But they've become bolder and more reckless recently according to Sepha and Crane. Reznor doesn't care about New Earth. All he's concerned about is staying in power. He's betting that people will tire of living in squalor and demand their old conveniences back. Which he tells people only *he* can provide. But of course, it's propaganda. We're keeping them alive. And New Earth is thriving. He feels threatened by that."

By the time we finally reached the cellar cave, my mind buzzed with all the new information Zander had imparted. I took a deep breath, trying to absorb it all. I wondered how much to believe.

I shivered in the damp, as my eyes adjusted to the gloom. I could just make out a big open area, enclosed by tan clay walls decorated with beautiful etchings and hieroglyphics that looked like they came right off an Egyptian pyramid.

Hushed voices muttered in a conspiratorial tone amidst the small groups scattered around the expanse. I caught Marshall's eye. He stared at me, a sneer forming on his lips. He leaned over to whisper something to the big burly guy next to him, starting a gossip chain, the news bouncing like fire, person to person. Daggered glares were cast in my direction, and I gulped nervously.

Zander placed his arm around my shoulders, leading me away from the hate-filled eyes. But as we walked deeper into the cave, I felt the stares boring into my back.

We sat against the southeast wall, everyone now in clear view. I squirmed uncomfortably on the hard floor as I recalled Marshall's words.

Don't you remember what happened to Sepha's old charge, Cosette? After she was freed from the game, she chose the government over us. Luna wants to find her parents. Connect the dots.

I straightened my back angrily; no way would I let those jerks win.

I would escape this godforsaken place and discover my real identity.

But first, I needed another memory—and fast. I counted back from one hundred, hoping the soothing sound of the numbers would take me back to a time when I was certain of everything.

No lies. No conspiracies. Just the truth.

Because the truth would set me free.

CHAPTER 12

ZANDER

"Sector three is in the clear. I repeat, sector three is in the clear. Diverting tactic successful. Report back to duty stations," Sepha said, her voice echoing through the intercom.

A cheer erupted from the crowd in the cave. "Anybody got a stash of Sepha's favorite German chocolate? The dame deserves it. Rot in hell dome keepers!" a baritone voice yelled from somewhere in the throng.

"Yeah, right," another piped in. "Like we make enough coin for chocolate, Bernstock. Don't be a dumb ass."

A laugh went up as people began to leave the underground sanctuary and head to higher ground.

I didn't move. Something didn't feel right. I closed my eyes, desperate to calm the swirling sensation enveloping me. But all I saw when I shut my eyes was smoke. Lots and lots of smoke.

I glanced over at Luna, who also hadn't moved despite the fact everyone else had bolted like their pants were on fire. She sat with her eyes closed, her slight form huddled over, shoulders hunched. I knew her well enough to know it had nothing to do with the stares and whispers—sure, it would annoy the crap out of her—but that would just make her fight harder.

And then I realized what she was attempting to do.

She was trying to remember.

Back up at main headquarters, things settled back down to their normal routine with everyone departing to their assigned duty stations. Luna and I joined Sepha down in the control room where she began explaining to us what happened when we escaped our glass cages.

But I couldn't concentrate. The nagging feeling I felt down in the caves wouldn't leave me—something was terribly wrong. What did all that smoke from my vision mean?

Would Luna be okay? I worried about this obsession over finding her parents. She had to be hiding something, but what? Why couldn't my new psychic abilities pick up anything? I wondered if what I'd told her about them had actually registered. I couldn't tell if she was simply acting like her usual stubborn self, or if she really didn't believe me.

"Zander! Are you even listening?" Sepha chastised, jolting me from my musings.

I looked at her sheepishly. "Sorry. I've been a bit preoccupied lately."

"I thought you wanted to know why your escape got so messed up."

"I do. Please go on. I promise to listen this time."

"Well, as I already explained to Luna, here—" she halted mid-sentence, pressing her earpiece closer to her ear, her mouth forming a grim line. "Hold on, guys. I've got an interference at the front entrance."

I frowned and leaned over Sepha's shoulder to view the monitor. She zoomed in on street level, but everything appeared quiet. One of the droids on guard could easily have been mistaken for a casual bystander. He leaned against the building, pretending to talk into his com.

She pressed a button on the dash. "Geo 12. Do you copy? Where's the interference coming from? This is 1330."

Sepha glanced over at Luna, who also peered at the screens. Probably endeavoring to glean any information she could from the monitor feed, then map out the entire place in her mind for safekeeping. "Everyone in the resistors has an ID," Sepha said. "Learn yours, Luna. If the security droids know your name and are captured, you can bet they'll extract all the data from them."

Luna shoved her hands into her jean pockets looking like a kid caught stealing a cookie. "What is my— " Luna was cut off by the droid.

"Good afternoon. How may I be of service, 1330?"

Sepha crushed the button under her thumb again, annoyed. "For bloody sake. Can't we get a droid with a little common sense?" she muttered.

"I'm sorry, I don't understand."

"The interference, Geo. Where's it coming from?"

"Feline domestic cat. Adult. Approximate age, three. Searching for sustenance in trash bin directly southeast of the perimeter of the building. No other interferences are detected on my radar."

"That's all Geo. Over."

"Glad to be of service, 1330. Over."

Sepha swung around in her chair. "Damn cat population on New Earth is getting out of control," she complained. She blew out a sigh, her beads jostling with a life all their own. "So, where were we? Oh, yes. The mission that fell apart, and we're still paying for."

She glanced at us. "You know how most of it went down by now. We didn't have time to hack into the system and transfer you to another energy outpost. Hell, we barely had time to unload the sleeping serum and help Crane unlock Luna's cage before the plan unraveled. Luckily Zander, you busted out of those shackles on your own."

She gave me a questioning look. She wanted to know if I had told Luna about the clock key I'd used to break out.

I shook my head slightly, hoping Luna wouldn't notice. Could I really add one more secret to the pile right now? I doubted it.

Luna abruptly leapt to her feet, staring accusingly at me. "You used some kind of tool to help me escape my enclosure. I meant to ask you about it. But with everything that happened, it slipped my mind. It allowed you to open my cage and release my restraints, didn't it?"

Sepha interjected. "Well technically, Crane released the lock on your glass cell, Zander only had to unseal it, but there was no way for him to know that." She smiled at Luna before continuing. "I dosed you with revival through the virtual system, but didn't have time to reach Zander. Crane had to manually inject the drug into Zander's bloodstream."

Sepha's attempt to distract Luna with facts wouldn't work. Sure, this was a proven tactic in the field. But we were dealing with the queen of all things sneaky. She was too smart. The gig was up.

"The cage may have been unlocked but you were right about the restraints, Luna. I used a powerful device called a clock key to free us."

"Clock key?" she queried dubiously.

"Yes. But in only works for the Elite."

She looked from Sepha to me, confused. "What the hell is a clock key? And is Sepha Elite too?"

"No, she isn't one of us. She's a protector."

A searing pain slashed through my skull, stopping me cold as the same smoke filled vision appeared again. Only this time, someone lay on the floor, face down, soaked in blood. I couldn't make out their identity—but suddenly all the pieces came together, unfolding like dominoes before me. I gasped, my knees buckling under the weight of what I'd witnessed.

"A raid. Sepha. They're coming. Please. Stop—"

"Zander? What the devil? Are you okay?"

I cradled my head in my hands. Luna crouched down beside me. "Zander, can you hear us? What's going on?"

In the far off distance, the voice of Sepha requesting a medic echoed in my ears.

"No. A raid." I managed to gasp again. Why weren't they listening? Was I speaking out loud? Or only in my head?

But too late, along with the pain, the vision disappeared, and just as surely, I knew the government henchman were here.

Shouts echoed down the hallway, and Sepha turned to the monitors, but they'd gone gray.

"Shit! Shit! Shit!"

With a flick of her fingers on the dash, a monotone voice drawled through the speakers. "Intruder alert. Security breach in process."

"Now you tell me?" she snapped. With a few more key swipes, she got the monitors up and running. She zoomed in on the main area.

Luna moved in closer. "Oh, God."

I dragged myself to my feet and leaned in to see what Sepha and Luna were gawking at on the vid screen.

"They've already breached the main door and are inside the atrium," Sepha breathed. I stared at the center monitor, a bit fuzzy, but you could still make out about a dozen men, weapons drawn, charging into the room. People scattering in every direction.

The resistors had trained for this. Their mission included wiping clean any data the government could use against us. But it was even more imperative not to get caught. The only ones officials cared to keep breathing were the Elite. However, with the low human battery status, keeping people alive would be in their best interest. At least I had that small sliver of hope to hold on to. Resistors could be saved if they became batteries.

Sepha barked orders at the screen. "Lockdown code nine. I repeat, lockdown code nine."

My heart constricted, Sepha had just initiated the gas order.

In seconds, smoky gas would release, infiltrating the entire area. My vision had become reality.

I'd almost bet money these guys were smart and carried special masks. But Sepha knew how to play her own game. If the creeps failed to put their masks on quickly enough, the noxious gas would invade their lungs, knocking them out for hours, gifting everyone precious time to do some damage control and make our escape.

"Lockdown nine has commenced. Preparing for shutdown."

Seconds later, we were plunged into darkness save for the blue backlight of the monitor screens, which were now completely void of data. Sepha handed Luna a small device and a mask shield which she pulled from a lower drawer of the kiosk. "Swipe the eratacon over the banks of drives, but make sure you put your facial protection on first. You're going to need it," she said as she handed me a gadget and mask too.

For once, Luna didn't hesitate, placing the mask over her face. Sepha did the same, then grabbed a flashlight from an alcove above the data station. Not wasting any time, she crossed the room and squatted in front of a tall plant in the back corner. She pushed it aside and began tugging at the floorboards with her bare hands.

I adjusted my gas shield and ran over to help.

The eratacon emitted a tinny hum, which reverberated around the room as Luna slid the device over the tech equipment. Jagged white lines flashed across the screen before snuffing out.

Luna gazed at the gadget in her hand. "It's an electromagnet. How clever," she whispered. "You're erasing your tracks."

"Luna," Sepha hissed. "Come and help us pull up this trap door. We have to get out of here fast."

Luna bounded over, dropping the eratacon to the floor.

"Ready?" I asked looking to them. They nodded, and together we gave one giant heave. It barely budged an inch. I sighed, as far as we knew, no one had ever used the emergency exit in this room. And it was stuck.

We glanced at each other. "Again," I panted. This time we managed to wrench it open, just as two uniformed government men burst into the room.

My muscles tensed, but I shook off my terror. The smell of acrid smoke and chemicals filled the air, but the mask did its job keeping me awake. Unfortunately, these guys were wearing masks too.

Damn it all to hell.

My eyes stung from the fumes, I blinked rapidly in an effort to clear them and get my bearings. Too late, the thugs were upon us, weapons drawn. One of the dudes aimed his gun at Luna, and without thinking, I launched myself in front of her just as he fired. Searing pain ricocheted through my leg as the laser beam struck. I fell on top of Luna, sending us both tumbling down into the hatch. I tried to reach out for Sepha as we plummeted past, but she darted aside and instead hurled herself toward the men—her own weapon cocked to intercept them—giving Luna and me a chance to escape. She was following the divine order of the protectors. Tears pricked my eyes but I didn't have time to think about it, as Luna and I crashed landed on the packed dirt at the bottom of the pit. Another gunshot echoed through the smoky haze, and I heard a small whimper as Sepha thudded to the hard floor above us. She'd been hit. A second later, a squeaky whine made me look up. Despite being wounded Sepha had somehow managed to close the trapdoor. Sealing her own fate. And ours.

Before I could react, I succumbed to the blackness.

CHAPTER 13

LUNA

The smell of blood filled my nose, making my stomach churn. What happened? I tried to make sense of my jumbled thoughts but my pounding head got in the way. A high-pitched moan filtered through my senses, small at first, then growing increasingly louder.

I strained, listening, not daring to move. There it went again. The sound reverberated through my ears.

Then I remembered. We had fallen. Escaped.

I attempted to open my eyes, but stopped, frozen in shock when I realized the noise I heard came from my own lips. I shut it down abruptly and concentrated on ungluing my eyelids.

Finally, I managed to pry them apart and take in my surroundings. We were in some kind of dark cave. I fumbled around—searching for Zander. When my fingers brushed the fabric of his shirt, I let out a breath I didn't realize I'd been holding. My relief however, was short-lived, when I felt the warm, sticky fluid that could only be blood, covering my hands.

My God. Zander must have been hit when he jumped in front of me.

I swallowed hard at the clear implications of his heroic act.

I forced myself up on one elbow, my vision adjusting to the

darkness. My entire body ached, especially my shoulder, but I gritted my teeth and pushed up to a sitting position, leaning over to look at Zander, barely able to see his outline in the shadowy gloom.

A thick red puddle pooled underneath his torso, and I licked my dry lips. *It's okay, Luna. Everything will be fine.*

I grasped his shoulder, gently shaking him. "Zander! Can you hear me? Wake up!" He remained still, his face ashen against the inky black. Panic gripped me; he needed a doctor, and fast.

"Somebody help," I croaked into the dusty void. "Help," I yelled again. This time louder. But no-one answered; we were completely alone. I turned back to Zander, I had to do something. I checked his pulse, that seemed okay, but I had to find the source of the blood loss before he bled out.

I recalled a book on wounds I'd stolen from a medic back on WI. I remembered thinking it might come in handy one day. Thank heavens for that memory. Fake or not.

When I patted down Zander's leg, he let out a cry, and I knew I'd hit pay dirt. I gently pulled at the torn bloody denim. He cried again. I bent over and touched his cheek to let him know I was there.

He lifted his arm and took hold of my hand. "Hey there, princess," he said, his voice barely above a whisper.

"Zander, listen to me, you were hurt, but you're going to be okay. I'm going to apply some pressure to your wound." I smiled cheerfully, trying to reassure him.

I gingerly pulled off my purple sweatshirt, and placed it beside me. It would make do as a bandage. "I'm sorry, I know this is going to hurt, but you need to raise your leg above your heart to slow the bleeding. Are you ready? On the count of three. One, two, three." I raised his leg and heard him suck in a breath, but he didn't complain. I gritted my teeth once more and ignored the pain of my own injured shoulder. If Zander managed to tough it out with a wound in his thigh, the least I could do was focus on the task at hand.

Ideally, his wound should be washed out, but that clearly wasn't an option down here. Instead, I grabbed my sweater with my free arm and began applying pressure.

My whole shoulder burned with a fiery intensity, but I didn't dare take the pressure off.

I wondered how long we'd been unconscious. Based on the volume of blood pooled on the floor, quite a while.

Out of the corner of my eye, I noticed a soft reddish blip of light headed towards us and realized this had to be one of the old metro tunnels. The never-ending passage made it difficult to estimate how close they were.

I gripped Zander's hand. "Zander, someone's coming. What if the government's found us? What if—"

I looked down at Zander; he had fallen unconscious again. I bit my lip, torn between staying with Zander and fighting off our intruder. I decided on the latter. He'd told me himself he would rather die than go back into a cage.

"Okay, Luna. You can handle this," I muttered, as I pressed my sweater against Zander's leg, securing it tightly with the sleeves. I rose up on shaky legs, taking a glance at my handiwork. It would have to do. I looked around the cavern, searching for something I could use as a weapon. A small rock lay not a foot from me, and I bent down to grab it, curling my fingers around the sharp edges.

Without warning, a hand clamped down hard on my shoulder. I stifled a yelp, spun around and stuck my leg out, swiftly flipping the intruder onto his back. I placed an unsteady but firm foot on his chest, ready to attack, rock in hand.

I couldn't identify him in this light, but the shadowy silhouette appeared lanky and tall. I could take him.

"Luna?"

I knew that voice.

"Crane? What the hell? Why did you sneak up on me like that? I could've killed you. How did you find us?"

"Well, I had light until you crushed the casing underfoot. You're lucky I brought a spare."

I crossed my arms and scowled at him. "You know what I mean."

"Okay. Okay. But can you take your great hoof off me?"

"Oops, sorry, just instinct—I didn't realize I still had you pinned." I held out my hand and helped him to his feet.

He brushed himself off. "I understand it's not exactly been an easy day. Is Zander here with you?"

"Oh my God, Zander. Yes, yes, he's right here." I stepped over and knelt down besides Zander's inert form, checking on the bandage before applying more pressure to the wound.

"Thank the stars," he interjected. "And to answer your question, it's my job to find you. I'm your protector, remember?"

"Well, protector," I said, "Here's your chance to be a hero. Zander needs your help. He's been shot."

Crane clipped an LED to his collar and handed one to me. "Roger that. Here put this on. The red light is part of the spectrum least likely to ruin your night vision."

I snapped the tiny contraption on my shirt and glanced up at Crane. "I applied pressure to the leg to try and stop the blood flow, but my sweater is a poor replacement for a clean bandage."

"Looks like it hit the upper right thigh. I've seen worse," Crane said, peering at the wound.

I'd never seen him look so serious. But I was grateful. For the first time, I began to understand why he got this job.

"I brought some supplies with me. Let's get the Z man stable."

I sat beside Zander while he worked. The eerie light drained Zander's face of any remaining color and darkened his normally chestnut brown hair. I pushed back a stray lock from his forehead, praying he would make it.

Crane folded up the sleeve of Zander's shirt, placed a tourniquet on his arm, and plunged a white liquid into his veins with a syringe. "This should bring him around and keep him awake, at least until we can get him to safer ground. But more importantly, it will ease his pain."

He ripped away the fabric around the gash and pulled off the bloody sweater. Then, delving into a small bag, he produced clean gauze. Under the red glow of light, I noticed a swelling around the wound, making it appear even more ugly and raw.

"The laser burned through to the bone. We're going to require a med tech." He procured something else from the bag which I now noticed was a hot-pink glitter fanny pack. I bit my lip, trying not to grin.

Crane caught my expression. "Hey, this baby is practical. And it looks pinker in this light. Not that pink isn't manly. And the glitter speaks for itself."

"I don't care what color you prefer, Crane. I'm just glad you're here."

"Thanks. I appreciate that," he said, beaming.

"What's the white stuff?" I asked, pointing to the pot of cream he pulled from his little pack.

He slathered it over Zander's wound and it immediately stopped bleeding. "Voila," he said. "Instant clotter. Pretty neat, huh?"

"Do you have something to clean the wound?" I asked.

"This cream will help, but it's not enough. The laceration needs to be washed properly before it's sealed, but I've done all I can for the moment."

"Now what?" I said.

"We wait for him to wake up. Should only take a minute or two more before the Aquaboom hits his bloodstream."

My eyes remained fixated on Zander, but I quietly asked Crane, "How bad is it up there?"

Crane hesitated before he spoke. "They're gone now. But they took Sepha and a few of the others."

"They weren't there to kill, so that's something. If we're lucky, they'll make them batteries, so we can attempt to rescue them later."

Zander's eyelids fluttered open so I stopped my questions, shifting full attention to my patient. "He's coming around, Crane."

"Perfect. No offense, but it's not my idea of a good time to hang out in an old metro tunnel. No matter who the company is."

"I take personal offense to that Crane," Zander said, voice haggard.

Crane grinned. "Sorry, buddy. I don't dig creepy, damp spaces."

Zander laughed. "Can't argue with you there."

I hugged Zander. "Thank goodness you're awake. You scared me to death," I said allowing myself to breathe in his familiar smell. He wrapped his arms around me as I whispered in his ear. "Thanks for saving my life. I owe you one."

"Anything for you, Luna. I'm just relieved they didn't get you."

My heart lurched a little, warring with my mind. *Don't trust him. Never trust anyone.*

Crane cleared his throat. "Not to interrupt you love birds, but we better skedaddle. We need to have that leg attended to, pronto. Besides, I'm sure that the government henchmen are still searching for you both. I'd bet good money they saw you two fall down that hole." He pointed up to the escape hatch. "Sepha really sacrificed herself for you guys. How she managed to stop them from following you, I'll never know."

I jumped to my feet, trying to play it cool, even as I swiped away the tears running down my cheeks. They meant nothing, of course, a simple biological reaction to the strain of the day.

"We're really appreciative of everything Sepha has done for us, Crane. Believe me, we won't forget it. And just FYI, we're just friends, not love birds. Now come help me prop Zander up."

Crane lifted his hands in surrender. "Whatever you say, boss. Nothing to report here in lovebird lane."

I cast him a warning look, and he smirked, prancing over to

the opposite side of me. The heat rose in my face, and I suddenly felt very grateful for the darkness. I avoided Zander's gaze as we lifted him to a sitting position. He groaned at the movement.

"Do you think you can walk with our assistance, buddy? The Aquaboom painkiller I gave you should kick in any minute, now you're awake."

"Yeah, I'm starting to feel better already," Zander replied.

"Okay. Luna do you think you are strong enough to take his right side? I'll take his left."

I snorted. "Of course I'm strong enough. I'm not a wuss, Crane." I omitted the little detail that my shoulder was probably dislocated. I would worry about that later.

Crane looked sheepish. "Sorry, you're just so short and—"

"Shut up, Crane. I can handle it all right?"

"Okay, okay, geez, so sensitive."

"Luna is tougher than she looks. In fact she's pretty amazing," Zander said smiling softly at me. And as much as I hated to admit it, my heart melted a little.

Damn hormones.

"Ready?" I said, ignoring my racing pulse.

"Yes. Let's get this over with," Zander said.

We heaved him to his feet, and with slow, tottering steps, headed down the tunnel.

As we inched our way along, Crane chattered endlessly about all his plans for the future. But my mind registered none of it, still reeling from the shock Zander had taken a hit protecting me. Not to mention the realization that I'd been beside myself at the thought Zander might die.

Still, despite all that, I worried he had an ulterior motive— and now had the power to break my heart into a million pieces.

But there was no way on earth I would allow that to happen.

CHAPTER 14
ZANDER

"Crane, can you get in touch with Madeline?"

Crane stopped digging through the pile of clothes in front of him and stared at me like I had three heads.

We'd left the tunnels and headed straight for Crane's bunk. We decided not to take the risk of returning to our own level to retrieve our things. Someone could be waiting for us there.

"Madeline? Dude, are you sure?" He glanced at Luna, then back to me as if searching for a clue as to why I would want to do such a thing.

I shifted awkwardly, trying to ignore the returning pain in my leg. The Aquaboom didn't last long. We needed to hurry.

I lay my head back against the pillow and closed my eyes. "Crane, I trust her. She's our best shot. This place is a ghost town thanks to the raid. Nobody will return here until tomorrow, and that includes the med unit staff."

"Why do you trust her? She called out Luna in front of everyone at that meeting."

"I know what she said. But she doesn't understand. I haven't had a chance to talk to her since everything went down. Besides she is a professional. She will put her personal feelings aside to help."

Crane snorted. "You put way too much faith in that chick, Z-man. I'm just glad it's you and not me. I wouldn't want her touching this divine specimen," He ran a hand down the side of his body as if to showcase his assets.

Luna ignored him, frowning. She sat at the other end of the bed, sorting through Crane's clothes, attempting to organize the jumbled mess into piles. "I don't get it, Zander. Somebody must have stayed behind for emergencies. She's not exactly on our side from the looks of things."

"No, everyone's gone. It's too risky for people to stay. Besides she's the medic I know best. I'd rather take a chance on her than anyone."

She narrowed her eyes at me. "You better know what you're doing."

"I do," I said, sounding more sure than I felt. "Find anything that would work to disguise us?" I ventured attempting to change the topic. It was a valid question. If we had to go outside into the daylight, we required camouflage.

"I'm not sure," Luna said, willing to let it go. Probably only because I was injured. I would take what I could get. She smiled as she held up a purple scarf decorated with yellow polka dots. She raised her eyebrows at me in question.

I grinned back at her.

Crane caught our silent exchange and whipped the scarf away from her, twirling it around his neck. "Never doubt the power of accessories, kids. This perfectly fabulous little beauty always brings me good luck. Now Zander, while I find you a hat, you can stop deflecting and explain to Luna who Madeline is, so she doesn't kill you before you get medical attention."

I winced. "Smooth, Crane."

He shrugged and went back to his rummaging. "Hey somebody needs to tell her."

Luna crossed her arms defiantly and glared at me. "What's going on? Why do you need to tell me about Madeline? I thought she was a medic. End of story. Spit it out before I kill you both."

"Ouch," Crane said. "Burn."

I grunted as I rose up on my elbows—big mistake—the room immediately started to spin. I dropped back against the pillow. "She's a girl from the program—an Elite like us. She always had a crush on me. But I didn't like her in that way, and let's just say she kinda got a little bit upset about it."

Luna lifted her chin and began casually picking through some of the other scarves on the bed. But I wasn't fooled, I knew how that mind of hers ticked. Curiosity ate at her like a rabid fox.

"Upset?" Crane scoffed. "That's an understatement. Madeline was more than a bit upset. She was crazy over you." He shuddered. "She didn't take it well."

Luna shrugged. "Why would I care about something like that? If she can help us, then I'm all for it."

"Well, Zander left out a tiny, but very important detail. She doesn't exactly like you. She viewed you as the competition for his affections. I think she figured if you were out of the way, he would be more interested in her. Of course, anybody with half a brain could see Zander only had eyes for you."

Luna busied herself to hide her discomfort, folding each item of clothing and stacking them in a neat pile. "That's garbage, Crane. Stop wasting time. Look, I think Zander's leg is bleeding again," she said pointing to my thigh. Sure enough, when I glanced down, I noticed a big red blotch covering the clean bandage.

Crane scrambled over and examined his handiwork. "Oh, sugar snaps. This isn't good. I can't give you another dose of Aquaboom for another hour. We better scoot."

He grabbed a bob-style blue wig from the pile and shoved it towards Luna. "Put this on."

She crinkled her nose in dismay. "Really?"

Crane ignored her, tossing aside garments in a frantic search for something. He finally found what he'd been after and held up his prize in triumph. "Voila." A gold glitter baseball cap with the letter C emblazed across the front dangled from his fingers. He reached across the bed and planted the hat on my head. "There, that will do."

"Crane, you just ruined all my hard work!" Luna exclaimed, staring at the mess of clothes no longer neatly piled.

"Hey, I have a process; now put your wig on, unless you want the government dudes to recognize you. And, I'll have you know, this is a top of the line wig." He reverently stroked the blue strands of hair as Luna rolled her eyes.

"This belonged to my old beau, Bogart. Such a romantic name, isn't it?"

"I thought you loved Ariel 5," Luna said teasingly.

"Oh, I love them all, honey," Crane said with a wink. "But that's a story for another time."

Luna twisted her ponytail into a bun and secured the wig on her head.

I grinned. She looked pretty hot with blue hair.

Crane danced a little jig around her and whistled. "You are stylin', girlfriend." He clapped his hands together. "Now let's move this train out."

"Aren't you forgetting something?" I asked Crane. He looked at me blankly. "Madeline?"

"Oh, right. Good thinking. Hold on two shakes."

Crane pulled out his com. "Find Madeline Bristow in contacts," he demanded.

"Searching, one moment. Found Madeline Bristow. What would you like to do?"

"Initiate text. Madeline, this is Crane. Zander needs medical attention. Can you meet us at the underground level 17 station? Respond A.S.A.P. Tell no one."

He pocketed his com. "Let's head over there, and hope she can—"

Before he could finish, his com beeped. He pulled it out

again and grinned. "She says she'll be waiting for us there. Fellow soldiers, we have lift off."

He stuffed the phone back in his pocket. "Okay Luna, take his right arm, I'll grab his left."

Together, they managed to ease me off the bed, but that's all I remembered before everything went black.

⚜

LUNA

The day had begun to fade into night as we approached the small row of brick buildings on the corner. A modest light burned in one of the windows. I squinted into the dusk, trying to get a better look.

Turned out the level 17 underground station was a small healing facility, more closely resembling a jumble of old doctors' offices than a hospital. Though I shouldn't have expected a hospital, that would have involved too many people.

My head sweated under the heavy wig, and I felt the perspiration slide down my forehead—this thing had been on for way too long. We'd taken public transport clear across the city to get here, and my heart pounded a million miles a minute the entire time, concerned we would be stopped and questioned about the unconscious boy we carried with us. But Crane's quick thinking solved that problem. His forced slurred words and obnoxious behavior made it obvious to passengers we were a bunch of drunks. Nobody bothered us.

I examined every billboard we passed on the way to the facility, worried one of them would display our faces with a big wanted sign on it. Not finding any did nothing to dispel my qualms.

Everything had been too easy. Too quiet. And it freaked me out.

My shoulder screamed in agony as I tried to shift Zander's weight. After my fall earlier and then helping support Zander, I had just about reached the end of my tether. His skin felt unbearably hot to the touch, which probably meant he had a fever. People on W1 had died of less. I found myself wishing my current reality was as fake as that one had been.

I kicked myself for all the time we wasted searching for the right disguises and our dumb conversation about Madeline.

I could deal with Madeline. As long as she fixed him.

As we neared the entrance to this secret location, I observed a lone woman standing by the clear glass doors. She appeared a bit out of breath like she'd been running. She wore a pair of white scrubs, and her glossy nutmeg hair was pulled back with a clip at the nape of her neck. Even in this so-called medical attire, she looked striking.

As we came closer, she spotted us with Zander and released a sigh of relief. We climbed the steps and she opened the door, ushering us inside. "Hurry before someone sees," she whispered.

"Thanks for doing this, Madeline," Crane said.

"Of course. Good to see you again, Luna," she said giving me a curt nod. Her tone remained neutral, revealing nothing of her true feelings.

I returned the nod, doing my best to avoid conversation. It would have been awkward to start talking with someone you didn't remember. Instead, I focused my attention on Zander as I struggled to keep him steady. As it was, Crane seemed to be bearing most of his weight.

Madeline led us down a hallway and into a back room. A short row of double cabinets lined the sterile white walls. Madeline crossed the small space and began scrubbing her hands at the sink.

"Put him down over there," she said pointing to the paper-covered bed in the middle of the room. We did as she instructed, easing his body onto the exam table.

Madeline dried her hands, then picked up a familiar-looking bottle. As she rubbed it on her skin, I realized this had to be the same stuff we used in the lab when we pulled our trackers out to create a protective coating and keep things sterile.

She approached the bed and began unwrapping the bandage. Blood immediately oozed from the gaping wound.

"I put sealing solvent on, but with all the movement getting him here, it's re-opened," Crane said apologetically.

Madeline nodded. "Another coat would have done the job. Looks like you didn't put enough around the edges. No matter. We can fix it. But do better next time."

"Sorry," Crane muttered. "I'm no medic."

Madeline ignored him, crossing to the cabinet, retrieving scissors and a small jar. She cut away the remaining fabric around the injury then scooped an iridescent powder from the little container, slathering it over the entire area.

"What's that?" I asked intrigued.

"It's transolve. It makes the skin translucent so the light can penetrate and heal the wound at the cellular level. It also encourages the tissue to knit back together."

I opened my mouth to ask what light, but she was already pressing a button above the gurney. A clear case snapped into place, attaching to the base of the bed encasing him in glass.

I lunged forward, but Crane caught hold of me. "What the hell are you doing? You can't put him in another glass cage. He—"

Crane cut me off. "Calm down, hellcat. It's not a cage for VR, but a healing prism. I promise you Zander is safe. Okay?"

I looked from one to the other. Crane seemed more concerned about me, but Madeline gave a smug smile.

"So, the rumors are true. You don't have your memories," she said.

My cheeks flushed, but Madeline didn't notice, she'd already turned to a palm pad on the wall and was busily checking something.

"I'm turning on the machine, Luna," she said without looking around. "I'm saving his life, not killing him. You can relax." She crouched down to look at something attached to the floor.

"Let me go, Crane," I said through clenched teeth. "I won't do anything."

Crane appeared doubtful but released my arm.

I stepped closer to the bed. "So, what's this thing going to do?"

Crane came up beside me and started to explain, while Madeline punched some numbers into the com pad. "She's setting up for a full-body scan. Every organ and cell in the body emits a distinct vibrational frequency that can be measured. They discovered that energy medicine can heal most illnesses, especially when there's an imbalance in the energy field. By rebalancing the field, health can be restored."

I stared at him. "How do you restore a gaping leg wound?"

Madeline glanced over at me. "The power of energy medicine is very real, Luna. And in my opinion took way too long to be taken seriously." She gave a small laugh. "I read about how archaic the system used to be. They used drugs that, more often than not, harmed people and merely masked the symptoms they were experiencing, instead of healing them. What on earth were they thinking?"

Madeline's words hit me hard. She talked about drugs as if they were nothing. I had stolen, risked everything so many times so that Mrs. Peters could have her life saving medication. My heart lurched, maybe it wasn't as life saving as I originally believed. Had I been hurting Dara more by giving her the pills? I shuddered. This "archaic system" as Madeline put it, didn't seem much different from the healthcare offered on W1. Maybe the gamer wanted some antiquated version of the truth.

I didn't get a chance to ask anything else because at that

moment the bed Zander lay on illuminated with a glowing white light, and a melodious hum emanated from the chamber.

I touched a fingertip to the glass, the vibration of the notes tickling my skin.

Crane copied me. "It sounds like a strange, beautiful song doesn't it?" Crane mused.

I nodded.

The sound soothed me, right down to my core. And I found myself wanting to somehow inhale the very essence of the weird harmony.

"Do you feel that?" I asked looking over at Crane—he swayed to the tune like he was at some reggae concert.

"Groovy, isn't it?" Crane asked, giving me a grin.

"It's sound healing." Madeline chimed in. "It uses a type of music that forms specific sound patterns to stimulate the brain, allow muscle relaxation, and improve lymphatic flow."

Crane sashayed around in a circle. "In other words —groovy."

I stifled a laugh. I had to be careful; I didn't want to upset Madeline, especially as she was the one in charge of this operation. But to be honest, she was acting a tad hoity-toity.

"The chart indicates an energy challenge in almost every area of his body which is not surprising with a wound this deep. Laser guns can be deadly; he got lucky. I'll have to reestablish the flow of energy to his chakras. I'm going to start at the crown, programing the light so all seven are reset. This will take a good thirty minutes. When everything is completed, the injury should be healed."

She peered up from her screen. "Zander is going to be fine. He'll need to rest and meditate to keep his chakras in alignment for a few days. But after that, he can return to his normal activities."

I looked at her, astonished. "Are you serious? You don't have to sew him up or anything?"

Madeline pursed her lips, obviously peeved she had to

explain so many things to such a simpleton. "This is cutting edge technology, Luna. Not the dark ages."

I was about to make a smart retort, but a flash coming from Zander's glass incubator distracted me. A dazzling rainbow prism of light beamed into his crown chakra, spreading down his body, filling the chamber. "How incredible," I whispered. "How's it doing that?"

Madeline sighed. "It's a complicated science, and I don't have time to waste explaining it to you. If you truly want to know, become a med tech."

"Ouch. That's harsh, Madeline. When did you get so cranky? I don't remember you being this moody when we worked together."

"A lot has happened since then, Crane. And people change."

"Yeah, no kidding."

"Luna, can you fetch some water for Zander? There's a fountain at the end of the hall. He'll be very thirsty when he wakes up."

Crane piped up. "I can get it, Mads."

"No. Let Luna. I need your help monitoring Zander. And please don't call me Mads. I'm not that girl anymore." I thought I heard her voice crack a little, but her face remained stony, void of emotion.

Crane's face said everything. He knew she was full of it. There was no way she would let go of that com port and allow him to monitor.

One thing I knew for sure. Madeline liked being in charge.

I shrugged. "No big deal. I can go. Don't worry about it, Crane."

I sauntered casually out of the room. Madeline followed slamming the door behind me. "Knock when you return. I don't want the light to be seen from the window," she called.

"Yeah, right," I growled to the closed door. "Pull the other one, it has bells on."

I turned and looked down the dark hall, shivering. It felt like something or someone was watching me. I remembered the red LED light attached to my shirt and turned it on.

Much better. Now to find Zander some water and get back here A.S.A.P.

A high-pitched voice filtered through the closed door—curious, I crept closer to listen. "For God's sake Crane, when are you going to grow up? You were useless as my protector, and clearly not much has changed. You placed Zander in real danger!"

"How do you figure that? I'm the one that brought him here, stopped him from bleeding to death, and made sure he didn't get caught," Crane barked.

I pressed my ear to the door, not wanting to miss a single word.

"And let's not forget about your little declaration at the meeting. Yeah. We all heard that loud and clear, girlfriend."

"Why are you so irritating, Crane? I was just stating what everyone was thinking. You should be thanking me instead of treating me like a criminal."

Crane huffed. "You do the crime, you do the time, Mads."

"Honestly, if you don't have anything constructive to say you can go."

"It's so obvious you still love Zander. Why don't you just admit it."

"How dare you," she seethed. "Zander and I are just friends. It's true I may have had a crush on him when we were young, but that was a long time ago. We've all grown up since then—well most of us anyway. And besides, he told you to call me, didn't he?"

"Yeah, and I also said it was a rotten idea. Why can't you just let go of all this bad blood between you and Luna? She's a great gal. You know her. Heck, you two were friends, remember?"

"We were never friends. We got along fine, but we were never close. Besides, people change. Sometimes not for the better."

"What does that even mean, Mads? What is going on with you?"

"Nothing. Look, let's just agree to disagree all right?" she snapped. "Move out of my way, I need to monitor Zander. I'm sure the toxic vibe of this room is ruining the healing process."

"Fine. I'm going to check on Luna, make sure she's okay."

"Why wouldn't she be? She's getting water Crane, not flying around the moon."

"I'm her protector, Madeline. It's my job. And besides, she's nice."

"I'm not sure who I feel sorrier for. At least she's not my problem anymore."

What did she mean? How did I used to be Madeline's problem? None of this made sense. Damn it, why didn't I remember anything?

"I'll be right back," Crane said resigned.

The squeak of the doorknob turning, sent me scurrying down the hall. Seeing the fountain, I dashed over and quickly grabbed a cup, pretending to be surprised when Crane walked up to me, his face flushed with emotion.

He gave me a wide smile, pretending to be his old happy go lucky self. But I knew better. Madeline had upset him. "Find the water okay?"

"Yeah, thanks. How's Zander doing?" I inquired, trying to act casual. I cursed myself, talk about a dumb question—of course he was fine, I'd only seen him like three minutes ago. But Crane didn't seem to notice.

"He's peachy keen, basking under the rays of the California sun. He'll be better in no time." He stepped closer. "Here, let me take that for you," he said grasping the full cup. Why don't you go sit in one of those chairs by the door? I'll join you as soon as I unload this water. It's much more comfortable out here."

He didn't want me with Madeline, and I couldn't blame him. I wanted to give her a piece of my mind.

I didn't dare though. Crane would know I'd listened in on their conversation. Besides, she was Zander's medic.

But it didn't mean I wouldn't kick her ass later, I thought.

"Hello? Earth to Luna?" Crane said waving a hand in front of my face.

I shook my head. "Sorry. I was thinking... what did you say?"

"Do you want to—" Crane's voice cut off and his eyes grew wide. He placed a finger to his lips.

I whirled around, looking down the blackened hallway.

That's when I heard it.

Two sets of footsteps.

We'd been found.

CHAPTER 15

LUNA

Another footstep. A snort. Then the glint of a gun. My hackles rose. Fighting back the instinct to freeze, I grabbed Crane by the arm and hauled him into Zander's room.

I glimpsed the flash of a uniform just before I shut the door and locked it.

I swallowed hard against the bile rising in my throat.

"You may as well give up, kids. You're surrounded. If you surrender peacefully, no one will get hurt," the harsh voice shouted, penetrating my shock.

I whirled around, searching for something to use as a weapon, then gasped in horror. Madeline and Zander were gone —even the bed was missing. The place lay empty and immaculate, not a trace of evidence that anyone had ever been in here.

I squeezed my eyes shut, then opened them again, not believing what I'd seen. Still empty. What the hell? What kind of weird voodoo crap had I got myself into?

Crane crossed the room and picked up the only chair in the place, hastily carrying it over to the door to wedge under the knob. Well, at least one of us had the good sense to act promptly. He grabbed hold of my hand and motioned me to follow him.

What was he doing?

Loud banging erupted on the other side of the door. I turned around. The chair shook violently against the pressure, but still held—for now.

This was it. There was nowhere to hide.

"Luna," Crane hissed tugging my arm. "Come on." With no other choice I followed him.

I inhaled deeply, filling my lungs with oxygen, ready to fight.

But Crane had other plans—hands and knees on the ground, he groped for something. I knelt down next to him to share my light. His fingers brushed what looked to be a magnetic strip.

We heard a splintered crash, and looked up to see a big crack in the door. We had only seconds to spare.

"Open up! You're both under..."

I tuned out the words, focusing on Crane.

With a shaking hand, he lifted the sleeve of his shirt and swiped his wrist against the strip he'd found embedded in the floor. The segment lit up, but then went dark, as a piece of the flooring rose up revealing a set of stairs.

Crane yanked me to my feet and signaled for me to go first. He followed, right on my heels. As soon as we'd cleared the threshold, the hatch receded, enveloping us in gloom.

And just in time.

The noise of the door smashing to the tile reverberated through the floor above us. Loud shouts echoed through the darkness, as we descended further into the underground maze.

We were back in the tunnels. But something didn't sit right. The sound of heavy breathing filled the atmosphere. And it definitely wasn't mine or Crane's.

My breath caught in my throat. We weren't alone.

Two shrouded figures stepped forward. I nearly jumped out of my skin in fright. Had we simply escaped one nightmare for another?

I reached for Crane. Too late. They were upon us. I slumped with relief as Madeline came into view with Zander draped against her shoulder for support.

I opened my mouth to speak, but Madeline shook her head and pointed above us.

Zander reached out and gave my hand a squeeze. Our eyes locked and relief flooded through me. He appeared to be okay.

The moment between us passed as Crane took hold of Zander's outstretched arm and placed it around his shoulder, relieving Madeline of some of the burden. In tandem and at a furious pace, they trekked down the entrenchment.

They knew exactly where they were going. A gazillion questions tumbled around my head, but I didn't say anything, too terrified I might give us away. So I remained silent, dutifully following behind.

With the adrenaline fading, I again felt the pain of my injured shoulder. I gritted my teeth and held my arm against my chest. A metal taste coated my tongue—the familiar tang of fear. But I ignored it—this was no place for a meltdown.

Mama's voice echoed in my head again. *Trust no one.*

I thought of my friend Dara, on W1. The last time I'd seen her she tried to warn me about all this. Repeatedly screaming something about a Cage of Glass before they silenced her for good.

I hadn't understood then.

But I did now.

I wondered if she was still at an energy outpost. If W1 was just a game, there was a strong possibility Dara might be alive and I could find her. I sighed. I'd escaped my so-called cage of glass—but replaced it with a cage of secrets—secrets I didn't recall—which was quite a big problem if I was being honest.

Dara must have somehow known it wasn't real. Did she remember everything? My thoughts wandered to my sister, Trinity. The other piece of my heart still missing in this equation.

I vowed to find them both. Along with my parents.

The answers were buried inside me. I knew it.

As if on cue, I felt a tightness in my head, a shift in perception indicating a memory was imminent. This time I was eager for the pain, knowing it would reveal to me another piece of this very complex puzzle. I gritted my teeth, hissing as the sting hit me, lancing through my skull like a brand. I clenched my fists and paused waiting for the throbbing to recede as the image materialized.

That man appeared again, the tall one with the weird star scar near his eye. But he wasn't with my parents this time. I strained to see what he was looking at. As it all came into view, I suddenly felt physically sick—almost out of body.

It was Mrs. Lennor—and me.

As if recognizing myself was some kind of trigger, I became part of the past, and was almost sucked into this body. I tried to calm my rapid pulse, watching in horror as the mystery man grabbed me by the waist holding me down. I tried to bite him but he was too quick for me. Mrs. Lennor forced some strange yellow liquid into my mouth. It tasted of anti-septic and burned all the way down. I slumped into an ornate red chair —I could feel my body going numb, succumbing to whatever elixir they forced into me. Despite all this, my mind was alert and I could see and hear everything. My eyes were open, and I scanned the room. I was in an opulent office, gild framed paintings hung on the walls. The light from the antique Tiffany lamps created a warm ambiance to my surroundings. Where had they taken me? Floor to ceiling windows took up the space facing me and I strained to look, but couldn't see outside. I wanted to close my eyelids, they felt so heavy—but I forced them to stay open determined not to miss a detail. My gaze returned to Mrs. Lennor. I realized she appeared slightly younger here, no longer sporting a brown bob, but had blonder, curlier hair that framed her face in pretty waves. Her appearance no longer prim, but pleasing. Her eyes dusted with a sprinkling of sparkling shadow, and her lips coated with coral pink gloss, softened her features. The man grabbed my face and turned it one way then the other. He got out a pen light and shone it directly into my eyes, before releasing me.

"Oh, that's wonderful work, Mummy. I couldn't have administered

the tonic better myself. It appears to have already taken effect. I appreciate the girl's spirit, but we need her still for her final examination. For obvious reasons, I want to examine her personally before she begins her quest." He pulled down my sleeve and smoothed down my tousled hair as if I was his pet.

"Of course you do darling, that's completely understandable," Mrs. Lennor cooed. "I'm so proud of the work you're doing. You're such a wonderful doctor and son."

Before I could figure out what was happening, I was pulled back from the scene. I resisted—but it was fruitless—and suddenly found myself back in the dingy underground.

Something brushed against my sneaker, and I jumped, startled, crashing back to reality. I looked down to witness a giant rat scuttling off into one of the dark recesses of the tunnel. I didn't so much as flinch. Rats didn't bother me, people and their buckets full of lies did. I pushed the rat from my mind and concentrated on what I'd just witnessed. My mind whirled with everything I had seen.

I shuddered.

Crane looked back at me. "You doing okay, Luna? I think we're far enough away that we can talk. How did you get so far behind?"

I scowled at him, but remained silent, not speaking of what I'd just seen. I needed to focus on getting out of my current mess before dredging up past mysteries. My legs felt weak, my gate uncertain as I hurried to catch up.

When I didn't answer, Crane continued on anyway. "No worries, I'm sure anyone would react the same without being prepared. You don't even have to say it. I know you want some answers about what just happened. Don't worry. I've got you covered. The short version is we just kicked government ass." Crane focused on his steps, but I caught the sheepish grin.

"I think she wants a little more explanation than that,

Crane," Zander interjected. "It's all about protocol," he said glancing at me. "We're trained to be able to exit any situation at a moment's notice, leaving no trace behind. It's how we were able to escape so fast and clear the room of nearly all its furniture before we left. You will remember all this soon enough. I know you will." Zander's voice rang with hope. He still had faith.

I was starting to lose mine. Why hadn't my memories returned?

"You can't compare us," he said, as if reading my mind. I had most of my memories to begin with when we returned here. You didn't. We didn't leave the game the usual way. Normally, the resistors are there to help restore memory loss. It's partly my fault, I didn't remember some things until I came back— including one essential component—namely, that it was virtual reality. If I had, I would never have put you in that kind of danger. I'm sorry."

Madeline interupted, shifting some of Zander's weight. "Let's worry about getting out of here alive, you can do all your apologizing later. Not that it's necessary. Since when did you become so sensitive, Luna? You used to understand sacrifices had to be made."

Zander turned his head angrily to Madeline. "You can't be serious. Why would you say that?"

"Ah, so you've met Madeline 2.0," Crane quipped. "Spoiler alert, she's a real witch."

"Both of you shut up and focus. We're going to need an aero taxi. Do you think you can handle that, Crane? There's a space elevator up ahead. Go back up to city level and hail one. We don't want to run the risk of these two being recognized by anyone."

"Where do you want to go?" Crane asked.

"The safe house in sector seven. Luna, come and take Crane's place."

Crane handed Zander off to me, and I winced as pain radiated up and down my arm from my shoulder, I cradled it closer to my body as I supported Zander's weight on my opposite side.

"Sorry," Zander whispered.

"Don't concern yourself about me. Madeline's right, there's more important things to worry about."

"No, I mean about being so heavy," he gave a grin, and I couldn't help smiling back.

Madeline frowned, her eyes narrowing. "When did you hurt your shoulder?"

I looked away uncomfortably. "Doesn't matter, it's fine."

She examined me more closely. "It's clearly dislocated. It doesn't pay to play martyr here, Luna. Not unless you want to become our weakest link."

Something in her tone made me look up. Her eyes sparked with challenge. She obviously didn't mind the thought of that at all.

Crane was right. She was a real witch.

"God, Lun. Why didn't you say something? Madeline could have fixed you up."

"With you out cold and all, it wasn't exactly the best time." *Not to mention the girl hates my guts,* I thought.

Zander pressed his lips into a firm line before meeting me square in the eye. "Are you injured anywhere else?" he asked.

"No."

"Promise me you won't hide something like that again."

Madeline didn't wait for me to answer. "Stop fussing, Zander. You're not her mother. I'll fix it when we get to base camp. Can we move on now?"

"Okay, with me," I said.

"Great," Madeline said sarcastically. "I must say it's been wonderful reuniting with you two, just like old times."

"Okaaaay..." Crane said. "On that touching note, I'm going to fetch us a taxi." And with that he disappeared, zipping away in the elevator.

I turned to Zander, trying to ignore Madeline's sour expression. "Is there a space elevator at every location? I could've used one when you got shot."

"We have a few scattered around, we just didn't happen to be close to one at the other safe house." He paused his face haggard. "Did they find Sepha yet?"

"Not that I've heard. But honestly, we haven't been anywhere but here."

"We'll try to collect some Intel once we make it to the safe house," Madeline said. "Of course, they took our best hacker out of the equation."

"Come on, Mads. You have to admit you're pretty good yourself."

She blushed, pleased with the compliment, but at the same time something warred in her eyes. No doubt fighting off her inner demons.

A whir sounded above us, and Madeline pushed us back against the wall, pulling a gun from her pocket.

Envy whirled up in me, as I stared at her weapon. I really could have used something like that after all these raids and fights.

The elevator screeched to a halt and Crane stepped out, Madeline's weapon trained on him.

"Whoa, Nelly," he said instantly putting his hands in the air. "I come in peace."

She pushed the firearm back in her pants and repositioned Zander who appeared a little pale.

"Did you find an aero taxi or not?"

"Yup. All ready and waiting."

Madeline marched Zander toward the elevator, giving me no choice but to keep up. She swiped her wrist and the doors closed, zipping us up toward the higher city level.

I glanced down at my own wrist, wondering if I had a working chip.

Zander caught me staring and as if guessing my question said, "I asked Sepha to reinstate your chip. But I'm not sure she had a chance before—" his voice wavered, filling with emotion.

"Do you think that was wise?" Madeline demanded.

I groaned. *Not this again.*

Zander looked at her puzzled. "Why wouldn't it be wise?"

"Never mind," she muttered. "Let's just get out of this hell-hole."

As if on cue, the doors opened to a back alley of the bustling city, the hum of battery-operated carts and the whiz of aero taxis above us filling the air. I never noticed the aero taxis before. Maybe they were in limited use or something. I remembered Zander saying cars weren't allowed down here due to pollution concerns, so they must run on some other type of Eco-friendly fuel.

I adjusted my wig, the hair underneath lay slick and sweaty to my scalp. I almost couldn't breathe with this thing on.

Zander unfortunately had lost his cap. So much for disguising ourselves—at least it was dark.

Crane ushered us into the aero taxi, and in a woosh, we whizzed up above the metropolis. I looked down at the rooftops, fascinated, the maze of buildings spiraling down into pyramids.

Zander leaned in close and gazed out over the city with me. "The aero taxi's design is based on the intercity rockets that are used to transport you anywhere in the world in under an hour. These are a smaller and more primitive version of them. The car is tethered to a line of invisible magnets that propel it forward and up. A genius idea." His excitement over the mechanics of the thing sounded clearly in his voice.

Zander's face still appeared sallow in the fake moonlight coming through the glass. I put a hand to his forehead. It still burned with fever. He moved my hand away and squeezed it in reassurance. "I'm fine. Stop worrying."

But I did worry. A sheen of sweat glistened on his temple, despite the cool evening.

"Madeline," I said. "Zander's burning up."

Madeline, sitting to his left, grabbed his face and peered into his eyes. "He'll be okay. His eyes aren't glassy, and he's coherent. We'll place him under the lights again as soon as we arrive."

"Thanks, guys," Zander said. "I'm right here, remember?"

I glanced towards the front of the aero taxi, looking for the driver, concerned he might overhear us. Only then did I realize this thing was driving itself. What a strange place.

Nobody spoke after that, each of us lost in our own worlds. Even Crane remained silent. I guess we were all exhausted. I watched through the window as brightly lit buildings flashed by. I attempted to count them in an effort to soothe my shattered nerves. When that failed to work, I stopped counting and tried to figure out my next move. But with nowhere to turn, I was stuck between a rock and a hard place.

Before my brain sparked any light bulb ideas, we arrived at our next safe house. It had taken us only ten minutes to reach quadrant seven, wherever the heck that was. I needed to figure out how these quadrants were laid out.

I stepped out onto the curb and found myself facing a cozy brick building adorned with window planters filled with a rainbow of flowers. It struck me as strangely familiar. My eyes traveled to the sign above the door, the rose-colored words lit up against the dark night sky.

Roselyn's Cafe and Bar.

The pink letters suddenly began to swim in wavy lines before me, and I found myself being pulled out of my physical body, into another time, becoming intertwined with some other version of myself.

The memory came, sharp and strong, as I inhaled the sweet perfume of flowers. The pleasure of a warm hand in mine mingled with the sheer joy of just being loved. I allowed myself the pleasure of the experience, which was definitely at odds with my present reality.

. . .

I was in front of the cafe—the sun warm on my skin, and I was laughing. The smell of gardenias wafted in the air as Zander wrapped me in his arms and whispered in my ear. "I love you, Luna."

I grabbed hold of his face and kissed him with an abandon I didn't know I could possess. Happiness flowed from my being, obliterating everything else around me.

But then Zander pulled away, reaching for my hand again. Men's shouts echoed down the street. Two men attacked us from behind, one grabbed me, ripping my pretty blue sundress. They wore the black and gray government issued uniforms I was somehow very familiar with.

Zander was torn from me, and I kicked and screamed as one of the officers tried to restrain me.

Another joined him, stabbing my arm with a huge syringe of crystal clear liquid.

Heat shot through my veins, and I was lost, all fight gone from me.

I succumbed to the darkness.

CHAPTER 16

ZANDER

I awoke from a nightmare in a cold sweat—where I'd witnessed Luna collapse to the ground, over and over again.

I thrashed around in a semi haze and my arm hit something hard—where was I? Back at the energy outpost? My heart raced in panic. I managed to open my eyes, only to be blinded by a glaring light.

Then I remembered where I was—and that my night terror had been real.

I was back under the energy healer. I eased my leg up slightly, but experienced no pain. My brain fog had cleared; the fever must have lifted. My clammy skin was probably the result of the nightmare. I wished the healing light could stop the sick dread I felt in my stomach.

Something had happened to Luna tonight—and I had a pretty good inkling she might have experienced a memory.

But why had she fainted? Was she physically reliving what she'd seen?

We'd rushed into the safe house after she crumpled to the ground, and immediately headed upstairs to a vacant room. I demanded Madeline attend to Luna first, despite everyone's protest. They finally relented, setting up a cot adjacent to my bed. Madeline lathered Luna's shoulder with a nerve blocker and with Crane's help, popped it back into place.

"She probably keeled over from the pain," she explained. "Shoulder dislocations are no joke. She's also very dehydrated, but the serum I injected into her veins will restore her cells back to their optimum level."

Madeline's reasoning sounded logical enough. However, I sensed something else caused her to pass out. I recalled nothing after that, as I must have collapsed myself.

I turned my head, relieved to see Luna still lay next to me, sleeping. Crane lounged in a chair by the door, snoring his head off.

I smiled. He would kick himself later for napping on the job.

A tap at the door had Crane bolting up ramrod straight in his chair, disoriented. "What? What happened? I swear, I didn't take the purple pony!"

I laughed. "Good dream, Crane?"

He blushed. "I must have fallen asleep, my bad." His creased cheek combined with the wild red hair spiking in all directions, made him appear even more boyish, far younger than the eigh-teen-year-old he was.

Madeline breezed in with her com port. "How are you feel-ing, Zander?"

"Great, but I'm ready to escape this contraption. Don't get me wrong, I'm grateful for everything, but it's not my idea of a swell time."

Madeline pressed a few keys on the com. "It looks like most of your energy balance has been restored. I would prefer to see more improvement in the sacral chakra region, but if you promise to meditate every day for the next week, I'll let you out. Deal?"

I smiled at her. "Deal," I said, relieved to notice a little piece of the old Madeline still lurked behind that frosty exterior. I wondered what caused the attitude—maybe if I hadn't been hijacked and stuck as a battery, I could have prevented it. I felt tempted to ask her if something happened while we were gone, but I doubted she would she tell me.

I watched as she started punching something into her com again, and I took the opportunity to glance over at Luna. Still laid out like a corpse.

I tapped my fingers, waiting for what seemed like eons for the hissing sound of the glass, letting me know the chamber had separated from the bed. I sucked in a deep breath of the cool air. Free at last.

"Crane, will you go to the kitchen and rustle up some water for Zander? We need to get him rehydrated as quickly as possible. I don't want to give him a hydro injection so soon after energy therapy."

"Sure thing." Crane hopped out of his chair like a spring bunny, obviously revitalized after his nap.

"Thanks."

"No problem. Do you want anything to eat?" Crane asked, looking to me.

"I'd kill for a sandwich. Whatever you can find. And if you don't mind, bring one for Luna? She's not picky. In fact, none of us have eaten in a while, so maybe you should get a bite, too. We can't have you fading away."

Crane grinned and rubbed his belly. "I'm never one to turn down a meal. Be back shortly," he said, leaving me, Madeline, and the sleeping Luna alone in the room.

I was about to check on her, but before I had a chance, Madeline pressed something hard and cold into my hand, closing my fingers around it.

I glanced down and opened my palm only to find a micro projector nestled there. I looked up at her, puzzled. "What's this?"

"You need to watch it. It will change everything." I detected an air of triumph in her eyes, as if she'd won some kind of war.

Curious, I flicked it open, revealing a tiny pinhole. A light beam shone through, projecting a small screen onto the wall in front of us.

Madeline closed her hand over the glow and snapped it shut. She eyed me fiercely. "Later, when you're alone."

But it was too late, I already knew what was on it. As soon as the micro projector powered on, it somehow triggered a vision. Flashing in front of my eyes like a movie—Luna forcing herself into a restricted government building by tricking the security guard. Though I felt no pain this time, I worried if Madeline detected something off about me, but I needn't have worried.

Madeline was peeking over at Luna, who was still dead asleep —which I found strange. The girl usually woke at the slightest sound—always on alert. She must be exhausted. I certainly hadn't helped, getting myself shot. I gritted my teeth in frustration.

Madeline's voice brought me out of my morbid musings. Her voice low and urgent. "This footage shows Luna is a traitor, Zander," she tapped the projector. I hacked into the governments system and combed through a lot of security vids to find this. It was well worth my time. You won't be able to deny the facts."

I snorted. "What's your point, Madeline?"

"Just watch it," she said again, warily. "What you do with the information is your business."

"What gives, Mads? You and Luna might not have been friends, but you always got along. Why would you throw her under the bus?"

"Rather than questioning my motives, you should worry more about the kind of company you keep. It's plain to everyone but you that ever since you two left the game Luna only tolerates you at best. She's using you, and it's obvious she doesn't trust you. I thought you'd be smart enough to dump her. The experience should have turned your blinders off."

"Blinders?"

"Yes, concerning Luna."

"Madeline, we've discussed this so many times. You're a good friend, but nothing more. You've always known how I felt about Luna, but that doesn't mean I don't care about you. Something's bothering you. If you'd like to talk to me, maybe—"

She tilted her head, confused. "Do you really think that highly of yourself? Believing I still carry a torch for you? That was ages ago. I don't give a flip what you do."

I pushed a hand through my hair in exasperation. "Come on, Mads, don't be like this. I appreciate everything you've done for me. Helping—"

Madeline cut me off, lifting the corner of her lip in a sneer. "Nobody calls me Mads anymore. I'm not a child. Examine the vid and contact me."

She turned to go, almost colliding with Crane balancing a tray piled high with sandwiches and drinks. She pushed passed him and stormed out into the corridor, disappearing.

He raised an eyebrow at me. "Tough crowd?"

"You can say that again," I muttered, stuffing the micro projector into my pocket.

He placed the tray down on the small side table, snagging a sandwich from the top of the pile as he did so. "Well, it's nothing an old-fashioned meal won't cure."

He handed me half. "Eat," he admonished.

I took the food from him and lifted the bread to check the contents. My gaze went to Crane. "What's in this?"

He took a bite of his own sandwich and grimaced, chasing the grub down with some hot pink fizzy drink. The cocktail appeared deadly enough to melt tar. "Don't you want to live with the mystery?"

I shrugged, taking a bite, not surprised to find the filling tasted like melted plastic. "Mmm..." I said sarcastically shoving the rest down. "Something I haven't missed, the taste of fake turkey."

I reached for the pitcher of water Crane brought, filling a cup, then gulping down the cool liquid.

"Ah look, sleeping beauty finally decided to honor us with her presence," Crane said, jumping to attention. Some of the mayonnaise from his sandwich splatted to the floor as he bowed irreverently to Luna, who had managed to push herself up to a sitting position. She stared at him, blinking.

I laughed. "I think waking up to you is a bit much for her."

"Whatever do you mean?" Crane scoffed in fake protest. "I bring gifts for the fair maiden."

He offered her his half-smooshed sandwich.

She wrinkled her nose and put up a hand. "What is that? It smells like old shoes."

"Me lady protests too much," Crane crooned. "Are my delicacies of faux turkey rejected?"

She grinned. "Yes, absolutely."

Crane exhaled in mock exaggeration, placing a hand on his chest. "Would madame prefer a nut spread with jam?"

"Sounds better," Luna said making a move to rise.

"Hey, you never offered me that option," I complained jokingly.

"Ladies first, Z. Ladies first."

"Right. Of course. Thank you for reminding me," I smirked.

Crane pushed Luna back down. "I will serve the lady."

"Pushy," Luna groused.

"I've been called worse," he said airily, producing a peanut butter and jam sandwich.

She took it, but still stood back up. "Sorry, Crane, but this lady is thirsty. I need a drink."

He quickly offered his pink liquid that had developed some kind of purple film on its surface.

Luna leaned back. "Is that even drinkable?"

Crane stared into the cup and shrugged. "The jury's still out. E-Z Energy claims it's a power beverage. The ad contends you'll be bursting with vitality after one sip."

"I think I'll have water."

"Allow me," I said, shifting off the bed to pour some. "How's your shoulder?"

She totally ignored my question and rushed over, pushing me aside. "Are you supposed to be moving? I can get my own damn water. What's with you boys, anyway? Have we gone back to the debutante era?"

I took her hand and pressed it to my chest ignoring the joke she used to mask her concern. Luna's fears for my safety broke my heart. "I'm fine. I got the all clear from Madeline. I'm glad you care though."

Luna's cheeks burned as she hastily pulled her hand away. She still distrusted me, and I had to admit it hurt. But to be fair, I could only imagine the hell she had been through. Crane told me he'd found out the gamers had her mother sell her back to the government on W1. Then she ended up in P8 with me. I understood the betrayal, to be disappointed by the one person who was supposed to take care of you. I had to be patient with her.

She was worth it.

"How are you doing?" I asked softly. "You gave us quite a scare back there," I said. "Do you remember what happened?"

She busied herself pouring water into the cup. "No. But I'm okay now, so you can stop fretting. Even my shoulder feels better."

"Madeline adjusted it while you were out."

"That was nice. I'll have to thank her."

I put a hand over her trembling one, and I knew instantly she'd lied. Not about her shoulder. But everything else. She remembered exactly what went down in front of the cafe. Like the micro projector, I seemed to get a vision just from the contact. I closed my eyes for a minute and a flash of white crossed my periphery. I focused all my energy into the object, until I deciphered what it was.

A syringe full of milky liquid.

And in an instant, it became clear to me what she'd recalled.

My God. Her first recollection of this place had been her

abduction? No wonder she hated being here. Then I began to consider another possibility. Maybe in a prior memory jolt, she'd seen her parents. Perhaps that explained her burning desire to meet them.

Luna whipped her hand back as if she sensed the intrusion.

"Geez, Zander," Crane said. "You're looking a little pasty. Maybe you should sit down."

"I'm fine," I said, a little more testily than I intended.

"Okay, okay. Someone has a case of the crankies."

Luna smirked. "Annoying, isn't it? Told you."

Just then, Madeline burst through the door, instantaneously wiping the cocky expression from Luna's face.

"What's happened?" I asked, crossing the room in two great strides.

She blinked innocently. "Why, nothing. Did I say anything was the matter?"

"Well you entered like a pack of werewolves were on your tail," Crane said. "If that doesn't say 'help my pants are on fire,' I don't know what does."

Madeline grimaced. "Don't be such a child, Crane. I came to fetch Luna. Now that she's awake she'll need her final checkup."

"I appreciate you fixing me up and everything, but I'm fine. I don't need a checkup," Luna retorted, a steely flint flashing in her green eyes.

Crane stepped between the two girls. "Have a sandwich, Madeline. You look hungry. Notice I didn't call you Mads? Aren't you proud of me?" He gave her a toothy grin.

She shuddered. "How do you eat that barbaric stuff? I tend towards a more health conscious diet." She motioned for Luna. "Come on, it won't take long—no excuses. I'm not concerned about your shoulder—I took care of that. You fainted on the pavement outside, and it's my job to ensure your energy centers are working. I'm just following procedure."

Luna turned to me for help. "It couldn't hurt to let her examine you. I'll come with you," I offered.

"No," Madeline interjected, way too quickly. "What I mean to say," she went on hurriedly, "is you're not family. Only family members can be present for a thorough examination."

"That's crap," I said.

"Leave it, Zander," Luna said. "We'll end up fighting all night if I don't go with Madame Madeline. Besides, my body's used to being poked and prodded. It's easier to just go."

I studied Luna for a minute, curious. Why was she giving up? I narrowed my eyes trying to read her. She was up to something.

She stuffed the rest of the sandwich in her mouth and wiped her hands against her jeans. With a mouthful of peanut butter, she said, "Lead the way," in a garbled tone to Madeline.

Before I could think of a way to stop them, they'd both disappeared.

"Is it just me, or do you think a full-on girl fight is about to go down?" Crane asked.

"I don't know about the fight. But something is definitely up."

And I was determined to find out what it was.

CHAPTER 17

LUNA

You'd think I would be smart enough to stay away from trouble by now, but here I was again, about to enter the lion's den with none other than Madame Madeline herself.

I traipsed after her down yet another long hallway. This place was a labyrinth of doors. The biggest safe house so far. Madeline didn't speak as she led me further away from the relative safety of Zander and Crane, down deep into the heart of the building. We descended two floors before we came to a door marked *Examination room one*.

She opened the door and ushered me inside. The small room held an exam table and some medical equipment that hung from hooks on the wall. The overhead light buzzed, reminding me of the interrogation room back on W1. God, that seemed like a lifetime ago.

Madeline shut the door behind us and whirled on me, eyes flashing fire. "You didn't honestly think I asked you here for a checkup, did you?"

"Do you think I'm that dumb? Of course, I knew you didn't want to examine me again. What do you know? You're hiding something. And wipe that sneer off your face, you don't frighten me. You're about as intimidating as a poodle."

Madeline stepped closer, she was a head taller than me, but I wasn't bluffing—this chick didn't scare me in the least.

She swallowed hard, uncertainty crossing her face. Obviously, I'd hit a nerve. Dear old Madeline surely must have mixed herself up in something she shouldn't. Now, she appeared confused.

Well, I was just about to unconfuse her.

"Look, Mads," I said sardonically, well aware she hated the nickname. "Apparently, we used to know each other, share some history or some nonsense like that. So, enlighten me, tell me the real story."

Madeline's harsh laugh echoed throught the cramped space. "Are you serious? Like I'm going to give you the lowdown on anything. Zander may be blind to your antics, but I'm not. Once he's watched the vid footage I gave him, he'll drop you like a hot ton of bricks."

"Drop me? What is this, third grade?" I snapped. I had no idea what she was talking about. What vid? Damn it, how long had I been out? She could be lying. The girl sounded desperate.

"Why are you acting so weird? Do you still carry a torch for Zander? If so, you can retract your claws. We aren't a couple."

"Do you think I care about that? What really concerns me is the probability you're a spy leaking information to the government. You told them where they could find me and Zander, didn't you? How clever of you to make it appear like you were an innocent bystander. Sorry, sweetheart, I don't buy it, the game's up."

I crossed my arms and stared at her. Was this girl for real? I wouldn't lead those government thugs to Zander.

"Get over yourself, Madeline. Like I would be that stupid."

She tossed her hair back over her shoulder. "You said it, not me."

I clenched my fist to my side, trying to resist the urge to punch her in the mouth.

She sighed like a bored child. "This was such a waste of my

time. I'm going to go. You'd better prepare yourself for life on your own little L, because once Zander wakes up to your game, the entire world will be against you."

She spun on her heels and left, slamming the door behind her. "Good riddance," I muttered.

Before I could analyze anything she'd spewed out, a pain ricocheted through my head again. Another memory from this life was coming at me like a barreling freight train.

I gritted my teeth, willing myself to stay conscious. I eased onto the exam table and shut my eyes, allowing whatever was about to unfold to come to me.

I sat on a bed in a spartan room with only a dresser equipped with a small mirror and an undersized wardrobe. I instinctively knew this microscopic space was where I slept, and that the government kept me here as a participant in their program.

I didn't understand what Zander had meant when he spoke of it earlier. Now, it was plain as day. The government collected the Elite like action figures and held us all in the same building so we could be trained in what they called *the program*. From what I gathered, we lived as a small community, taking our meals, exercising, doing pretty much everything together. Unfortunately, this still didn't give me any clue as to the whereabouts of my parents—but I wouldn't give up.

My attention was brought back to the room. I watched it unfold like a movie in front of me as Madeline came and sat down beside me on the bed. I shivered with cold.

She put her arm around me as if trying to comfort me. "Sorry to hear about your diagnosis, Luna. That's a real bummer."

I gave her a probing stare. My gut instinct told me she felt sorry for me, but only a fraction—and even then—it wasn't quite sincere.

I shifted uncomfortably, moving a bit away from her. "Why are you being nice to me?" I asked in a strained voice, clearly unhappy.

"Look, I realize we've never been close, but I wouldn't wish a P.A.S. diagnosis on my worst enemy. You've heard the stories."

I stiffened and stood up, desperate to distance myself from her. Pacing the small room.

"How is this happening? I was so careful."

"Exactly. Complete injustice. The way they treat the nine of us is cruel, especially considering how valuable we are to them. Poor Zander. I sure will miss him. They didn't even bother to give a reason for his punishment."

Sincerity rang in her voice, and I studied her carefully, understanding that Madeline did love Zander after all—it wasn't merely a silly teenage infatuation.

Tears spilled down Madeline's cheeks. "You don't grasp how lucky you are, Luna. I would do anything to have him look at me the way he looks at you."

I stopped pacing and stared at her. Nobody was supposed to know we were an item. It was part of a plan we'd hatched to keep us safe. "What are you talking about? Zander and I are just friends."

She wanted me to tip my hand. I wasn't that gullible.

Madeline scoffed. "Please. I've known for months. Don't look so worried. If I was going to tattle, I would have done so by now."

She was never this honest, she usually just gave me the cold shoulder. What was her deal?

"Why do you believe that? You're mistaken."

Madeline shrugged. "The time for lies is over, little L. You're leaving. You got diagnosed with Personal Ambition Syndrome for a reason. You put your ambition and desires ahead of the government's. I doubt you'll come out of VR prison in the same shape you went in. The least I can do is level with you."

"Wow, thanks for comforting me, Madeline." I began pacing again, trying to think what to do. My gaze drifted to the ceiling where I started counting tiles in an attempt to calm down.

Madeline continued, "I didn't keep my mouth shut for you. It was for Zander's benefit. Besides—once they plug you into the program, you'll *become their little lab rat; they want to see how you respond to certain pressures and stimuli in the game." She couldn't resist a smirk.*

I laughed harshly. "You don't think we're in a test now? Seriously? I mean we're in 'the program' for crying out loud," I said, air quoting with my fingers.

"Ah, yes, but when you go to virtual prison, there's a chance they could wipe your memories to do it. Then you won't remember dear old Zander. You'll be lucky if you even end up in the same simulation." She stood up and traced a finger down the bed post. "Of course, I will be there to pick up the pieces of his shattered heart."

I snorted. "Like that will work. In your happy little scenario, Zander will lose his memories too, and then he won't remember you either."

She grinned like a Cheshire cat that had just licked up all the cream. "Oh, don't you worry, Luna. I always have a plan."

CHAPTER 18

ZANDER

After waiting over an hour, I went in search of Luna, finally finding her in a level seven exam room—Madeline nowhere in sight.

My breath caught in my throat at the sight of her, crumpled up on the bed like a rag doll. I rushed over, shaking her. "Luna, are you all right?"

Her jade eyes flickered open, and she stared at me. I lifted my hand and pushed her hair back from her face, emotional turmoil written all over her features. Something had shifted in her, I could sense it somehow.

I closed my eyes, tuning in to her energy field, hoping for a vision, something to tell me what had happened. Only one person appeared in front of me—Madeline. My lids flew open and I stared down at Luna. Only then did I realize how close I'd come to her face. My gaze lowered to her mouth—I so desperately wanted to kiss her—but I didn't move—both of us locked in a hypnotic trance, bound by her memory.

I only wish I knew which one.

Luna broke the silence first. She licked her dry lips, as if attempting to muster up some courage. In a croaky voice, she said, "Did you really love me?"

I smiled, leaning down, my head touching hers. "I don't take a laser to the leg for just anyone."

She pulled away and sat up. "Be serious."

I settled next to her on the exam table and turned to face her. "Since the first day we met, it's been you. I don't know what I have to do to make you trust me again, but I'll figure it out and I swear I'll do it. I love you, Luna, always have, always will. There is no one else in the world for me but you."

She turned away and stared up at the ceiling. "I don't know what to believe anymore."

Those seven words were all it took to crush my heart.

I covered her hand with mine. "Before being forced into the games, we talked a lot about how our memories might be taken. So, we drew up a plan. When they threw us into VR prison for our so-called insubordination, we were ready. We made a pact that if either of us somehow retained our memories, we would find each other and discover a way out. The ironic part is, you lost your memory—yet you're the one who found me in P8. It must have been fate, since neither of us remembered that we made a pact."

Luna smirked.

"What's so funny?"

"I may have found you, but I kicked your ass."

I laughed. "I expected no less."

"What did we do to deserve VR prison?" she asked her voice turning somber.

My heart lifted, encouraged by the question—maybe I stood a chance.

I dug in my pocket. "Let me show you. Madeline gave me something."

I felt her stiffen beside me. "Let me guess, it's some kind of vid."

I held up the micro projector. "Bingo." I frowned at her, puzzled. "How did you know?"

"Oh, your friend Madeline happened to mention it when she brought me down here."

Annoyed, I pressed my lips together. Concerns over Madeline's trustworthiness still lingered in my mind. But I couldn't forget that Madeline had healed me, immediately coming to my aid when I needed her.

"Hello? Did you check out on me?" Luna said, breaking through my thoughts.

"Sorry, just thinking. Don't worry about what Madeline said. She thinks I'm clueless regarding what's on this. But I remember what occurred that night. She doesn't know I was there, too."

Puzzled, Luna scrunched up her face. "Where?"

I shut off the lights and sat back down next to Luna, flipping open the micro projector and pressing play. The video appeared on the blank wall in front of us—the images familiar and haunting, and precisely what I expected.

I tried to explain. "This took place about a week before you went into VR prison. We worked for months with the resistors to set up a heist to steal the clock key."

"You told me a little about the key before, but how does it work exactly?"

"I'll get to that." I pointed to the scene unfolding before us on the wall. "We broke curfew, which alone was grounds enough for us to be locked up, but we managed to sneak out and took the last shuttle to the capital headquarters. Scott and Beth gave us fake IDs and enough credits for transport. They received intel that the clock key was being stored in the lab facility occasionally used for Elite med checkups—which made us familiar with the premises. We were pretty confident we could infiltrate the building easily. Once we arrived on site, you hacked into the security system, so we could sneak inside."

"I hacked into a government facility?"

"Yes, of course. You're a great hacker. Why?"

"That explains a few things."

"What do you mean?" I asked.

"Back on W1, I hacked a computer system to free myself from a locked interrogation room. That was right before my transport to P8. Unfortunately, I ended up being caught before I could escape the building."

She shook her head as if to break something loose. "I need to stop acting like W1 was real! It's only a stupid game."

"Hey." I squeezed her hand. "It was real to you. And those memories are as important as anything you remember here—you have every right to keep them."

"I always thought it a little strange that I could hack out of such a top-line security system from reading a book. I guess they didn't erase everything."

"They can't take everything, Luna. They can never take your mind, your soul. That belongs to you and no one else. We're going to fight them and win. We will stop this, I promise."

"Still, we must be able to retain something. Otherwise, I wouldn't have that ability anymore," she reasoned.

"You may have retained some reflexive skills. Perhaps they only took memories that linked you back to this place. Like you could keep the skill, but not how you acquired it. They did all kinds of strange tests on us, so anything is possible."

Luna didn't reply, her attention focused on the images flashing before her on the wall. I watched with her, as the shadowy image of Luna all in black came onto the screen. She ran past a distracted droid working security on the building and quickly scanned her stolen ID to get inside. Before anymore could be seen, the image scrambled and cut out. Madeline must have assumed since Luna had an entry badge, she was working for the government. I suppose to the outside eye that's exactly what it looked like.

Luna's head whipped around. "If we cut the security feed, why do we have footage of me entering the building? And where were you?"

"We didn't realize that a droid would be at the door. All the times we'd been before we'd never seen one—and were worried someone was on to us. But in the end, we decided to move forward. It had taken so long to get everything lined up we didn't want to wait any longer. There was too much at stake. You'd cut the security by the time we arrived, but didn't count on this guy. We knew he probably had his own camera built into his eye—most security droids do—and would capture us going in. We decided we would create a distraction."

"Couldn't I just cut the feed from the droid?"

"We had dropped the gear about a block back. And we only had about fifteen minutes until the security camera came on. We knew it was now or never."

"What about you?"

I grimaced. "You tricked me. I threw a rock to distract the droid, he went after the noise, and before I could stop you, you took off like a shot, headed for the door. I had insisted I go first in case there was any trouble. If there were more security hiding somewhere I didn't want you to get caught.

"I chased after you, but I must have been out of the line of vision of this guy by the time I made it over there."

Luna smirked. "Glad to know not much has changed."

"Ha ha. Very funny. Do you want to hear what happened after that or not?"

She sobered. "Tell me."

I cast my eyes back to the wall mentally revisiting what played out afterwards. "Once inside we headed straight for the lab. The clock key was hidden in a cabinet marked with skull and crossbones and a caution sign on it. I think they wanted to scare people away, make them think whatever was in there was dangerous."

"According to Scott and Beth's information we knew there would be a secret compartment hidden in the back where they stored the clock key. They liked to keep the device handy when they ran experiments to see the effects the key would have on us and vice versa. None of us suspected that's where they kept it. It was all very hush hush. Do you remember how I told you the

Black Mark wants to use us to send us back to certain events in history?"

Luna nodded.

"Well the clock key is how we get there. So, when they lost it, they freaked."

Luna visibly gulped. "Things went south didn't they?"

I sighed. "You could say that. Right after you grabbed the key, we heard shouting somewhere in the distance. I was keeping guard some distance away. You locked eyes on me, and I understood what you wanted me to do—but I deliberately dragged my feet. We made a pact I instantly regretted. In fact, I remember we argued about it—you were going to steal the key without my help, insisting you had the better skills to do the job."

Luna shrugged. "That does sound like something I would say. And it's true."

I ignored her jab and continued. "I felt really uncomfortable with the idea of leaving you behind in the event we got caught. But you made me promise, declaring it was for the greater good of the Elite. No matter what I said, I couldn't talk you out of it. In the end, we compromised and you allowed me to come along as lookout."

I paused remembering the haunted look on Luna's face when she recognized our gamble had failed. Luna nudged me. "Hey you okay?"

"Yeah, I was just thinking about the look on your face once you realized you'd been captured, you were so pale." I smiled a little. "But of course, you being you, went into warrior Luna mode within moments, your lips pressing together in that determined way of yours. You decided to transfer the clock key to me, kicking the device in my direction—but so discreetly no one noticed. You blended the movement of crouching to the floor, with booting the key over. And with that one move, you probably saved our necks."

"What happened after that?"

"I grabbed the clock key and ran, and believe me, leaving you behind was the hardest thing I've ever done. I know we agreed to separate if things went wrong. On an intellectual level, I got that, but it didn't make it any easier to do."

"What happened after you ran?"

"The guards had already nabbed you when I took off. I didn't stick around—but knowing you, you probably didn't go down without a fight."

Luna nodded her approval. "I agree, I'm sure I gave them a run for their money. Stupid bastards."

I got up and crouched down in front of her, taking both her hands in mine. "I don't want you to think I abandoned you, Luna. I planned on breaking you out with the clock key just as soon as I'd contacted the resistors for help."

She shrugged. "Zander, that was a long time ago. Like you said, getting the clock key helped us later on."

I narrowed my eyes. "That's it? No, I can't trust you Zander, you betrayed me, Zander?"

Luna rolled her eyes. "I suppose I can offer you a little leeway, considering you took a laser for me."

I grinned, leaping up and wrapping my arms around her, whooping. "I'm so relieved. I was terrified I would tell you this and you wouldn't—"

Luna pried me off her. "Get a grip Barringer. You've been hanging out with Crane for too long. No need to share in his flamboyant enthusiasm. Just sit down and tell me what happened next."

I eagerly took her through the story. "Well I had the key, but the problem was, within hours of all this, I was ordered into a glass cage. They put quite a few of us under glass with no explanation. The government panicked over the loss of the clock key. They couldn't pin anything on you because you didn't have it. Believe me, they searched everywhere. And I mean *everywhere*."

Luna blanched. "I think I get the point."

"Anyway, even though they couldn't label you guilty for trespassing, they did the next best thing and diagnosed you with

P.A.S. Basically, they made up a syndrome to suit themselves. If you don't bend to their whims, you're accused of having a mysterious syndrome, whose only symptom is common sense and having your own mind.

"After they found you in the lab with the cabinet open, they figured out you were after the clock key. Hell, they even waited 48 hours to see if you'd swallowed it. But no luck. We deliberately kept our dating a secret, in case we were ever pared against each other if caught—and it paid off."

I paused as I let Luna process everything I'd told her. She poked me in the ribs with her elbow impatiently. "Then what?"

"I didn't remember the key until we jumped out of P8. But as soon as Crane revived me, I remembered details I'd forgotten. They never bothered to frisk me before they sent me to P8, so the clock key remained hidden in my sock the entire time."

"How did you keep your memories?"

I paused. How much should I reveal? I decided to stick with the facts. My hunch that my psychic ability helped me was only a theory.

"I told you almost everything back on P8. My memories slowly returned. By the time you came along, I'd cobbled together most of my past, but there were still a few loopholes in the picture. Do you recall how I told you about how my friends disappeared back in P8? First Billie, then Dafina? After Dafina vanished, the next day I woke up with two sets of fresh memories, some from this place and some of what supposedly happened to me on P8. But the biggest factor—that we were in a game—eluded me. At least until we were back here. For you, it was different. You only remembered W1 and P8."

"But I didn't wake up one day in P8 and just know, like you did," Luna interrupted. "In my case, I think there was a glitch." She shifted to face me. "When I stepped through the gates from W1 to P8, something flickered, like there was a microsecond power short. From the very first moment I woke up, I remembered my life on W1. And on top of that, new memories—that weren't mine—surfaced. But there weren't enough details, I had huge gaps in my knowledge for this new life."

Luna's words made me wonder—perhaps I'd been mistaken in thinking that my psychic abilities gave me an edge. Maybe the resistor leader's theory had merit.

"Interesting. Scott and Beth theorized that the mineral in Elite bodies may help retain or even restore some memories."

I got up and began to pace the small room as I recollected more of the details. "Back on P8 when sleep alluded me, I would lie in bed and sometimes hear a blipping sound. Now I realize these were most likely game updates." I stopped pacing and turned to Luna. "Think about it. When someone disappeared, they had to make everyone believe they'd never existed. How else would they do that, but with an update? That's the only way people would forget the missing players, with no questions asked. Updates would also explain why I would receive more memories every time I slept."

"That makes sense. I'm surprised that my P8 father wasn't just erased. Wouldn't they not want me to ask questions? What did Scott and Beth think?"

"There's been no time to contact them—what with running from safehouse to safehouse and trying to keep ahead of the feds. You're the first person I've spoken to about my theory. I don't want to start a rumor that isn't true. I'll wait until I get their input before deciding what to do next. And as for your Dad, well I can only assume it was another one of their sick tests for us. To see how we would perform. Kind of like what they did to us when we were in the program."

"So why didn't we wipe out the feed so that this vid wouldn't exist?" Luna asked, switching topics.

"We didn't believe we would both be sent off to VR so close together. One of us was supposed to come back and obliterate the video. But with me going into the game right away and you being watched so closely, there wasn't an opportunity. We decided there would be too many red flags if we cut the security cameras before we finished the deed."

"Couldn't Beth and what's his name do it?"

"Scott."

"What?"

"His name's Scott. And no, neither one could. Not without jeopardizing everything. By that time, you'd already been caught and the government was on guard twenty-four seven."

"This certainly is complicated," she murmured, cinching her eyebrows together in thought.

"I think it's about to get more complicated."

She rolled her eyes. "What now? Let me guess we're about to be hit by a meteorite."

I shook my head, ignoring the sarcasm. "No. Luna. Think about it. You are forgetting something major."

She frowned, staring at me puzzled. "What?"

"How did Madeline acquire the footage? It is government property. I'd like to know how many other people have access to this video. I don't trust her, Lun. Not anymore. I don't think we are out of the woods. Not by a long shot.

CHAPTER 19

LUNA

The faux moonlight coming through the window cast shadows on the wall, and I counted the long fingered lines that looked more like monster talons than the shadow of the blinds.

One...two...three...

I sighed; this was pointless. I couldn't sleep. Everything Zander had told me today ran around in my head like a washing machine set to spin.

I wanted to understand more about the clock key. For example, why did it only work with the Elite? My fingers itched to mess around with the device's inner mechanism. If I figured out how it operated, maybe I could untangle this whole crazy scenario—and get out of it.

I rubbed my eyes. Unanswered questions weren't the only thing keeping me awake. My stomach burned with guilt as I thought of my own secrets Zander still knew nothing about. I clung to my few precious memories I'd acquired, unable to share them with him. Something held me back.

But what?

I groaned. Sleep didn't appear to be in the cards tonight. I pulled back the covers, letting my feet hit the cold tiles of the bunk room

—a small space with only about half a dozen beds. Crane snored softly in the corner, while Zander slept in the bed next to mine. His chest rose and fell slowly and evenly, indicating he was sound asleep.

I would have preferred my own digs, but this was the only room available in the safe house. All hands were on deck due to the recent attacks. I stretched my neck to ease the crick in it—but froze when Zander rolled over. When he stilled and continued sleeping, I breathed a sigh of relief. I allowed myself to study him for a moment. His skin still held that familiar tan glow, but his brown hair was a little longer now, curling up at the edges and sticking up at the back of his head. I wanted to jump inside his mind, to be sure everything he told me was true—but of course, that was impossible.

My eyes caught on something gold and shiny under his pillow. I hopped off the bed and tiptoed over to attempt a better look.

What was he hiding?

I soundlessly plucked it out from beneath his head—he didn't move. I grinned. I still had the magic touch.

I tread carefully over to the window, taking a look at the small device in my palm. At first, I thought it might be the micro projector, but this was larger. I leaned in to get a better look and almost gasped in surprise.

The clock key.

I never had the chance to examine the piece up close before. The tool measured about two inches in diameter with two elongated snakelike shapes cut into its sides. Obvious spiral grooves ran along the center, spiraling out from what appeared to be a natural fire opal set in the middle. I turned the clock key over, but the back looked identical to the front, warming my palm. Could it give off heat? But how? Why?

I tiptoed over to the new pack of supplies I'd received from Crane earlier this evening—remembering the red light, like the one we used in the caves. I let my hand search the front pouch of the bag in the darkness. When my fingers hit pay dirt, I pulled out the light and returned to the window.

I strained my eyes, looking for any detail I might have missed. And then I saw it—a second groove along the lip of the device. I ran my finger over the edge, attempting to force the scal open, but it wouldn't budge.

Something must trigger the mechanism to separate, but what?

I bit my lip, trying to think. Should I borrow the clock key? Zander would never be the wiser if I returned the gadget before morning. My mind raced with possibilities. Zander said the Elite were hunted for their time travel abilities and the clock key would help to that end. So, what if I tried to manipulate the key to find my parents? That wouldn't be such a stretch. They possessed something important that might change everything. I felt it in my bones.

My pulse raced. What if I took it a step further and attempted to have the clock key send me to Dara? Or Trinity? I swallowed the lump in my throat. The possibility of seeing either of them again made my chest burn with a hope that I didn't dare dream of.

It wouldn't hurt to examine the thing further while Zander slept. I would learn the mechanics, see if the key connected to any kind of system I could hack into.

I noted a small chair by the door and silently crossed the room to grab it, along with the com Crane gave me.

I tapped my fingers against my forehead, trying to think. Normally, you could type in a brand or model of whatever you were endeavoring to hack into and retrieve all sorts of intel, but this device was clearly one of a kind. Which led to another question—wouldn't there be a tracker on something as precious as this? I imagine Zander would have already removed anything that garnered suspicion. But what if the tracker was undetectable? Carrying this thing around, Zander unknowingly might bring the government henchmen right to us.

With more resolve than ever, I got to work searching the web. A lot of government and criminal organizations back on W1 used user/password combos to mine data or spy. But there was nowhere to input a password into this thing, not as far as I could tell anyway. Perhaps it was newer, better technology. I wasn't in W1 or P8 anymore.

I fiddled on my com for about an hour searching and discovered that there were infinite ways this thing could be encrypted. The trigger to unlock it could be something as simple as using cloud based iris recognition or as complex as an electric cardiac signature. Bottom line, there were no backdoors to open it, and I was back to where I started.

With frustration, I put down the com and rubbed my eyes. *Think. Luna. Think.*

When nothing came to mind, I looked at the device again. I needed something to pry it open. My eyes lit upon the meal schedule for the main mess hall, pinned up by a thumbtack. I pulled the flier down and snapped up the pin. I took my prize back over to the window and ran the sharp edge under the seal, that seemed to connect the two portions of the key together.

I met with resistance at first, but I pushed harder, then heard a pop. To my dismay the instrument came apart, hanging only by a small hinge.

My skin grew clammy, a sheen of sweat formed on my forehead as I panicked. *Oh, my god I broke the key.* With shaking hands, I tried to return it to its original form, pressing the pieces together, willing them to seal. I realized now the opal was actually an encasing of some sort, filled with a liquid running the spectrum of colors—red, orange, yellow, blue, and violet.

Mesmerized, I stared at the rainbow, momentarily forgetting I should be attempting to fix this thing. The energy from the clock key ran from the palm of my hand up my arm in a flash of vibration, making me feel alive in a way I never thought possible.

But what's more, it granted me another gift—certainty. My mind cleared, no longer clouded by questions of what I should do or who I should trust. I knew my own heart. And it was intoxicating.

I became so engrossed in the emotions the clock key stirred in me, I didn't notice Zander sneak up behind me.

"Luna what are you doing?" Zander hissed, keeping his voice low, so as not to wake Crane.

I spun around, the mutilated apparatus still in my hand.

He caught sight of the object in my open palm and his face visibly paled in the red light. "My God, what have you done?"

"Nothing," I hedged, my voice laced with guilt. "I was just figuring out how this thing worked. I couldn't sleep and I saw the clock key under your pillow and thought I would take a look."

Zander snatched the key carefully from me trying to examine it. "It's not supposed to be opened. The entire system might be comprised." Not caring if he woke Crane or not, he barked. "Lights on."

He squinted against the bright light, letting his eyes adjust. "You pressed the seam too hard, creating a hairline fracture at one edge." He came closer and ran his pinky finger down the crack in the structure, to show me the damage.

"I'm sorry Zander, I thought the clock key opened. I assumed it was difficult to pry apart because the government didn't want to make the clock key easy to get into."

"Damn it, Luna. This isn't a game. Why couldn't you ask me how the key worked instead of going behind my back? I would've told you everything I know." He went over to the lamp by his bed and examined the device further. "I think the ampule is still intact. But with the casing broken, it's vulnerable."

"What's in there?" I asked hesitantly. Zander never got this freaked, even when we were about to jump into an unknown abyss in P8. I wrung my hands together, praying the contents were easily replaceable. But I knew in my bones that wasn't true.

Zander turned, casting a glance in Crane's direction, who unbelievably was still asleep, then looked to me. "The liquid inside is the mineral Elite 9 in a very concentrated form. The same stuff that bonded to our DNA is in this ampule. If you'd broken the glass, you would have destroyed some of the last rare compound that exists. Then we would have no leverage against the government. No chance to make things right."

Great. "Well give it back. I'm sure I can fix it."

Zander looked at me with sad eyes. "What will it take for you to start believing that I'm on your side? That you don't need to creep around at night and figure things out on your own? I'll answer any questions you have."

"Tell me how that clock key works with us."

Zander pushed a hand through his hair, working the muscle in his jaw. "Fine. You want to do this now. We'll do it now." He sat on his bed and placed the clock key delicately on the night-stand, his fingers tracing the edge of the delicate apparatus.

I moved and sank down on my own bed to face him.

"This is the first time we've had the clock key in our posses-sion. Scott and Beth haven't even seen it in person yet."

I winced. If that was meant to be a dig at me, it worked. Thanks to my genius efforts, they would never see the instru-ment in its original form. At the first opportunity, I had to try to fix the damn thing.

I didn't interrupt Zander, afraid if I did, he might stop talking altogether. The more I understood about the key, the better chance I would have at repairing it.

Zander continued. "According to research and a spy network of resistors, we discovered top-secret files that explained how the time travel would work. The mineral conforms to the energy locked within the brass circle and can be transmuted from the disk into the body of an Elite member—and then the mineral bonds to itself."

"Bonds to itself?" I asked, not quite understanding.

"Yes—the portion from our bodies and the portion held in the ampule of this clock key bond together to produce incred-ible amounts of power, much more than a normal human. Essentially, the Elite can be batteries, but on a much bigger scale. Let's face it, the government is never going to want to get rid of batteries, elite or otherwise, not if they can help it anyway. But with us we can get to the point where we could contain enough energy to eliminate the time barrier, without the use of any outside help. They called the instrument the clock key because it's literally the key to manipulating the clock."

"Wow. And you're sure about all this?"

"The files obtained through the resistors show years of testing and experiments done on us and the rest of the Elite while we were in the program, including some before we even entered their school. They've acquired the data. All that's left to do is put what they learned into practice."

"And they're just nine of us?"

Zander looked up at me for the first time. "Yes, as far as I'm aware, only nine. Probably why they named the mineral, Elite 9."

"Why wouldn't they create more?"

"I think by the time they realized how powerful we could truly be, the Elite mineral was already heading toward extinction. The last found traces were placed into this clock key."

The silence stretched out between us as I tried to comprehend everything Zander had just revealed.

Finally, Zander spoke. "Why don't we get some sleep? You can let me know if you believe me or not in the morning."

"Zander I—"

"Not tonight, Luna. Okay? It's been a long day. I just want to go to bed." With that, he barked, "Lights out."

Zander didn't say another word, only closed his eyes, and turned his back to me to go to sleep. Not knowing what else to do, I returned to my own bed in an attempt to get some rest.

As I shut my eyes, I realized something. For the first time, I trusted Zander. Completely and fully. I was unsure of what triggered that trust. Maybe it was the look in his eyes when comprehension dawned that I'd broken the key—you couldn't fake that horror. Or perhaps it had been a slow build leading to this moment. Or more probable—the clock key had changed me.

Either way, the timing sucked. I lay awake for a long time thinking about how the moment I believed in Zander, he'd lost his faith in me. The universe was a cruel mistress.

I vowed I would make this right.

I would have to open up to Zander about my true motivations to find my parents. But what if telling him about the disk put him in danger? And he had the right to turn me away after everything I'd put him through. Could I handle that?

One thing however was for certain, once I discovered the truth—I would unleash the true power I realized had always been inside me—revealed when I connected with that clock key.

The force of the key stimulated every cell in my body, and I responded to its pull.

Even now, the buzz remained, coursing through my veins like sparks.

I wondered how long it would be until the government caught up with us. And if somehow my existence would be quietly erased from the world without anyone really caring.

I'd pushed everyone away.

And was now very much alone.

CHAPTER 20

LUNA

The next morning Zander was up and out of bed before sunrise. Somewhere in my sleepy fog, I heard him leave, muttering something to a half comatose Crane about heading to the engineering center to see if he could make a repair. I noticed he didn't tell Crane exactly what repair that was.

He didn't come over and try to speak with me, and I kept my eyes shut. If he didn't want to talk, well, I deserved that, I supposed. His disappointment in me was apparent last night—I would give him some space.

After he'd gone, I feigned sleep for as long as possible, but soon gave up, rising just before the fake sun rose on the horizon. By the time I got back from the bathroom, Crane was up, dressed and ready to go. His purple t-shirt had the words *Rock On* emblazoned across the chest, with a glitter guitar underneath. His skin-tight black jeans and boots completed the look.

"Good morning, sunshine. Ready to get this day started? I have some plans for us. But first, breakfast!"

"Are you always this cheerful in the morning," I grumbled.

He pulled me in for a side hug. "You bet. Consider it a perk of working with the C-man. Now come on. The early bird catches the worm."

"What about Zander? Shouldn't we wait for him?" I asked.

"Nah. He had something to do first thing. I'm sure he'll catch up with us later."

Not knowing what else to say, I let him lead me out of the bunk room and down to the cafeteria.

After an uneventful breakfast, Crane dragged me down to basement level to a computer room. The walls almost hummed from all the tech equipment crammed in here. Surveillance cameras covered every surface, and security programs ran data through a loop at an enormous rate. I spent all day listening to Crane go on and on about how good I used to be at hacking and how much they needed my help.

Translation—Zander asked him to keep me busy.

After a day of running codes and scanning vids for malicious activity, my eyes burned with fatigue. I was dying to know what happened to the clock key. Had Zander been able to fix it? To my dismay, he didn't come to dinner, and by the time I got back to my room, he was already asleep or pretending to be.

"Great," I muttered. "Now what?" I was never going to find out about the clock key at this rate.

"Hey, if you can't beat em' join em' right?" Crane said, throwing himself down on his bed. "Man, I'm stuffed. They outdid themselves tonight with those fake sausages. I think they're..." he trailed off mid-sentence, a snore emanating from his corner of the room. I rolled my eyes. How did he fall asleep so fast? I swear the kid was some kind of weird mutant.

I crossed to my own bed and noticed Zander had left the clock key on the bedside table. Since he really did appear to be flaked out, I tiptoed over and took a peek.

I gently picked up the device, and my heart sank when I realized it was still broken. I straightened, determined to fix this problem—I'd been thinking about it all day, all I had to do was close the two pieces back together and seal the crack. I usually made it my business to figure out how things worked and would find a solution for this, too.

Then maybe Zander would forgive me.

The only problem was I didn't have what I needed to fix it. Could there be another way that I wasn't aware of? My fingers tingled in delight at the small object in my hand. Even damaged, I felt it's pull—the desire to keep it close.

I glanced up—Zander's eyes remained closed, but for how long was anybody's guess. I needed to leave the safehouse away from prying eyes and Zander's judgment. I wanted to feel the power of the clock key just a little longer. Maybe if I kept it with me for a while the answers I sought for finding another way to repair the device would come.

I placed the clock key carefully into a small container I'd pinched from the tech room before popping it into my jeans. I checked my other pocket for my com then pulled on a black hat I stole from Crane. He wouldn't miss it—I never saw him in the same thing twice. Without turning back, I slipped out of the room.

Earlier that day, down in the computer room, Crane made sure my ID chip worked, so I was free to come and go without the Resistor squad coming at me full throttle for trespassing. Still, even with that security in place, I decided to keep to the back halls. In a matter of minutes, I found myself outside. I paused, leaning heavily against the brick building, taking in the cool night breeze. The atmosphere held a different quality down here, recycled and modified air from above ground circulated through the streets, filling it with a musty fragrance, but I didn't mind, letting it be a balm on my sweaty skin. Besides, this air was incredible compared to some slums of W1.

I started down the main road surprised that, despite the late hour, the noise of the city never abated. Vendors called out selling their soy hot dogs and sausages, billboards played their looped ads overhead, and the pedal bikes swooshed by me, pushing the foot traffic to the side.

I grinned. It felt good to blend into a crowd again. For a minute, I pretended to be the girl of W1 I remembered—off to steal some food for my family. Finally, alone and free, after constantly being surrounded by people since I arrived, I allowed myself to think of Dara and Trinity. Holding their faces in my mind's eye, I wondered where they were. They could be in any of the many energy outposts scattered throughout the city. Even if I did find them, would they know me? I pushed that down. Now wasn't the time to worry about that.

I followed the throng about a half mile before making a quick detour down a side street. No helpful road signs marked the avenues here, as the metropolis divided itself into sectors. I tried to mentally count every step and map out my location in my head, to remember how to find my way back—if necessary, I could always use the sat nav on my com.

The odd smell of wet garbage and fried food hit my nostrils as I turned a corner. Wrappers lined the street here, and I resisted the urge to tidy up. My life had become very chaotic, and my fingers itched to create order. I headed east, discovering a falafel cart along the way that smelled like heaven on wheels. My stomach grumbled despite having eaten dinner. I pushed on. The last thing I needed was to attract unwanted attention to myself by not having enough funds. Sure, the ID worked, but that didn't mean there was coin on it. Besides, I was on a mission—I didn't need to pilfer. I had food in my belly. I had to have some standards.

A few more streets over, I found the perfect spot to collect myself and breathe. I stopped abruptly and almost crashed into a cyclist delivering takeout. I avoided him just in time and leaned up against the wall. The wail of sirens in the back alley were quieter, and I let myself rest in the comfort of the shadows, behind a row of apartments. A hovering halo lamp gave me enough light to examine the clock key again. I marveled at the strange light fixtures just for a moment. They seemed suspended in the air like mini UFO's, with nothing tethered to them to hold them in place. The advanced technology blew my mind. Most of the life I remembered didn't even involve electricity.

I sat down on a semi-clean part of the street and got down to business. The hinge itself appeared intact, but I had nothing to recreate the seal. I wondered how much heat could be applied without compromising the ampule?

I let myself get lost in math equations, trying to figure out the exact amount of pressure and heat required on a device only two inches across. Just when I believed I was close to solving the calculation, the vibration of multiple sets of boots pounding the pavement brought me to attention. I scrambled up, shoving the clock key back in my pocket.

Then the surrounding silence exploded into chaos.

Loud knocking on doors rappelled down either side of the main thoroughfare. Men's voices rose, and babies began to cry.

With a sinking dread, I realized what was happening.

Another raid.

And I was right in the middle of it.

I pushed myself from the wall but remained in the shadows, not sure which way to run, as screaming came from both ends of the backstreet. Whichever way I went, I would be headed right toward the government henchmen.

The alleyway practically pulsed with the thunder of a thousand heartbeats as the wails of the people of New Earth multiplied in the streets. I turned and strode closer to the mouth of the alley, just making out the pristine black and gray uniforms of the officials, dragging men, women, and children into the street like they were less than animals. I pressed back again into the shadows—inhaling a shaky breath before stealing another glance.

I squinted, unsure if what I witnessed was really happening. Bile rose in my throat as I watched them line people up like cattle—one by one, forming a long chain. The uniformed men yelled in their faces, rage contorting their features into something grotesque. A baby wailed and the uniform smacked the mother, telling her to shut the kid up. An elderly woman crumbled to her knees in exhaustion, and another guard dragged her back to her feet and spit in her face. I covered my mouth, horrified. Flashbacks of the fateful night with Dara came screaming back to me. The syringe plunging into her neck before she crumpled to the ground played again and again in my mind. That was the last time I saw her. Would they do the same to these people?

What were they going to do after they collected everyone? Shuttle them away somewhere to be batteries? That hardly seemed legal. There were too many of them. It would raise countless questions they wouldn't want to answer.

Some people from the adjacent building came into the alleyway in an attempt to hide, hoping they wouldn't be next.

I needed to run. Now. They hadn't seen me yet—but once the chaos died down, they certainly would. I was about to turn and stride back down the alley when fingers tightened around my waist. A hand slammed over my mouth muffling my startled cry.

I froze, rooted to the spot, unable to breathe or form a single thought. All I heard was the dim roaring in my ears as the horrifying truth washed over me.

I'd been found.

CHAPTER 21
ZANDER

The press of Luna's body against mine caused my breath to catch in my throat. Her hair tickled my nose, but I forced myself to focus.

We needed to get out of here. Now.

Luna stood rigid, waiting for me to make the first move, so she could use my own weight against me. I wasn't in the mood for a face full of dirt and trash—time to tell her it was me.

"Luna, it's Zander. Don't scream, okay?" She nodded, and I let her go.

She spun around, eyes full of emerald fire. "What the hell—"

I cut her off, pointing to some officers over her shoulder that had come way to close. She took one glance, her face turning ashen in the moonlight. She visibly swallowed, her eyes looking at me as if to say, *now what?*

I grabbed her hand and quietly led her further into the recesses of darkness, deeper into the alleyway. Both ends of the road now teemed with officials. Sepha wasn't kidding when she'd said the raids were getting out of hand. The government had never gone this far before. They had to be desperate for batteries. Something had sparked a fire that burned the agreement between the capital and New Earth all the way to hell.

"There's only one way out," I whispered. "Follow me."

We crept down the alley until we got to a large grate I'd passed on the way in. I let go of her hand and knelt to peer inside the drain. "These grates lead back to the old train tunnels. If we remove the barrier, we can escape this way." I grabbed the iron bars, and pulled, but I was still a bit weaker than I liked. My body needed more time for complete healing. Wordlessly, Luna crouched next to me to assist. Together, we moved the heavy cover to one side, and it made a loud clang as it hit the pavement. We were instantly caught in the crosshairs of a flashlight. The beam blinded me, and I held up my hand to block it.

The agent hollered. "I found two more down here!"

Three other men joined him as they raced toward us, their feet pounding the pavement in a sickening syncopated beat.

They inched closer every second.

"You need to jump!" I shouted. "Hurry!"

Without a moment's hesitation, Luna launched herself into the unknown blackness. I heard her groan as she fell hard on the concrete below. Without waiting, I hurled myself through the opening right behind her. Luna was already up, grabbing my hand and dragging me to my feet. The pain of the fall was masked by my adrenaline. Only steps behind us, the agents hovered above us like hungry seagulls.

"Run!" she yelled.

Together, we sprinted down the old tunnel. The space was beyond dark, but the sound of our footsteps gave away our location.

It was only a matter of minutes before they would catch up to us, but we had a lead for now. I held firm to Luna's hand as we raced through a maze of dizzying tunnels, often stumbling in the blackness, but managing to stay on our feet. I held my arm out as we ran, making sure we didn't run into walls or corners. I mostly let my senses guide me, intuitively taking turns at every opportunity to lose our unwelcome guests.

We were quicker than they were but not by much. I quickly

hooked a right, dragging Luna with me—before the agents could spot us. My fingers searched the wall, hoping beyond reason what I was searching for would be there.

Come on, I thought to myself. My thumb fell into a hidden notch; I pushed, and a door opened. Without thinking, I shoved Luna inside. The room was tiny, and I realized it must be one of the old storage rooms off the tracks.

It was musty, and the itch of spiderwebs prickled the back of my neck. I didn't dare move, holding on to Luna's hand like a lifeline, to ensure she was safe beside me.

The agents trampled past us. From the noise they made, there had to be at least six. Why would they send so many for two people? I supposed I already knew the answer to that question. We were special—and with only nine Elite, it wouldn't be hard for us to be recognized.

An ache materialized in my chest at the mere thought.

We waited about five minutes in silence, before either of us spoke. Our breath slowly evened out, coming to some sort of normal rhythm again as we crowded together.

Luna rested her head against my chest; I could feel her entire body trembling. "That was close."

"Tell me about it. I'm never letting you out of my sight again," I joked, attempting to ease the tension.

She tilted her head toward me, I could scarcely make out the outline of her face. I lifted my hand and cupped her cheek, reveling in the warmth, her closeness.

Luna turned on the red light attached to her jacket, casting the room in an odd, eerie pink.

"Why do you care about me so much, Zander? All I do is make more trouble for you. I mean, look where we are now for goodness' sake."

Her words were a burden sitting on top of the grief and guilt already weighing on me so hard I worried my knees might buckle. I failed her in so many ways. There was no point in trying to tap into whatever she felt for me once upon a time. I needed to appeal to the steely determination that lived inside her now and had gotten her this far. The girl she had become.

"Luna, you're no trouble to me. We're keeping our promise to protect each other. That's what we do. We aren't quitters. We never were and we never will be." I allowed myself the luxury of tucking a wayward lock of hair behind her ear that came loose from her ponytail. I licked my dry lips, not believing what I was about to say.

"We need to see our way out of this mess together. It's the only way to help those poor people we witnessed being pulled from their homes and being treated worse than rabid animals. We can stop the government from doing whatever the hell they want and thinking they can get away with it. They have no right to control anyone, and it's time they learned that lesson. I believe the Elite are one of the few groups who can fight them and win." I searched her face, unable to read her—her green eyes smooth as a Caribbean ocean.

I took both her hands in mine and took a deep breath. "Fight with me, Luna. Fight with the resistors and I vow to you after that, if it's what you want, I will never come near you again."

She dropped my hands and fixed her gaze over my shoulder as if something besides old cleaning supplies sat on the shelf behind us.

I swallowed hard, locked on her profile. Waiting for her to say something. Finally, after what seemed like an eternity, she turned to look at me again, and said, "What about my parents?"

"I'll help you find them. We can go, just us, and see what happened to them. But know, you probably won't like what we uncover. We'll have to go on our own. Nobody else will want to risk the danger it involves." I pushed a hand through my hair and sighed. "If we're going to do this, there's one more thing you should know about me. And I don't think you're going to like it."

CHAPTER 22

LUNA

"What is it?" I asked.

He stared at me, looking as ragged as I felt, his chestnut hair, now stuck out in all directions from where he'd run his fingers through it. I crossed my arms to prevent myself from smoothing down the stray locks.

He didn't know I trusted him, otherwise he wouldn't be acting this nervous. Not even his proclamation of another secret had ruffled me.

I still wasn't sure where my certainty came from. Perhaps my theory about bonding with the clock key had been accurate, or maybe outrunning death on a daily basis changed a person.

Whatever the reason, I could be patient for once and wait until he was comfortable enough to take me into his confidence —and I would be sure to listen calmly. Besides, he didn't realize I had secrets of my own. It would be nice to share them with someone. The crease in Zander's forehead deepened, and I became even more certain he was freaking out about how to explain things to me.

The old me would take advantage of his apprehension. Work the angles until I had gleaned all possible information from him

—without giving a thought for his welfare. I liked having the upper hand. Mama had taught me well.

After a few more minutes of impenetrable silence, Zander finally worked up the courage to speak. His voice wobbled a bit, but he hung in there.

"I discovered something about myself inside the P8 game; it came on gradually at first, but since I got home the knowing has increased. I think I'm developing psychic ability." He shook his head, as if arguing with himself. "No that's not true. I'm positive I'm psychic. Especially after my experiences tonight."

My brow furrowed, puzzled. This was not what I expected. "Psychic? What do you mean, like telling the future or something?"

"I'm not sure—more like hunches, or feelings about things. But today was different. I suddenly woke up and realized you were in danger, and I knew exactly where to find you. Not only that but how we would escape. I didn't question anything, I got dressed and went after you. The entire scenario just sort of downloaded into my mind, even though none of it had actually happened yet."

Well, that explained how Zander was able to locate me in that alley, I mused.

"It's happened before," Zander continued. "Do you remember the break-in at the safe house where Sepha was captured?" His voice broke a little, saying her name.

I nodded.

"Well, I had a prophetic vision where I glimpsed smoke, but couldn't figure out what that meant—or what I was supposed to do. The rest I discerned only moments before the feds showed up and I realized we were under attack—by then it was too late."

"I remember that," I exclaimed. "You were acting so weird, holding your head and mumbling something about Sepha, but I couldn't understand you."

"That vision hurt like hell, but this time, the revelation came more as a dream. Leading up to the premonition, a million other little things popped up that didn't seem to add up to much, but put together, it makes me wonder. I keep asking myself why me? Why now?"

He stared at me in bewilderment. This was the first time I had seen him without answers. It made him more vulnerable, more open. I took both his hands in mine. They were clammy with sweat.

Had I been that much of a jerk that he would be so scared to tell me something like this?

Don't answer that, I admonished myself.

"If you ask me it's pretty cool," I said. "I wish I had that kind of insight. Why didn't you want to tell me?"

"It's not that." He hesitated, glancing away before continuing. "I considered saying something, but then I thought you might be upset because this would be one more thing I hadn't told you about. I didn't want to put any more distance between us than there already was."

"Look, clearly I've been a bit of a pill," I said with some reluctance.

Zander looked back at me, his lips twitching, obviously trying not to laugh.

I swatted him. "Hey, it's not funny."

He put his hands up defensively, a huge grin now plastered across his face. "I didn't say a word."

"Fine. So I'm a big pain in the neck, okay? I have my reasons."

Zander sobered, fingering a lock of my hair. "I get it, Lun. You've been through the wars. We all have. I understand if you're not ready to talk about your experience in the W1 simulation, but if you ever want to, I'm here."

I cleared my throat. "Since we're confessing, I need to own up to something."

"Look Luna, you don't have to explain anything. I want you to feel comfortable around me. If this isn't what you want to—"

I placed a hand on his chest. "Stop right there. It's important you hear this."

He nodded, his crystal blue eyes filled with anxiety. "All right. I'm listening."

I took a deep breath and dove right in. "I've had a few small memories return."

Relief flooded his face, and he reached down to hug me. "That's amazing."

I pulled back to meet his gaze. "Look, before you get over excited, they aren't much—if anything they leave me even more confused. But there's one memory in particular that bothers me a lot. My first one."

"What happened?" Zander asked, cupping my shoulder. His gentle touch made me wonder if he still held concerns that he might somehow shatter the line of communication that had arisen between us.

I pressed my palms together, remembering. "Do you recall when we escaped the capital and met up with Crane? I freaked you out when I fell. We blamed it on the poor air quality and demolecularizing, but I was receiving a memory."

"You were in pain," Zander said. "I worried we wouldn't make it to the underground city before they caught us."

"Yeah, you and me both." I shook my head. "Anyway, that's not what I wanted to talk about. I have to tell you about what I witnessed."

He didn't speak, simply rubbed his thumb over my hand in a soothing gesture.

"I saw my parents, Zander. My real ones, from here. My father held some kind of disk or memory card. I haven't figured out what's on the device, but it must be important—the way they both stared at the thing made me think they were hiding something colossal." I tugged at my ponytail and with an agitated flourish twisted the hair around my fingertips. "I'm positive it will help us. If we can find out what's on the disk, it might change everything."

He reached over and brushed away a tear I didn't realize had fallen. "Ssshhh. So that's why you wanted to find your parents. I should have guessed there was more to the story than you were letting on. So you believe if you locate them, you'll also find the mysterious disk."

I nodded and looked down, ashamed I'd hidden such vital information from him—but at the same time still worried my confession would somehow put him in greater peril. I inhaled a deep shuddering breath. "I realize it sounds stupid, and it's probably a long shot. If I were you, I wouldn't believe me. But my gut tells me this is worth pursuing."

"Hey," he took me by the shoulders. "It's not stupid. And I'm a big believer in divine timing. I found out exactly when I was meant to."

I rolled my eyes but couldn't help but smile a little. "You seriously believe in all that woo woo crap?"

Zander grinned ruefully, lifting his hand to gently tug my ponytail. "It's not woo woo, it's very scientific. Now do me a favor. Shut your eyes."

I shot him a wary look. "Why?"

"Because I want to put a spider down your shirt," he said, teasing.

"Haha. What's your angle, Barringer?"

He sobered. "No angles. Promise. Trust me okay? I swear to you, no funny business."

I sighed. "Fine," I closed my eyes, relaxing.

"Good. Now, picture the scene with your parents. Are you there?"

"Yes."

"Now hone in on what they're holding. What does the gadget look like? Any distinguishing characteristics? Big? Small? Anything notable to help us identify it?"

"The disk is silver and small, but not as tiny as the micro projector. And there's something engraved on the front. Maybe a N? I can't tell because my Dad's holding the mechanism in his palm. My parents are staring at each other, and I know they're hiding something."

My temple began to throb, and I held my hands to my head trying to hold onto the image. But despite my best efforts, the picture faded, clouding at the edges. "Hey, there. Pull back now. That's enough. You all right?"

I opened my eyes. Zander peered at me, his face so close I felt his warm breath on my skin. He lifted my chin, his big blue eyes piercing right through to my soul. I stared back with a naked longing, my heart burning with desire. Then, without a second thought, I leaned in and pressed my lips to his.

I had been alone so long. I wanted this.

Once our mouths met, the sparks flew, setting my blood aflame.

In that moment, I realized I was lost to Zander and his touch. Forever.

And there was no going back.

CHAPTER 23
ZANDER

I turned and gazed up at the air tram starting its ascent into the clouds, just as the first flush of dawn lit the sky. Soon the streets would be bustling with traffic from the morning commute. The day arrived like any other in the underground city—yet somehow the world seemed different, because for the first time in a long while, I was happy. The taste of Luna's warm lips on mine, still lingering on my mouth.

We'd paused in a back alley to make sure no guards were prowling in the vicinity. I slipped a quick glance in her direction, her emerald eyes reflecting the golden light of the sun. Our fingers were still laced together, both of us unwilling to let go of our newly discovered connection. It had only been a few minutes since we'd come up from the underground tunnels, and already I felt so incredibly gratefully to have her here beside me.

It was going to be okay. We were reunited at last.

"I think the coast is clear," Luna whispered. "Shall we go?"

A male voice cut in from the platform across the street, announcing a new arrival. "Air tram approaching. Please keep a safe distance from the loading zone. Thank you."

We exchanged a silent look. Neither of us wanted to take any chances by sticking around the terminal to find out who was on the incoming air tram. So we took off, making our way east, towards the safe house, all the while keeping a beady eye out for any loitering officials.

When we reached the central hub of the metropolis, heading into the suburbs, the crowds thinned. Which unfortunately, made us sitting ducks for any henchman patrolling this area.

After what happened last night, it appeared Scott and Beth were losing control of the city. It was imperative I meet with them as soon as possible. It infuriated me nothing had been done to stop this nonsense—it was time to change that. But first, I had to get Luna back to the safe house. Crane would be there, and he'd take care of her until I returned. Once I'd sorted things out, maybe Luna and I could come up with a plan to remove ourselves from the government's cross-hairs.

I had to figure out how to prevent her from protesting when I told her I was going to see Scott and Beth. Alone. It was far too dangerous for both of us to go.

As we hastened down the main thoroughfare, heading into the seventh sector of the city, an idea formed in my mind. "Hey Luna, stop for a minute," I tugged her hand to slow down. She halted mid-stride and stared at me expectantly. I dove in before I could chicken out. "We can't allow the Black Mark and their government cronies to carry out their dire plans for the Elite."

"You mean to send us back in time?"

"Yes. But I think there's more to it. They should be worried about our safety, yet they're chasing us down like dogs. Either they don't realize who we are or something is askew in the capital. What's more, they're getting desperate."

"So how are we supposed to find out?"

"Well first, we need to return—" My voice died in my throat as flashing lights from a government vehicle came into view. It was one of those illegal gas-fueled cars. I instantly grabbed Luna's hand and dragged her behind a dumpster, just in the nick of time. It drove past slowly, almost as if they were looking for us. A human form moved in the rear of the transport. My breath quickened. I would recognize that red hair anywhere.

Crane.

He stared out the window and our eyes locked, caught in silent communication. He gave a curt nod, and I returned the gesture, knowing what I must do.

I watched in numb horror as the car disappeared around a corner, out of sight.

I closed my eyes and prayed to God it wasn't the last time I saw my friend.

CHAPTER 24

LUNA

Something unspoken had passed between Zander and Crane. A lost secret? A brotherhood pact? What? It made me uneasy, and instinctively I wanted to get defensive, demand he explain what was going on. But I had decided to trust Zander. I couldn't let my fears interfere. If I did, we'd both die.

Besides, this was definitely not the time to ask questions. As soon as the government vehicle with Crane aboard vanished from view, Zander pulled me away from our hiding place behind the smelly dumpster and made a U-turn, backtracking the way we came. "Hurry up, Luna, before it all falls apart. Run!"

I didn't answer—it took all my energy to keep up with Zander. He gripped my hand, squeezing tight. My arm stretched out to its max as he pulled me forward. I did my best to keep up with his long strides. We whizzed past food carts and people opening their shops for the day. I almost ran into a delivery cyclist but managed to dodge him at the last minute.

We followed the main road all the way to the city square, not even bothering with back alleys anymore. Whatever was going down—remaining hidden had become a low priority. Just when I thought my arm might snap, Zander finally slowed down and gave a brief glance around. Satisfied the coast was clear, he led me across the street to a nondescript warehouse constructed of flimsy sheet metal. It looked like it would only take a strong wind for the entire building to collapse. I wrinkled my nose at the stench that assaulted my senses as Zander scanned his ID chip and opened the bay door. Moist air gushed out, sweeping my hair back from my face. I tried not to gag. We were definitely in the ghetto.

Without a word, he pulled me inside and slapped a green button on the hanger, closing the door behind us. Before the daylight winked out, Zander grabbed a flashlight hanging on the wall.

"Come on, this way," he said, hustling me toward the back of the large structure. The space sat mostly empty save for a few old pieces of abandoned equipment. One filthy window high in the rafters sliced a single streak of light through the darkness, like a lightning bolt cast down from the heavens.

But this place was far from heaven.

As we neared the rear of the building, we stayed close to the interior wall, covered in peeling green paint. A row of metal cubbies lined the entire back facade, reminding me of my classroom at school on W1. Though Mama never did give me food for lunch, so my cubby remained empty. I started stealing not long after that. Starvation being a major motivation.

I stopped short, realization striking me. I never lived that life. According to Zander, we went into the game as teenagers. They had given me that horrible memory.

"Those sick bastards," I muttered.

Zander didn't hear me. He had crouched down to examine one of the small compartments, holding his flashlight high, exposing all the dirt and dust around us. Obviously, no one had set foot in here for a long time.

After the noisy city, the silence was palpable. If I had to hazard a guess, I'd have said the place was soundproof, which surprised me, considering the condition of the structure. I tapped my foot impatiently against the rough wood floor. I knew

Zander was concentrating, but before we went further, there was still one thing I had to find out. My voice cut through the dead air like shattered glass.

"Um, Zander, why didn't we follow Crane and find out where they were taking him—try to get him back?"

"The oath of the Elite and their protectors includes the promise of secrecy. Crane knows too much. And in government hands, he's a weapon."

I nodded in understanding. Zander was trying to stop important information from getting into the wrong hands. That had to be our priority.

I watched as he put a hand into one of the alcoves and pushed on the wood backing. The panel made a loud click, then disappeared, revealing an optical scanner and keypad. He pressed his thumb to the pad and leaned down for the camera to scan his retinas.

The only indication that anything was happening was a barely audible beep. Seconds later, the entire line of cubbyholes folded up like an accordion, revealing a scrubby, narrow room brimming with first-class electronic equipment. A wall of security screens filled one side of the room. The space had no furniture, save for a tattered chair sitting in front of the vid cameras —it looked out of place with all the expensive tech.

Zander raced over to the bank of monitors and pulled down a keyboard from the mainframe. He didn't bother to sit down, his fingers already flying over the keys. A live security feed lit up the screens, and a man, probably in his early forties, filled the viewer. His brown hair had been stylishly tied back at the nape of his neck, and his meticulously trimmed beard made him appear older than his years. His silver-grey eyes lit with warmth when he saw Zander.

"Zander, how lovely—" his voice broke off, his eyes now sharp, on full alert. "What's happened?"

"Luna is with me Scott. We barely escaped some agents over in sector six; we were there when a serious raid went down. They spotted us, but we managed to escape. We caught sight of Crane on our way to quadrant seven—in the back of a government vehicle—so I initiated code twenty-seven. We lost about ten minutes en route, and now I'm afraid we're out of time. And Scott..." Zander paused, taking a breath. "They were using a gas-fueled vehicle—they broke the agreement—and then some. You don't know the half of it."

Scott glanced off-screen for a minute. "I have their coordinates. They've breached the city and are above ground, but not yet inside the capital. There's still time, Zander. Do what you can from your end. I'm initiating a shutdown on all the safe houses Crane has knowledge of. We can do this. I'm counting on you. Now go!"

With that, Scott disappeared from the feed. Zander immediately began shutting down all the equipment. "Hey, what's happening? Talk to me," I demanded. He picked up a duffel and started stuffing drives, and a few other electronics into the bag, including a com screen, and began to explain. "Crane hasn't arrived at the capital yet. But as soon as he gets there, he will be injected with a truth serum that will allow the government to access all of the memories stored in his brain. Everything the resistors have worked so hard to achieve, will be compromised. Scott's going to make sure everyone vacates the safe houses Crane's recently been to, and move them to a more secure location before the administration catches on. Our job is to delete all the data in this fortification because this was his designated emergency hatch. It's ours, too. But we'll be assigned a new one soon enough. All the records here are backed up at other hatches throughout the city. Nothing will be lost."

"What about a VR simulation? He could reveal information that way."

"Yes. But they don't have the time they need to do that. The gamers would have to cobble something together first. They want answers immediately and the truth serum does that."

Before I could ask any more questions, he handed me a pint-size device that emitted a low hum. "You remember what to do with this?"

I nodded, recognizing the eratacon. I immediately started to swipe up and down the drives, causing the security screens to flicker, before blacking out completely. All information now deleted.

"Grab that blue duffel over in the corner. We're almost ready to go." He turned the chair upside down and retrieved a drive hidden in the base, set it straight and scanned the room. I went to lift the bag he'd instructed me to fetch, and let out a groan. "What's in this thing? It weighs a ton," I complained.

"Just open it up and check everything's there. Should be a few microchips, ID's, some documents, and other miscellaneous items we need."

He stepped over to help me take inventory. "This looks good..." Zander was still talking, but I didn't hear him. My eye caught something familiar glinting in the crook of the tote. I went to remove the object and realized it had been pinned to a simple white shirt. I grabbed hold of the fabric and tugged it free, my gaze still riveted on the diamond-shaped pendant with the engraved symbol of an oak tree, a keyhole stretching around its roots.

Zander touched my shoulder, jolting me from my reverie. "Oh good, you found a shirt. Let's hope there's some pants in there too. An extra set of clothes is always useful," he said. I didn't even look at him, the memory of this insignia suddenly hitting me. I gasped.

Mrs. Lennor.

Her prim face swam before my eyes. The pendant clipped to her tailored navy blue blazer. How did it get here?

"What is it, Luna? Why are you staring at that shirt?"

"Zander, I've seen this pendant before."

He frowned and took the blouse from me, studying the design. "It's definitely unusual. Where have you seen it?"

GENEVIEVE CROWNSON

I swallowed hard. "On P8. That teacher, sorry spy, Mrs. Lennor."

"You mean Elia Watford?"

I nodded fingering the edges of the pin. "One and the same."

The question became, if P8 had been a game, how was this pendant real?

"How is that possible?" Zander probed.

I frowned. "I wish I knew."

My heart thudded in my chest as another recollection came to me. I gripped Zander's arm. "Back on P8. One of the officers we saw, right before we jumped from the game, wore a strange medal on his lapel, next to all his other military insignia. At the time, I couldn't work out where I'd seen it before, and I dismissed it since I was too far away to be sure. But now I am almost positive he had on the same symbol."

Zander brushed his fingers over the pendant and became very still. He closed his eyes not saying a word.

"Zander?"

He didn't respond and silence descended on us for a few moments, until finally he began to hum, so low at first, I could barely make it out. But he kept going, louder now, and my heart froze.

I knew that melody.

It was the one I sang to Trinity as she drifted off to sleep. How in the world did Zander know it?

I stood up and shook him hard, his eyes popped open in surprise, like he had been in a deep sleep. He looked at me strangely for a minute as if to orient himself.

"How do you know that song? What the hell is going on?"

He shook his head. "Sorry, I kind of spaced out there for a minute."

I put my hands on my hips. "You don't say?" I said sarcastically.

He held his head for a minute and winced. "I had a vision. I

194

think I just saw my mother, Luna. She was holding me as a baby singing that song."

I stepped closer. "What?"

Zander turned to me, face pale. "And that's not all." He lifted the shirt holding the pendant. "She was wearing this. These were hers."

I pressed a hand to my head trying to wrap my head around what he was telling me. "But that song, Zander. That's the one I wrote for Trinity while I was in W1, how is that possible?"

"Before we went into the game, I would hum that melody to you when you were sad. It's my favorite song. But I never knew where it came from until that vision. You must have brought it with you somehow and put it to words for your sister." He put a shaking hand to my hair and looked at me with such intensity. "I'm glad you had a small piece of me with you."

He turned away quickly then, but not before I saw tears in his eyes.

I put a hand to his shoulder. "It's a good thing, right? You saw your Mom. I bet you've wondered about her."

Zander quickly wiped away his tears and handed me back the shirt. "Yeah. But it's a lot. Let's just focus on the job for now okay?"

"Sure." I placed the shirt carefully in the bag, knowing Zander would want it later and zipped it up.

"We need to leave. Crane's probably already reached the capital, and they'll search this place once they give him the truth serum."

I shuddered. I couldn't imagine being forced to give away secrets against your will.

"We're lucky, Luna. The truth serum doesn't work on the Elite. They think the mineral interacts with our DNA, blocking the effects. But the government considers it a pesky side effect. One of the many reasons they prefer us locked away. Now come on, we better go."

We left the secret room, each with a bag in hand. With one

touch of Zander's palm on the inner wall, the computer chamber receded and the cubbies returned to their original position.

Zander picked up the pace and headed back toward the front of the structure. When we reached the door, he hit the green button, once more allowing the bright morning light to penetrate the warehouse. I squinted, my eyes adjusting to the brightness after the dark interior of the complex.

Before we stepped from the shadow of the building, Zander rummaged quickly through the bag hanging off my shoulder. He pulled out what appeared to be a little scanner and tapped his wrist with it, and then asked for mine. He nodded approvingly at the sound of the beep.

"What is it? What are you doing?"

"I loaded our chips with a fake ID and enough credits for us to survive for a while. If anyone asks, your name is Eden Avery. Here, put these on." He drew out a baseball cap and sunglasses, and I took them from him. I pulled my hair through the back and settled it snug on my head, then covered my eyes with the shades. Next, he took a beanie from the same pack, encasing his chestnut locks, and yanked on a green denim jacket over his black sweatshirt.

"There, that will have to do," he said appraising us.

"So, what's your new ID?" I asked curiously.

He grimaced. "It's Eugene Flanner."

I snorted. "How did you come up with that one?"

He frowned at me. "I didn't create the names. A database of fake ID's curated by Scott selects a name at random."

"Well, whoever came up with those monikers should clearly be assigned to another task," I giggled, unable to help myself.

"Come on, Redwood, move it on out," he said pushing me onto the pavement.

"Of course, Flanner. Or should I call you Eugene?"

He grinned as he ducked under the shutting door. "You're not going to let this go, are you?"

"Oh, hell no," I said, glad to see him smiling again.

Zander's smile was fleeting, his face turning solemn as soon as we hit the pavement, putting himself on high alert. He propelled me forward, grabbing hold of my elbow and gently leading me down the alley towards the main road. "Not too far from here is an isolated park on the north quadrant of the city—we can talk safely there. I don't think anyone will bother us."

I nodded, following close behind him as we worked our way through the trash-littered streets and out of the slums. We didn't dare take any transport as our disguises were weak at best. Zander feared that Crane had already divulged our last hiding spot to the authorities and handed over a current composite of us. As we headed north into the less dangerous quarter of town, houses with well-tended front yards began to appear, leaving behind the stench of trash and fried food. I breathed in deeply, taking in the fragrant smell of roses, lilacs, and other flowers that people had planted in their gardens.

We bought some crepes and water from a corner vendor with a jaunty red and white striped umbrella covering his cart. The man manning the wagon had greying hair and wore an apron that matched his awning. His mustache curled up at the edges, reminding me of a distinguished gentleman from the late 1800s. He smiled kindly as he served us, seemingly far from threatening, yet I still breathed a sigh of relief when we'd put some distance between us. I ate hungrily, the aroma of the fresh dough and strawberries almost my undoing. I hadn't realized how famished I was.

After the crepes were devoured, we walked along quietly, each lost in our own thoughts. I think we were both worried about Crane and thinking about the vision Zander had back at the warehouse. Crane had endangered his own life to help us. I couldn't live with myself if anything terrible happened to him because of me. I also feared Zander might be next on the list to be taken.

The grounds were quiet, and we easily found a secluded spot

to sit behind a fountain in the shape of two fish, spewing water from their mouths.

"This feels familiar," I said, remembering our chat in the P8 park.

"Yeah, at least here, we don't have to worry about listening devices or trackers like we did back then. We have a lot more control over what happens to us in the real world."

I laughed sharply. "It doesn't seem like it. We've been on the run ever since we escaped those horrible glass coffins."

Zander picked at some grass, not looking me in the eye. "Yeah, true. But here on New Earth, protections are put in place against listening devices. Thanks to Scott's software update our chip IDs contain sensors that will set off an alarm if any are detected."

I shrugged, not convinced. "I guess. When am I going to meet this famous Scott in person, anyway? You certainly talk about him enough. He looked to be an interesting character on the vid call."

"He's going to be busy locking down all Crane's haunts. But maybe after that..." His voice trailed off.

I sat up straighter. "What is it? What aren't you telling me?"

Zander ran a hand through his hair. "Luna, we have to talk."

I winced. "Nothing good has ever come from 'we have to talk'..."

Zander covered my fidgeting hands with his. "No. I don't mean it like that. I just meant we need to discuss what to do if we get separated or if something happens to—"

I got to my feet, raising my hands in protest. "Nothing is going to happen to us. We've got this. We've come this far, haven't we?"

Zander stood, watching me pace. The air between us hung thick and heavy. "Luna if I die, you..." his voice cracked. "There are things you need to be aware of."

I covered my ears, tears unexpectedly pricking my eyes. "I

can't lose anyone else!" The words tumbled out of their own volition, uncontrolled, and forceful.

Zander gently grasped my shoulders, turning me to face him. "Hey. It's just precautionary. We have to cover all our bases. Okay?"

I didn't respond, my body going numb. What would happen if something happened to Zander? Who would I turn to then? I'd be left on my own again. I cleared my throat and licked my dry lips. Mama would be ashamed of me. Her grating voice echoed in my head.

Let no one see your weakness.

I closed my eyes and spun away from his grasp. "Maybe it would be smarter if I found my parents on my own."

He took hold of me in a surprisingly powerful gesture, fire burning in his blue eyes. "Like hell, you will. We didn't come this far to give up, Luna Redwood. We're a team. And way better together."

"What's the point, Zander? Someone always gets hurt. Or taken away. Look at Sepha. Crane."

He exhaled sharply. "We owe it to them, don't we? To stop this? Find your parents? And figure out a solution? We can only do that together. Separated, we don't stand a chance. You of all people should know what the government is capable of."

He was right. It was one thing for me to play martyr, but quite another to mess with the lives of Sepha and Crane. They had helped us. And they deserved our full effort.

I stared at Zander, searching for something. I wasn't sure what. Hope? Reassurance? Whatever it was, I couldn't find it. His face held as many questions as mine. Still, I knew I couldn't ask for a better partner in crime, even if he did stink at being stealthy.

"What are you smirking at?" Zander demanded, still sounding mad. "Does that mean you're in?"

"Yeah, I'm in."

His shoulders sagged with relief as he drew me to him. His

voice filled with emotion as he whispered in my ear. "Thank God."

He pulled back, and looked at me so intently I couldn't breathe. I stepped away and playfully punched his arm. "So, what you're telling me is that you didn't receive any psychic hits on how we're going to achieve this?"

He smiled at me, rubbing his thumb across my cheek. "Sorry, princess. Not this time."

I returned the smile. We needed this connection—for what we were about to embark on, could be deadly for both of us.

We joined hands and left the park.

Our fates sealed.

CHAPTER 25
LUNA

The border shimmered before us in the wan sunlight like a labyrinth of rainbows, the arches connecting in a wave of angling prisms across the causeway. Beyond it, the domed capital sparkled like a white snow globe, so gigantic I couldn't take in its circumference all at once.

I swallowed hard against the bile that rose in my throat. The last thing I wanted to do was go back inside the walled city; to me it seemed like yet another prison. I felt grateful for the face covering Zander had insisted I wear when we got above ground. I didn't want him to witness my freaked-out expression. We had work to do.

The air lay thick and heavy as we trudged forward, my lungs seemingly drowning in water despite the mask providing low levels of oxygen. Part of me wished this was a game too, so I wouldn't have to face the truth—that our planet had been destroyed by our own human hands.

Zander touched my shoulder, bringing my attention back to the present. "We need to leave these bags here, Luna. I texted headquarters—someone's going to come pick them up."

We were at the edge of the woods, if you could call them that. It looked more like a haunted forest that had been decimated by an evil sorcerer who brought fire and brimstone to earth, leaving nothing but charred timber in their wake. Still, I guess the broken trunks provided some cover.

"What are you doing?" I asked, staring as Zander pressed his foot back and forth against the base of an old tree trunk. He didn't answer, concentrating. Seconds later, a faint pop echoed from where he bore down with his sneaker.

My heart froze, wondering if it had been a booby trap. But when he knelt to brush away some dead leaves, I realized he was searching for something. His thumb latched on to a loop disguised as a root and tugged at it. I gasped when a huge chunk of earth dislodged, revealing an empty cavernous hollow under the tree, obviously dug out by someone. Zander rifled through his pack and withdrew an odd-looking box, crystal-clear with a numerical symbol on the front.

He finally spoke, his soft voice sounding off a warning through the dank undergrowth. "We can't take any of this with us. The border patrol scanners will pick up on any equipment. But we will need one thing."

I frowned at him puzzled. "What?"

Zander looked at me eyes solemn, his voice strained. "The clock key. Tell me you have it."

My hands shook as I searched my pocket, praying that in all the chaos it hadn't fallen out. I sighed with relief as my fingers grasped hold of it. "Got it."

He exhaled loudly. "Thank God, I was afraid we'd lost it. Or that Crane..." He trailed off unable to complete the thought.

I remembered Crane was supposed to take the device to another quadrant of the city in the hopes a well-known engineer there could repair it, but I'd snitched it from Zander's night-stand last night before that happened. Just the idea of the clock key landing in the government's clutches gave me the shivers. If I was Zander, I would have been freaking out, too.

"Why didn't you just ask me before? I actually forgot about

it, we've been so caught up in all this mess. I feel like we've been on the run since we got here."

"I didn't want you to think I only came to save the clock key. I needed you to understand I was here for you," he explained.

"But Zander, what if Crane had it in his possession? What would you have done?" Damn, I must have been a real pain in the neck for him to keep this from me.

"There's nothing anyone could have done. Besides, the plan is to get Crane out, right? And anyway, I had a gut feeling you had the key." He grinned then. "You can't resist a challenge. I assume you were trying to fix it?"

I shrugged nonchalantly, fingering the small device, even as the tingling sensation of power radiated through my skin and up my body. "I don't know what you're talking about."

"Sure," Zander said in an amused voice.

"What's that?" I asked changing the subject, and pointing to the mysterious box.

"This is a brand-new experiment a few resistors have been working on in the lab. And we're about to ascertain if it works."

I reached out and touched the side of the vessel, but my fingers instantly recoiled as they hit the ice-cold surface.

"It's a magnetism box," Zander explained. "Designed to make any item you put inside undetectable to high-performance security systems."

I traced the numerical seal on the front. Despite learning that my past was a lie, some things didn't change. I loved numerology, the black and white world of math. And this symbol etched into the glass intrigued me.

As if Zander sensed my question he said, "The number identifies what test study this box comes from. There are numerous versions of this, each one an improvement on the last. This particular one may not even be the latest and greatest."

"Why is it so cold?"

"The magnets perform better at cool temperatures. The atoms that comprise the magnets vibrate more slowly and less randomly when chilled. The result is an enhanced alignment of the atoms that generate the magnetic field, boosting its strength."

I stared at him for a minute, blinking. "So, when did you become a complete science nerd?"

Zander shrugged. "I told you, I like to figure out how things work. And besides, in training we're taught how everything in the emergency kit operates."

I cast my gaze down, picking up a twig, tapping it into my palm—trying to pare down the anger I had toward myself for not remembering this. I knew that I too had this instruction, and should be able to comprehend this stuff at least as well as Zander.

"Hey, are you okay?"

I dropped the twig to the ground, snapping it into two pieces under foot. "If you must know, I'm really annoyed I can't recollect any of this when I know that I should."

Zander rose and gingerly put an arm around me, as if he half expected me to bite. "It doesn't matter, Luna. What's important now is that we save the people that helped us. Plus, we have to find out what your parents are hiding. You'll get your memories back, give yourself time."

I sighed. "It's so aggravating. I hate it when you make sense."

Zander grinned. "I'm growing on you, aren't I?"

"Anyway," I said, ignoring his gloating demeanor, "let's get on with it." I tapped the lid of the cold container.

He didn't move or say anything for a beat, grinning at me like a fool, hoping I would acknowledge his comment.

I waited patiently, not giving an inch. Finally, he surrendered. "Okay, okay. Obviously, you're never going to admit you find me adorable."

I pretended to gag, and he looked at me bemused. "Are you done? Be careful with the clock key, you don't want to drop it."

I immediately sobered, and stared at the small object, it appeared so inconsequential, who would guess it held so much power? I swallowed hard and gazed up into Zander's face. "I'm really sorry I broke it."

"I know. We'll do our best to fix it. But right now, we need to focus on getting Crane and Sepha out of Dodge."

"Any plans on how we're going to do that?"

"I've got a few ideas, but I won't know for sure what the next best step is until we're inside the dome. I checked with Scott; he hasn't seen our mugshots on any data screens around the capital, but we must keep our guard up."

I frowned, puzzled. "When did you chat with Scott?"

Zander toed the bag of goods he'd brought with him, now at his feet. "Burner phone. I texted him as we walked."

I crossed my arms. "Okay, smarty-pants. Do you plan on sharing what your ideas are or what?"

Zander's brow furrowed. "I'll explain the details once we're safely inside. No point in getting tactical moves down that aren't going to work."

"Fine. Let's go, then."

Zander looked at me sheepishly. "I need the clock key first."

"Oh, right." I placed the small circular device in his outstretched palm and felt a little bereft as I handed it over. Almost immediately, an overwhelming sense of exhaustion overtook me. The key must have been masking my fatigue. A big part of me longed to snatch it back so I could investigate. It looked like I was a bit of a science nerd myself.

"I'm going to place the clock key in the box, shut the lid, and let it rip," he said.

"Is that the technical terminology?"

He didn't look up but carefully placed the clock key in the vessel, and I had a fleeting thought that this place was full of secret glass cages.

"How do you know it's functioning?" I asked, peering closely at the mysterious container.

"Easy. Place your hands on the box."

Gently, I allowed my fingertips to brush the sealed lid. I frowned. "I don't feel anything."

Zander nodded in approval. "That's perfect. If you can't detect the clock key's energy, it's working."

He offered me the box. "Do you want to be the guinea pig, or should I?"

I hesitated. The old part of me stirred to life, hackles rising. *Trust no one.* But this time I shut the voice down. I took the case, almost as if to prove to myself I believed in him. "Let me carry it, I'll take the bullet this time," I said. I placed the container into my boot, where I normally stored a knife. When I looked up, Zander was shaking his head at me.

"Don't even joke about guns. Too soon."

I winced. "Sorry."

"Don't worry, you can make it up to me later."

I was about to ask what he meant but then caught the mischievous twinkle in his eye. My cheeks flushed with embarrassment, and I hastily picked up the bag and swung it into the empty cavern under the tree. Zander followed with his pack and then pressed the seal back down.

He offered me his hand. "Are you ready, Eden Avery of quadrant seven?"

"As ready as I'll ever be," I said lacing my trembling fingers through his. I hoped he didn't pick up on how nervous I felt. He gave no indication he had, his eyes solely on our destination, determination in his step. I took a deep breath, following him into whatever loomed ahead, relieved that at least we were together.

⚜

The atmosphere became lighter closer to the dome, thanks to a system of fans humming like small insects above us.

"They're not trying to improve air circulation," Zander said catching me watching them. "It's to help maintain an optimal temperature for the scanners and robots. The humans stay out of sight unless there's trouble afoot."

I didn't respond, too busy concentrating on the dusty dirt trail that led toward the rainbow arches.

"Remember, you don't have to do anything except scan your ID," Zander continued. "A voice will verify your name and quadrant; all you do is simply confirm with a yes. Then the bar beyond the arch will lift and you'll be able to walk through. A droid will be manning the entrance into the dome. Once you pass through, wait for me by the white pillars that say, 'Welcome to the Capital.'"

I nodded. "Doesn't look like many people are returning," I said in an ironic tone.

"Yes, the rules are pretty strict for re-entry. And most citizens don't want to come back after experiencing the freedom of New Earth. But there are a select few that can't handle living underground that may want to return. After last night's raid, we might see a rise in numbers."

I shuddered, recalling those poor people being lined up like up like cattle, then spit on. Before I could reflect any further, a droid approached us.

"ID please," the bot said in a droll monotone.

I glanced at Zander, but he looked as surprised as me. Had they changed the rules and now required two scans? Unsure of what else to do, I allowed the robot to scan my wrist with his glowing orange fingertip. He pointed to the archway directing me to a gate. "Please continue to gateway B and wait for instruction."

I gave Zander another look before leaving, and he nodded for me to go ahead. I made my way down to the arch, paused and took a deep breath. "Here goes nothing," I muttered.

I scanned my ID under the brass plate that said *scan here*. A voice came out of nowhere, making me jump. "Eden Avery of quadrant seven, do you swear that this is your true identity and that you promise to uphold all the laws of the capital herein? Confirm yes or no."

I swallowed the large lump in my throat. It was too late for backtracking. This could be the lie that changed everything. "Yes."

"Please proceed forward, do not stop. The light sweeping over you scans for potentially harmful substances or unidentifiable objects. If you're clear, the bar will lift. Thank you for your cooperation."

I glanced around, searching for Zander. At first, I couldn't find him. I pivoted on my toes, my eyes frantically darting in all directions. Then I spotted him, all the way down on gateway M. A few passengers were passing through other gateways, their arches lit up with gaudy neon lights, reflecting against the grey sky. I sucked in a deep breath. This would be easy. It had to be.

I stepped forward, the small box containing the clock key burning a hole in my boot. What if they detected it? All would be lost. I pushed the thought away.

"Just focus on the job, Luna," I muttered. When I crossed the arched threshold, a light blinded me, and I lifted a hand to shield my eyes. As instructed, I kept moving, my eyes never leaving the metal bar, willing it to rise. After an agonizing moment, the bar came up and I jumped as another bare bones robot swished forward. He seemed far from human, more a mix of compressed alloy and various assorted parts—giving the appearance he was indestructible. Maybe that had been the point.

He bowed. "Welcome to the capital. The happiest of sanctuaries. Enjoy your stay." He gestured with a tin arm toward the dome entrance. For the first time, I gazed upon the inner sanctum of the metropolis. Talk about breathtaking.

A vast open-air pavilion greeted me, a soaring space with a massive crystal chandelier hanging from a high ceiling that looked as though it had been pulled from the heavens. A curved archway of gilded gold led up to a platform filled with awaiting air trams. On the left wall hung a bold painting of the president in vivid colors. His slick gray eyes seemed to follow me as I made my way further into what I now realized was an entry station. My boots tread silently along the stone floor entrance hall as I headed toward a set of white pillars near the middle of the cavernous room. My fingers gripped one of the colonnades for support as I scanned the area looking for Zander, as well as any potential threats.

My heart calmed when no one took heed of me, and I caught a glimpse of Zander's black hat. He waved and grinned, his face awash with relief. He crossed over to me and hugged me tight. And odd time for affection, I thought, but then his voice rang low in my ear.

"Thank, God. We made it," he breathed. "One more hurdle. We need to take the air tram to get to the city center. There is no way around it. Just act casual and follow my lead. Okay?"

I nodded. Zander took hold of my hand and led me to the stairs. We hurried up the right side, a sign on the wall read *Inner-City tram this way*. Zander followed the arrows, and we ended up on a platform where our IDs were scanned yet again by another droid. Fortunately, this one was friendly. Characterized as an older gentleman, he wore a crisp white uniform with a badge that identified him as Fred. His eyes might have appeared kind if you hadn't noticed the faint circling of a processor behind the fake blue irises. "Inner-city tram. Four credits for the full loop. Two for half," he touted in a baritone smooth as butter. Fred actually sounded human. I couldn't help but be impressed, but Zander seemed indifferent to his perfect diction. "Two for the half-loop please."

"Scan your ID's and board. Thank you for taking Capital Airway. Have a pleasant trip." He gave a stiff smile before moving his attention to the next person in line. We stepped up and scanned our IDs at the kiosk next to the train—a compartment door slid open and we quickly passed through.

I gasped in surprise. This was the nicest transport I'd ever seen. Rich wood paneling covered the walls and lux fabric curtains draped the sides of a large window. It would probably show off an aerial view of the city once in flight. We sat down, and I sank back, enjoying the plushness of the red velvet seat.

"Is this first class?" I hissed in his ear.

Zander leaned closer. "No. This is the first train that leads into the city. They're trying to impress you with the wonder of the capital. You'll recall, the one we took to the border wasn't quite this grand."

I'd almost forgotten about that. It seemed like a lifetime ago. I was about to ask why we didn't just demolecularize again. But then remembered Zander's warning, about sacrificing ten percent of our lifespan. Not that it would matter if we didn't survive this trip.

"Do you have a plan yet?" I whispered, as the air tram pulled away from the platform.

"I'll pick up a burner once we reach the inner city, then inform Scott we got in. He'll be able to advise us on the weakest point of entry into the government facilities, but after that, we're on our own."

I shivered, turning my head away. My gaze wandered to the window and out over the domed city as we rose higher and higher above the skyscrapers. The air smelled fresh and clean inside the train, but when I looked out, I noticed black particles floating in the atmosphere. I bet they had to scrub the dark muck off the train every day. Now I understood why the government was so desperate to make this work. Even inside this dome with semi filtered air, the conditions were far from ideal. If they went back in time using us as guinea pigs, they might have a chance of saving the planet. But that was a *big* if. There were no guarantees. That was the thing about the human race, we did the stupidest stuff and to heck with the consequences.

A faint bell rang overhead and a few people started to collect their bags. "This is the end of the half loop," Zander said. "Are you ready?"

"As ready as I'll ever be."

"Follow me." Zander rose and grabbed one of the roof rack bars to steady himself as we landed. The hustle and bustle of the city, along with the sound of honking horns, filtered through the air tram walls.

"Welcome to the inner city. The half loop is complete. Watch your step as you disembark," a pleasant female voice said, echoing through the speakers. The only thing in my possession was the clock key, everything else had been left behind under the tree outside the border, so I easily flowed with the crowd as we made our way up to street level.

We passed interactive billboards that changed scenes with every person that went by. Fascinated, I slowed down to take a look. A man walked by, coughing heavily, and an advertisement for cough drops filled the screen. Next on the video monitor, a classic clutch that doubled as a briefcase was shown to a woman, impeccably attired in a smart business suit. As I neared the bill-board, Zander took my arm and steered me away.

"Hey, I wanted to—"

Zander cut me off. "We can't risk it, Luna. They have programmed cameras in them that will scan you. We may have safely passed security, but I don't want to take any unnecessary chances."

"I've never seen those before. Or at least I don't remember them. Is that the only one?"

Zander frowned looking back over his shoulder at the over-sized screen. "Unfortunately, no, they're all over the city. Try to avoid them if you can."

By the time we reached the crowded street, with its familiar view of the White House building, the noonday sun was already peeking through the patchy clouds. Zander and I didn't speak, but kept our heads low, blending in as much possible. I think we were both eager to do our job and get out of this place. But that was easier said than done. I had no clue where my parents might be, let alone Crane and Sepha.

Zander stopped when we came to a corner coffee shop. A sign out front boasted it had the best coffee in town. A faint breeze carrying the scent of fresh pastries wafted through the open door, and my stomach rumbled. I hadn't eaten anything but the crepe early this morning. I'd gotten soft in P8. Hunger was harder to ignore now.

As if hearing my growling stomach, Zander said, "I'm just going over to the quick mart across the street." He pointed to a storefront across the crowded thoroughfare that displayed a flashing red sign, reading *24-hour mart*. "I need to buy a burner so I can call Scott and ask if he has a location on Crane and Sepha. Maybe he'll even have some leads on your parents. Why don't you grab us a couple of coffees and something to eat? We're going to need our strength."

My mouth went dry, and I gripped his arm, my hunger temporarily forgotten. "You're going to tell him what I told you about my mom and dad?"

A passerby with wild pink hair gave us a strange look but kept walking. Zander pulled me into the shadows of a side street. "It's the only way we'll get any leads, otherwise we have nothing to go on. Scott may know something about the disk they had in their possession."

I snorted—it was one thing to trust Zander, but I had never met this Scott guy. "No way, Zander. I don't like it. How do you know for sure we can trust him?"

"Luna, he's helped us on numerous occasions. Remember Eden Avery and Eugene Flanner?"

The fake ID's. They'd come from him. So, if he was a traitor and knew our identities, we'd be screwed.

"Luna, are you okay? You look as white as a sheet. Maybe you should—"

I interrupted him before he could say anything else. "Please, Zander. Don't. You can ask him about Crane and Sepha, but not my parents."

Zander pushed a hand through his hair, causing it to stand up at a funny angle. "Luna, you can trust him."

I shook my head, adamant. "You have an idea about where my parents live, right? I mean isn't there a directory or something? What about your family? Were they acquainted with mine?"

It was Zander's turn to go pale. And with sickening horror I suddenly remembered that he'd mentioned he was an orphan.

"I'm so sorry, Zander, I completely forgot for a moment."

He patted my hand. "It doesn't matter, it happened a long time ago."

Pain lashed through his voice. And I knew the truth. You didn't just get over losing your parents, whether you had a relationship with them or not. He sighed resigned. "Look, I won't tell him about your memory. At least for now. Maybe we can attempt to hack into the system and find an address. I don't have a clue where your parents live. You were pretty tight-lipped about your background when you came to the program, and I didn't press you on it. But I wish I had now."

I winced. "You know me. I'm a great one for secrets."

Zander grinned. "Yeah, I know."

I playfully swatted him away. "Don't you have a phone to buy?"

"Right. Okay. I'll meet you back here in five minutes."

"What type of coffee do you like?" I asked, feeling stupid I didn't remember what he preferred.

"Anything with caffeine. Ever since real coffee beans winked out of existence about ten years ago, I don't care. I had a few sips of the good stuff when I was a kid. The fake junk doesn't even cut it. Just surprise me." And with that, he jogged across the street toward the quick mart.

I watched him for a second, then turned and entered the shop. The aroma of roasting beans and sweet sugar confectionaries hit me full on. I inhaled deeply, filling my senses with the exotic spices. I stepped over to the counter, then realized I

GENEVIEVE CROWNSON

had no idea what to order. Everything seemed so fancy. They had
done an amazing job creating fake coffee bean scents, and I
wondered what they were made from. The taste however, must
leave something to be desired, especially if Zander didn't care
what he got. I ended up ordering a couple of black coffees and
two apple-filled donuts. I added a ton of soy cream, the only
option, and plenty of mock sugar to drown out the flavor.

I decided not to wait for Zander and sunk my teeth into the
piping hot donut. *Oh, sweet heaven.* I sighed with pleasure, as the
gooey caramel apple melted in my mouth. Unable to contain
myself, I polished off my donut on the spot then headed back
outside, carefully balancing the tray of steaming hot coffee.

Zander was already out front, the new burner phone plastered to his ear. He was pacing—talking and nodding as he
spoke. When he saw me, he waved. I walked up to him, just
catching the tail end of the conversation. "Thanks, Scott. I'll
keep you posted."

I handed over the coffee and was about to ask him what he
found out when all hell broke loose. A dark unmarked car,
flashing red and blue lights, careened around the corner onto the
street.

The siren's piercing shriek jangled my nerves as everything
went into slow motion. Zander dropped his coffee and grabbed
my hand, telling me to run, but the shrill cries of the siren
drowned him out.

This low sleek car wasn't for regular use, I'd never seen one
like it before. It didn't take an idiot to figure out this vehicle had
one mission only, pursuit and capture.

I could almost see Zander's mind in overdrive, trying desperately to come up with a solution, as we pushed away from the
sidewalk into the lunchtime throng.

But suddenly it seemed like everyone knew we were the
prize. The crowd parted like the Red Sea, exposing us to the
bloodhounds behind the wheel.

The car had stopped, but we kept going. A bright yellow light beamed right in our faces.

"Don't stop no matter what, do you hear me?" Zander said.

"Yes," I gasped breathlessly, trying to keep up with his long strides.

A car door slammed somewhere behind us, and two sets of footsteps that could only belong to the government henchmen clattered on the pavement. Everyone else appeared frozen to the spot as they checked out the pursuit.

"I'm so sorry, Luna," Zander said panting dragging me off the main thoroughfare and into an alley that cut through to another avenue. "I blew it."

"Don't you dare say your goodbyes, Zander Barringer," I muttered through gritted teeth. "We're going to—"

My words were swallowed up by a booming voice echoing from the megaphone. "Halt. Under the order of the capital. If you don't stop, we will shoot. I repeat, we will shoot."

"Run faster, Zander!" I yelled.

My lungs burned and my legs turned to jelly as we pressed on, racing down yet another street.

I thought we'd established a good lead, when out of nowhere a uniformed man appeared. With a smooth face completely devoid of stubble, he looked much too young to have any authority. He stepped out about ten feet ahead of us and regarded us with cold dark eyes, his mouth twisted into a cruel line.

We backed up and cut through a different side street. But two more men lay waiting for us, their weapons drawn.

Before I could think what to do, the taller of the men fired two shots right at us. I saw Zander fall, and then before I had time to react, I felt a sharp sting in my neck and the world exploded in front of me.

Everything went dark.

CHAPTER 26
ZANDER

I groaned. The intense throbbing in my temple made my stomach roil. I gritted my teeth against the nausea that hit me like a tsunami.

What happened?

Then I remembered. I'd been shot.

When I forced my lids open, my eyes watered from the bright light coming from the buzzing bulb hanging overhead. There were bars in front of me and the outline of a room beyond. *Where was I?*

Sweat pooled on my forehead as recognition dawned on me. I knew this place—the prison located underneath the energy post where we'd been held during the game. How had I ended up back where we started? And what about Luna?

"Luna?" I croaked in desperation, attempting to rise from the cold floor. My body wouldn't co-operate, and I barely moved an inch. I tried my arm and managed to stretch it out a little. Maybe she was nearby. As my fingers extended to the max, I bit back a cry as a searing spasm of pain shot down from my shoulder. I pushed past the discomfort, not willing to give up. She had to be here. But wait—what if she escaped? After all, she'd still been standing when I took the hit. My heart lifted a bit at the thought.

Just as quickly, my hopes turned to ash as my hand brushed the edge of her jacket. "Luna?" I said again, this time a little louder.

No response.

I set my jaw, willing myself to move, but nothing happened. My bones felt as though they were held down with weights.

I took a couple of deep breaths, gathering my strength. Based on the pain levels, I would hazard a guess that the government thugs had hit me with a high voltage stun gun, known to leave victims utterly incapacitated for at least a full day.

If I had been out twenty-four hours, Crane had been held in custody way too long. We should have already gotten him out. I realized with sudden clarity that Scott might have also given us up for lost.

We were on our own.

I took a few deep breaths, then with a calmer mind, assessed my situation. Nothing would be achieved if I panicked. The good news was the effects from the stun gun were wearing off. A faint rustle nearby jolted me from my musings. Was someone down here with us?

"Hello? Is anybody there?"

"You ssshoulllld not be here."

The voice arose out of the darkness from somewhere outside our cell.

I began wiggling my fingers and toes back and forth, desperate to get my blood circulating again. Once I could move without pain, I would be able to protect Luna. "Who are you?" I hoped I sounded authoritative. But my voice shook.

A shrouded figure appeared out of the gloom, pressing themselves against the cell bars across from us. As I peered closer, I realized it wasn't an apparition, but an elderly woman with kind green eyes. Her filthy clothes indicated she'd been living here a while. Her hands trembled as she clutched the barricade, her gnarled fingers clawing at the iron railings as if it was the only thing keeping her upright.

"I'm Ddddara Peters," she said huskily, her voice quivering in the damp cold.

"Dara Peters. Why does that sound so familiar?" I asked, more to myself than to her. I scrutinized her. Had we met before? Her chalky, withered face was framed by snow-white hair that fell to her waist in a knotted tangle. But nothing about her features triggered any memories.

"This wasn't how it wwwwaaaasss supposed to beeee," she whispered, her teeth chattering.

A small keening to my left made me jerk and I glanced back over my shoulder. I hissed as pain coursed through my limbs, quick and sharp—then dissipated. Determined not to be defeated, I slowly rose and started the three-yard crawl towards Luna. It felt like I had a ten-ton bus on my back, but I toughed it out.

"Luna."

A moan escaped her lips as I put a hand to her shoulder and rolled her over to face me. A large shiny bump protruded from her forehead, and I swallowed hard against the fear rising up in me. I told myself to calm down, she probably just picked it up when she fell. I ran my fingers lightly over her body, checking for other injuries. I detected a swelling on the left side of her neck—that must have come from where they shot her with the stun gun. No wonder it took a little longer for her to come around.

I patted her cheek. "Luna? Can you hear me?"

For what seemed like an eternity, she just lay there, but then finally her lids began to flutter and she slowly opened her eyes.

She gazed at me and smiled, but instantly regretted the action as she grimaced in pain.

"You'll be okay soon. The government shot us with stun guns. At first, every time you try to move it will feel like bricks crushing your body, but you must exercise those muscles, Luna. Once the blood flow increases, the pain will ease."

"I'm going to kill those bastards," she said her voice a little slurred. A nasty side effect of where they'd hit her. Still, I smiled at her, glad to know they hadn't broken her spirit.

"Luna? Child, are you all right?"

Luna giggled, then winced again. "I think I'm losing my mind, Zander. I swear I just heard Dara's voice."

Of course. She had been Luna's neighbor and friend on W1.

I brushed the hair away from her face and grinned. "Don't worry. You're not crazy. Dara's in the cell opposite us. We're in a jail block under the energy center."

Luna gave an incredulous gasp before attempting to maneuver herself to peer in the direction of Dara's voice. I tried to warn her about moving too fast, but I was too late. She let out an almighty yelp as her nerve endings fired together.

My pain had eased considerably, so I helped her sit up, albeit at a much slower pace. She gripped the iron barricade, pulled herself forward, and squinted into the darkness. "Dara? Is that really you?"

"It's me, child. I'm so sooorrry to seeee you here," her voice shook more with emotion than cold this time.

Luna's eyes pricked with tears, as she stretched out her arms trying to reach her. Dara also took a shaking hand and pushed it through the bars, but they were too far apart to connect.

"What are you doing here?" Luna breathed. "I thought you were dead. It wasn't until recently, when I found out W1 was a game, that I began to hope..." she trailed off.

"It maaay have only been a game, but our friendship was very real. Don't yooouu forget thaaat."

Luna looked to her, concerned. "How long have you been down here?"

"I'm fine, never you mind about that. You have bigger worries."

"I have so many questions. Did you remember this place when we were in W1? Was that why you tried to warn me? I can still recall your last words, cautioning me about the cage of glass."

Dara's eyes misted over. "I'm sorry. I should have explained earlier, but I thought you were going to be okay. And if they found out...well..."

"Well what, Dara? How did you know those things?"

I placed a hand on Luna's shoulder and leaned down to whisper in her ear. "Hey, be careful, there might be surveillance cameras down here."

She immediately glanced around, biting her lip. I noticed the swelling in her neck had lessened, but it still looked bright red. "It doesn't matter, Zander. This is important." She shrugged. "Besides, aren't we pretty much screwed anyway?"

Dara's sharp voice startled us both. "Don't you dare give up, Luna Redwood. You will get out of here. There are things you're meant to do."

Her hands gripped the cell door so tightly, her knuckles turned white. "What things? Tell me Dara. I need to remember. Help me."

Tears fell in earnest down Luna's face, a rare show of emotion for her.

Dara's face softened. "Don't cry, child. It will be alright. Now why don't you introduce me to your young man?"

She deflected, wanting Luna off her tail, but why? She locked eyes with me, almost pleading. I sensed, whatever the secret, she didn't want to share it here where she might be overheard.

I huddled closer to Luna. "Yeah Lun, where are your manners?"

Dara's face filled with gratitude as I flicked my gaze to Luna, who briskly wiped away her tears and returned to business mode. She saw me watching her and rolled her eyes. "For goodness' sake, Zander, you know this is Dara."

I raised my eyebrows at her.

She held up her hands. "Fine, you win. Zander, this is Dara. Dara, Zander."

"Nice to meet you, son," she said. She stood taller now, and her voice had lost its shaking edge. As if protecting Luna had renewed her strength.

When she spoke again, she sounded determined. "There's one thing I must tell you while I still have the chance."

Luna's voice rose in panic. "I'm going to get you out of here, don't talk like that."

Dara sighed. "I'm an old woman, and I've done my time. We talked about it in our little chats. I do miss those..." she trailed off wistfully.

"So do I," Luna choked. "You were a good friend to me."

"It's okay to express your feelings, dear. Lucky for you, I can read between the lines—and I love you too. Don't ever be afraid to love." She glanced meaningfully at me, then back to Luna. I stared down at my hands, almost afraid to discover what I would find in Luna's expression.

Dara's voice pierced the silence. "You're going to have to support each other if you want to survive what lies ahead."

"What do you know? Tell us. Anything. Please," Luna pleaded.

"They've discovered who you are. Be mindful of that."

I frowned puzzled. "What do you mean, Dara? Everyone knows we're Elite," I said.

"It goes beyond that, Zander. Deeper. More personal."

"What do they have on her?" I demanded. Suddenly, I didn't care who heard us. If Luna was in even more danger than I realized, I needed to be made aware of it.

"I possess the sight, Zander. But it's not always clear what I'm given. I can only tell you what I see."

"That's how you knew about the cage of glass," Luna murmured. "Why you tried to warn me."

"Yes. And why they removed me from the game. When they found out I might spoil all the fun, I became a liability. They pulled me out and put me in here until they could figure out what to do with me. The only reason I'm not dead is because they wanted answers. But the truth serum doesn't work on me." She smiled mischievously as if it were a personal victory. "They need batteries badly, and my vision revealed I will end up at a far-off energy outpost, providing whatever vitality remains in me. I don't care now if they find out I have the sight; I've lived a long life. And your fate is already set in motion."

"No!" she shouted. "They can't do that to you. We're going to find a way out of here."

Dara looked at Luna with compassion. "I did what I came here to do."

"But I don't know anything about you. I want to hear about your real life. Please let me help."

"You know all the important things. We know each other's hearts, and we know how to love. I'm the same woman you knew on W1. It may have been a game, but no matter, they can't take away who we are. Sure, they can manipulate you, but they can't ever destroy what resides in your soul. Never forget that."

"All right therapy session's over. You're annoying the surveillance guys upstairs with all your yapping. It's time for a little Q&A."

My head whipped around to discern who had descended into our dungeon. A big burly man with dark skin and brown eyes headed towards us. His crisp black and gray government-issued uniform strained against his huge biceps. He scanned his wrist and opened our jail door. I staggered to my feet, but Luna struggled to even move. I went to help her, but the hulking giant shoved me aside.

"Don't worry," he said, "I'll take care of the little lady."

He took hold of Luna's arm and lifted her up as if she were little more than a doll. She cried out in pain, and I leapt to her defense.

"Take your hands off her, she's still hurting."

The man chuckled—a hearty laugh that came from deep in his chest. "Calm down, lover boy. The boss just wants a little chat with her. When she's done, I'll bring her right back down to you, okay?"

"No!" I yelled. "Take me instead, let me answer your questions." I pushed up against him, attempting to slide between him and Luna.

"Zander, it's fine. I can handle it," Luna said between clenched teeth trying to keep her pain under control.

"But Luna."

"Listen to the little lady, Romeo, unless you want to be separated from her permanently. Because if you interfere with the boss's orders, she might very well arrange it."

I swallowed hard but didn't move. Finally, he just pushed me off as if I were an insignificant fly. "God damn kids. Why do they never listen?" he muttered under his breath.

I cursed as I hit the floor. "You stay put," he warned with a flick of his finger.

Luna looked at me pleadingly as he dragged her along the hard concrete and out of the cell, locking the door behind him. I hauled myself to my feet and threw myself at the rails, but he'd already reached Dara's chamber.

"Tell you what, since you two are so chummy, you can come upstairs together. How's that? I think it's time the old lady goes on her next adventure. Don't you agent Brick?"

I turned my head, peering down the narrow corridor and saw another man appear, smaller than the brute that held Luna, but similar in build, with strong stocky limbs. I could take the small one, but I had no chance against them both, especially after being tranquilized.

"Great idea, Oscar. Come on, I'll take you up old broad. You've troubled me enough these past few weeks. I'll be glad to see the last of you." He scanned his wrist and opened the cell. "Let's go." He gave her leg a quick kick with his heavy boot, grabbed hold of her hair, and began dragging her through the exit.

Luna screamed, her legs and arms flailing as she struggled

against Oscar. I could almost see the adrenaline coursing through her body—pain forgotten, as her entire being focused on saving her friend.

I stood helpless; my arms stretched through the bars in a pathetic attempt to somehow grab one of the agents as they passed. Instead, my hand grazed the back of Dara's foot as Brick hauled her away.

As our skin made contact, pain clamped down on my skull and a vision roared through me like a freight train.

Disoriented, I felt myself losing consciousness as the stark truth cut through me.

A truth that changed everything.

Dara had lied to everyone.

My mind spun, trying to make sense of it all. But it was too late. The blackness crowded in and I lurched forward, falling hard to the ground.

Right before I passed out, Dara's eyes met mine.

And she realized I knew her secret.

CHAPTER 27

LUNA

"Why am I here?" I demanded, gripping the small table separating myself and the warden. It took everything in me to maintain an upright position, but I refused to allow the government to see my weakness. The interrogation room, windowless and barely bigger than a closet, made me feel more than a little claustrophobic. The whir of a recording camera overhead under normal circumstances would bother me, but today, I ignored it, my eyes laser-focused on the woman before me.

Detective Jardin and I were alone, but I wasn't stupid, I knew others surveyed us from afar. Tall with taunt muscles and pallid skin, she hardly appeared threatening. Her watery grey eyes gave her an almost ethereal quality as she tapped delicate fingers on her com screen, her face impassive. Finally, after an interminable silence, she lifted her gaze. "I will be the one to ask the questions, Luna, especially since it is you and your friend Zander that are the ones that appear to be in a bit of trouble."

"We were doing just fine until you came along," I spat, temper flaring.

"Do you wish to explain how you exited the virtual reality simulation assigned to you and left our facility?"

I frowned, crossing my arms. "Not particularly."

"Miss Redwood, let me remind you that you and Zander have committed a criminal offense. And I assure you, the less you cooperate, the more severe the punishment."

My pulse raced, but I kept my features schooled. If the detective had done her homework, she should realize interrogation wasn't a new concept to me. I understood the stakes. I bit back all the questions I longed to ask—namely, how I managed to keep the clock key that now burned a hole in my boot. Why hadn't they searched me when they captured us?

"Miss Redwood?"

I leaned forward, putting on my best scowl. "Look, I don't know what you want from me. I ran because I woke up and found myself in a glass cell, having been placed there against my will. Anyone else would have done the same."

"How did you escape—walk away so easily? You must have had some assistance."

"What are you going to do to Dara?" I countered, changing tack. "Why don't you release her? She's an old lady."

"Dara Peters is not the person we're here to discuss."

"Well, she should be. She was in the game with me after all."

Detective Jardin regarded me with a tolerant expression, but her eye twitched like an irritated cat's tail. "We have many simulations, Miss Redwood, but we're here to address how you escaped—not to rehash your experiences in W1. At least for now."

"I want a meeting with my parents before I answer any more questions. I have rights."

She leaned back in her chair a shocked expression on her face. "Your parents? Why would we involve them?"

I rolled my eyes. This lady needed to get a life. "Because they're my Mom and Dad. And I'm under eighteen."

Jardin regarded me coolly for a minute, as if trying to access what my angle was. It would be a cold day in hell before I gave her any information, no matter how long she stared down that owlish nose at me.

Time to throw down the gauntlet, I thought. I needed to act dumb and play this out to the best of my ability. Even as I plotted, I prayed they left Zander alone. "If you let me see my parents, I will answer any questions you want."

Sure, it was a bold-faced lie. But I was a damned good liar. I would worry about step two when the time came.

Jardin stared at me with a blank expression, before turning to her com pad and setting it to sleep mode. She rose from her chair. "All right, Miss Redwood. We'll do this your way. I'll bring your parents, but you better hold up your side of the bargain." She strode briskly to the door and knocked. The guard appeared almost instantly, awaiting instructions. She turned and gave me a last look. "If you burn me on this, you will live to regret it. Are we clear?"

"Crystal," I said trying not to sound gleeful. This was my opportunity.

Jardin looked doubtful but said nothing more. "Warden, take Miss Redwood back down to her cell, then contact the Redwoods. I need to speak with them."

"Yes, boss."

So she was the boss. Intriguing. Before I had time to process this new piece of information, the guard snagged me by the arm and railroaded me into the hallway. "Ouch. Watch it," I hissed.

"Shut your mouth girl, or I'll do far worse."

I decided to keep quiet after that, no sense in causing unnecessary trouble. However, I remained vigilant of my surroundings as we made our way back down to the basement, mapping the place out in my head. As far as I could tell, the labs holding the glass cages must be located upstairs, on the floors above the interrogation center, which also held other administrative offices. Below that was what I now called the dungeon. The warden shoved me into a small elevator, and pushed a chubby finger to the digits on the wall. Trapped in the confined space there was no escape from the stench of sweat and cigarette smoke radiating off him in waves. I held my breath as much as possible, until the chime dinged, telling us we were back on the lower level. By the time we arrived at my dank cell, I felt satisfied I had a pretty good layout of the area. But all my plans flew out the window when I looked inside the jail and saw Zander lying unmoving on the cold cement floor.

"Zander!"

He didn't respond and I turned to the officer. "You need to help him!"

He sneered, displaying a set of yellow stained teeth. "I don't have to do nothin', little lady. Didn't I already tell you to keep quiet?" He turned to the opposite cell, the one where Dara had been held, and swiped his wrist key. "Get in there." Swinging the door open he shoved me forward, clanging it shut behind me before I even made it fully inside. As he started to walk away, I called out.

"Wait! Where's Dara?"

He turned and grinned, spitting on the floor in front of him. "Don't you worry your pretty head about Dara. You're about to have enough problems of your own without worrying about that old hag."

I wanted to ask him what the hell he meant by that, but he disappeared into the gloom before I even opened my mouth.

The sound of groans emanating from the opposite cell made me whip my head around. Zander still lay on the ground, but his eyelids were fluttering. He lifted his hand, and rubbed at a large bump swelling on his forehead.

I rushed to the bars and frantically stuck my arms through in a desperate attempt to reach him—a wasted effort.

"Zander? What happened? Are you hurt?"

"Luna? Where are you?" He sounded disorientated, and I started to panic. What had they done to him? Zander claimed the truth serum didn't work on us, but perhaps they had some other vile remedy to torture us with. But if that were true, the smug detective would have saved herself some time by giving me a dose.

Before my thoughts completely spiraled out of control, Zander sat up, still looking confused.

"I'm over here," I called out. "In the other cell."

He rubbed a hand over his face, attempting to collect himself.

"Did they do something to you?" I whispered.

Finally, he spoke, his voice a little shaky. "No. Something else happened...wait, why did they put you in the other holding area?" he asked blinking rapidly, eyebrows furrowed.

"The jerk face that brought me back placed me here. Probably because I screamed at him to help you when I saw you lying on the floor."

He winced. "Sorry to freak you out. I had an episode."

His eyes bored into mine, as if pleading with me to understand. An episode? Another psychic vision? Because the last one left him pretty messed up. It made sense.

I studied him. He looked rattled. Whatever he'd seen shocked him, or at the very least taken him by surprise. I couldn't exactly ask. Not with the gooney surveillance team upstairs charting our every move.

"Are you okay now?" A lame question, but the best I could do.

"I will be. I found out something interesting. But we can talk about that later."

Translation—he had definitely seen something worth mentioning, but too many ears listened in. Why had that annoying guard put me in a different cell? We couldn't communicate now. I slammed my hands against the bars in frustration. "I hate this!"

I ignored the pain that shot through my body and let the rage fuel my energy. There had to be a way out of this mess.

"What happened upstairs?"

"They asked me a bunch of questions about why I ran away. I wasn't much help."

Zander smirked. "I bet."

"They're going to collect my parents and bring me back up when they arrive."

Zander's eyebrows rose up in question. "How did you manage that?"

"Let's just say we struck a deal."

His eyes filled with concern. "Luna, you shouldn't have—"

I interrupted him. "I'll be fine. I need to ask them some questions. You should understand that better than anyone."

I hoped he got my meaning. We needed to figure out the contents of that disk.

"I bet you wish you possessed a memento of theirs," Zander said. "It's always nice to hold onto a keepsake from the people you love. Just so you have a little token to remember them by when you can't be with them."

I frowned at Zander. Something didn't add up. He knew I didn't recall anything about my parents. So what was he trying to tell me?

"Yeah, that would be nice," I said hastily to fill the void. "At least I can see them today. They'll help us Zander. I know it."

A part of me hoped it was true. Despite all that happened, I wanted to believe they were good people who cared about me.

"I wish I had a small keepsake to remember my parents by," Zander continued, along the same vein. "Even something as insignificant as a hairpin from my mother or a handkerchief from my father. Maybe then I could recall some memories of them."

I swallowed hard. Comprehension dawning. Zander wanted me to steal something of theirs. But why?

I softened my facial features and looked to Zander with compassion. "It must be terrible to not know who your parents are. I'm sorry, I shouldn't complain." It was true, Zander had a raw deal. And I realized how selfish I'd been that I never asked him what it was like for him growing up. I vowed to rectify that when we escaped this dump.

"No. I—" He pulled up short when he caught my gaze, realizing I got the memo or maybe he picked up a psychic hit.

He changed tack. "Thanks, Luna."

It was the weirdest conversation we'd ever had, but whoever watched us now wouldn't understand that. They didn't know us.

And if I had my way, they never would.

If my hunch was right, Zander wanted to pry information from whatever object I could steal from dear old Mom and Dad. I wasn't sure how all this psychic stuff worked, but if he found any new evidence that could help us, we would be better off than we were now.

Deep in my gut, I sensed my parents knew something important.

And I needed to uncover exactly what that was.

◈

Several hours later, the same creepy warden from last time was now winging me back toward Detective Jardin and my only blood relatives. I kept a check of the route, and all the exit signs, just to make certain the directions I mentally squirreled away earlier were accurate. Soon we arrived at the same interrogation room as before. I wiped the sweat from my palms and swallowed hard.

Time for another performance. Beyond those doors my parents—who I had almost zero memories of—waited. And I had to pretend as if nothing had changed between us—that our shared history remained intact.

To complicate things, I had to undergo the biggest pilfer of my life.

If I failed—Crane, Sepha, Zander, and I would be trapped in this rathole indefinitely.

I took a deep breath. I could do this. The guard opened the door and dragged me roughly inside. His unforgiving fingers dug into my arm, and I cursed him under my breath, knowing there would be a big bruise from his brute force. However, when I laid eyes on the two strangers in the room, any thoughts of skin injuries were quickly forgotten. I recalled my memory flashes; these people looked exactly the same, right down to the clothing. Mom, attired in a periwinkle blue designer dress with a cream blouse, definitely looked the part of a wealthy woman. Her hair had been pulled back into a tight bun at the nape of her neck. The severe style accentuated the hard lines around her red colored lips and sharp eagle-blue eyes. Dad's outfit seemed just as conservative with his pressed gray slacks and button-down forest green shirt. He wore an expensive gold ring on his pinky finger which sported an unusual insignia. A family crest perhaps?

They stood together, a tight unit, only their faces etched with tension gave them away. Mom touched a hand to her hair, and I caught a slight tremble in her fingertips. Dad's mouth twitched in a weak effort to smile at me.

Whatever delusions I'd had about these people possibly helping me suddenly disappeared. These two were definitely the kind of parents that would put me in a cage and throw away the key. But I had to be sure.

I plastered on my own fake smile and rushed over to greet them. I concentrated on bringing crocodile tears to my eyes, they rose effortlessly to the surface, thanks to my recent injury. My body still ached, though it had become more bearable.

"I missed you both so much, I'm so glad you're here," I exclaimed wrapping my arms around them in a bear hug. Mom reeked of expensive perfume, and Dad smelled of musky aftershave.

Dad stood stiff as a board, but managed to reach out and give me a quick pat on the back. As for my mother, I could almost feel her skin crawl at my touch.

To be fair, I imagine I looked pretty awful. More like a dirty brown rat, than a human daughter with my filthy clothes and tangled hair which had long since escaped the confines of my ponytail.

"Yes, well it's good to see you too, I suppose," Mom said in a clipped tone. Dad made a grunting noise that I think meant he agreed with her.

I held on to them a tad longer than normal—time to collect my little mementoes.

"All right, Miss Redwood, that is quite enough," Detective Jardin said. I knew she'd been there all along but chose to ignore her. And that's where I found my opportunity.

I did my best at pretending to be surprised, giving a small jump at the sound of her voice. That allowed me to trip and fall into Mother, creating the perfect chaos for my little slip of the hand. I deftly nipped one of the many clips holding Mom's bun in place, and slipped it under my sleeve.

Dad caught the both of us, preventing us from crashing onto the hard floor. As I gripped his arm, I swiped one of his cufflinks and slid it into my pocket. I hid the smirk that threatened to escape; it was like taking candy from a baby.

Ironically, Zander would get the hairpin he requested and more.

"Please, everyone sit down," Detective Jardin barked. Seriously this woman needed to relax. Would she bring a whistle out next to try and corral the troops?

I sat down at the long silver metal table, my parents opposite me.

I reached across for my father's hand, allowing my bottom lip to wobble. "Daddy, please get me out of here. They put me in a game against my will, and now they're keeping me locked up in a cell. They're asking all sorts of questions about why I escaped." I gave Detective Jardin a meaningful glance then turned back to face dear old dad. "Tell her I was just trying to return to you."

Mom scoffed. "That's a bit farfetched, Luna, even for you. Last time we saw you, I believe you told us we could rot in hell and that you never wanted to see our faces again."

Jardin leaned forward, peering at me closely. "Now, that piece of information seems to be something you omitted, Miss Redwood. Is it true you had a falling out with your parents?"

My heart hammered in my throat. Of course, I had no recollection of the things I'd said, but it sure sounded like me. It put a real kink in my plans, but I would just have to work with it. I quickly changed tactics.

I shrugged. "That was ages ago. Besides, you were a teenager once, you must know what an emotional roller coaster it can be. One minute you're in love with life, the next it feels like the end of the world."

"Yes, well," Dad interjected. "What you said was hurtful, Luna. Your mother wept for days after you left."

Bull crap. Zander had been right. They didn't give a flying fig what happened to me.

I furiously blinked away tears. "I'm so sorry I hurt you both."

Mom nodded and Dad patted my hand, his palms clammy. "Well, it was a difficult time, but I think your Mother and I can forgive you," he said in his deep baritone voice.

They were saying all the right things in the wrong way. Decidedly not adept liars, they were hiding something. If only I could access another memory. I'd hoped seeing them in person would trigger another.

But all I received from these two were bad vibes.

Definitely not good people.

I always came back to the same conclusion. I would be okay on my own, I didn't need anybody. I could take care of myself.

Detective Jardin said something to my parents, and I tried to focus.

"Do you have any idea why Luna would want to contact you after all this time?"

"You don't need to talk about me like I'm not here," I snapped, irritated.

Jardin raised a pointy eyebrow at me. "You'll get your turn, Miss Redwood, don't worry."

I frowned at her but didn't say anything else.

"Honestly, I don't understand her at all. She's acting so strange," Mom said adjusting the bow at her neck, eyeing me suspiciously.

"Our girl was never one for affection," Dad added. "The hug she gave us earlier was out of character."

I groaned inwardly. It looked as though I'd have to intercept this conversation before it got out of control. I held up a hand. "People change. I realized after you left..." I paused, letting my voice hitch a little. "What a mistake I made in pushing you away."

Jardin almost snorted but managed to clamp her lips shut in time.

"What I don't understand is why you wanted to see us," Dad said. "We explained to you previously that you went into the program because Tyrone believed you to be special. And as a loyal family friend, we trusted him to do what's best."

"Tyrone Harrison?" I yelped.

Dad looked at me, puzzled. "Of course, who else?"

Mom frowned, deepening the crease in her forehead. "Why are you acting like you're so surprised? You know, Tyrone's always been very kind to you, to all of us."

Zander's words echoed in my ears. Tyrone was the leader of the Black Mark. The brainchild behind the idea to send the Elite back in time and most likely to our deaths. They had no plan in place to ensure our safe return. *Oh my God.* He was their *friend.*

A sudden sense of urgency gripped me. I needed to put feelers out about the disk. Was it possible that the disk was from Tyrone? The idea seemed a bit farfetched, yet at the same time made sense. Only one way to find out.

"So why do you think he's always been so kind?" I pressed. "Did he do something for you? Share secrets? Give you a gift what?" I leaned forward watching their expressions.

Mom's eye twitched a little, while Dad looked away, as if something on the wall intrigued him.

"You don't become friends with someone just for what they

can do for you. Honestly, I thought I raised you better than that." Mom crossed her arms, her hands fidgety.

Interesting. There was a connection here. Sure, it was a stretch, since I couldn't come right out and ask them about the disk. But it was definitely something to think about. I wasn't going to get any more out of them. That much was certain. As far as I was concerned this game was over. I stood, the chair scraping against the cold tiles. "I think we're done here."

I understood perfectly well I was showing my hand, but I couldn't be with them in this tiny room a second longer. My parents. My flesh and blood had sent me on a trajectory that would eventually end in my destruction. It was beyond disgusting.

"Luna, sit down. This session isn't over," Detective Jardin commanded, pointing to the seat I just vacated.

I threw my hands up in the air, exasperated. "You wanted to know why I ran away? I was looking for my parents. But it turns out that was a mistake. Okay? Now you have your answer, can I go?"

Jardin frowned and tapped something into her port screen before looking at me with cold eyes. "I decide when the discussion is over, Miss Redwood, not you. But it's clear to me in your present frame of mind, it might preferable to change the subject. Perhaps another approach may suit you better."

I seethed inwardly, clenching my fists into tight balls to prevent myself from lashing out at her. This woman was getting on my last nerve. "What else is there to know? I ran away from a game. It's not that big a deal."

Mom and Dad glanced at each other in silent agreement, then rose from their seats. "We'd best be going Detective Jardin, it's obvious our presence here isn't required," Mom said. She turned to me. "We made the right decision placing you in the program, Luna. You clearly need more discipline in your life. And quite frankly, your father and I have had enough of your ridiculous outbursts."

Seeing them standing there together, made my mind flash to an old memory. The one I'd received not long after arriving here —when they'd been with the mysterious tall man sporting the trademark scar. I remembered the three of them had been staring at me. I swallowed dryly. Was it possible that this stranger had been Tyrone Harrison? Had I been witnessing the moment they shipped me off to the program? Words, whispers of voices crowded my head. *He's a loyal family friend, Luna. We trust him.* I'd heard these words from my parents before. They had told me that the day I'd been taken away. If my hunch was correct—and all signs pointed that way—that meant Mrs. Lennor's son was the one and only Dr. Tyrone Harrison. Bile rose in my throat, and I tried not to vomit.

I wasn't sure I could move. The shock too much.

I must have been openly staring at my parents because Jardin, assuming I was ready for battle, interrupted my whirling thoughts, her voice cutting the thick tension in the air.

"Please, allow me see you out," Jardin said rising swiftly to her feet, as if trying to placate them. "Boyd, return the girl to her cell. We'll deal with her later," she snapped at the guard as she exited the room.

As Boyd dragged me unceremoniously back down to the holding quarters, my mind raced with the implication of all this. I could never have imagined what was in store for me.

We were on a sinking ship, falling into an endless sea, and I didn't know how any of us would survive.

CHAPTER 28
ZANDER

The jail remained quiet save for the sound of Luna's soft, even breathing coming from the opposite cell, telling me she was asleep. I ached to hold her and tell her everything would be all right—but that was a promise I wasn't sure I could keep.

A small sliver of moonlight cast a shadow over Luna's still frame. The only light in this hellhole since the government henchmen snuffed out the overhead bulb about an hour after bringing Luna back down.

Luna had been tight-lipped about the meeting with her parents. When she'd returned, her face had been pale, but also triumphant as if she couldn't decide which emotion to go with. All I'd managed to squeeze out of her was a muttering about mementos being overrated, and how her parents disappointed her.

Despite her proclamation, I intuitively gathered Luna had stolen something. Which meant she had understood my cryptic message. I hoped to God when I touched whatever she managed to snag, I would receive a hit. I vaguely remembered reading something about this when I began researching psychic abilities in an effort to figure out what was going on with me. According to what I learned, getting a "vibe" or psychic impression from an object was a real thing. I think it was called psychometry, or something like that anyway. Whatever its name, right now, we were too far apart for me to get any sort of information. How could I gain access to the object? I silently wondered if getting an impression from a person, like I did with Dara, fell under this category or if that was a whole new level of weird.

Before I could come up with a solution, or figure any of this out, the faint sound of scraping from the outer door alerted me.

Someone was coming.

I jumped off the bed, heart hammering in my chest, and rushed to the front lock, straining to catch sight of who'd come in. The noise must have awoken Luna because her face was already pressed to the iron rails. Even in the wan light, I noticed her white knuckles as she gripped the metal bars. She would see who came around the corner first. Her face turned ashen when they came into view.

"Who is it?" I hissed.

Her mouth opened to speak, but I saw who it was before she had a chance to respond.

"Well, well, well, fancy meeting you two down here."

"Madeline?" I asked incredulously. "Did they catch you too? What are you doing here?" I looked past her to scope out if an officer had hold of her. But instead found two kids I recognized from the program, Arliss and Tansy. They were Elite, but I'd always kept my distance—they were always so gung-ho about what the government wanted us to do. I didn't trust them.

"So, it appears you've gotten yourself into a bit of trouble," Madeline sneered at Luna, ignoring my questions. She leaned towards her so closely, Luna probably felt her breath on her skin.

"Come on Mads. No need to rub it in," I said.

She whipped around to face me eyes flashing. "Nobody calls me Mads anymore. You would do well to remember that."

"What do you want, Madeline? Why did you sneak down here?" Luna sounded bored, but I was conscious of the fact she had to be freaking out inside.

Madeline slowly stepped back over to Luna, her movement akin to a prowling cat. "This doesn't concern you little L. I came to warn Zander. You, I could care less about."

"Who are your goons?" Luna said jutting her chin towards Arliss and Tansy.

"Never you mind about that, pet. Why don't you scram?" She laughed then, a startling inhuman laugh, and my gut twisted.

"Oh, right. I forgot, you can't go anywhere because you're locked up." She scrutinized Luna as if examining a flea. "Well, that's too bad for you isn't it, kitten?"

"Madeline, what's gotten into you? You're acting really weird."

Madeline spun around again and glared at me. Her silver eyes squinted in disapproval. "I'm trying to do you a favor. Watch it."

"I don't wish for that kind of favor, Madeline. What we need is to break out of here."

She stepped closer and ran a finger down my cheek, the tip of her tongue sticking out at the corner of her mouth. "Don't concern yourself with that, darling boy. If you follow the rules, we'll have you out of here in no time. Oh, and by the way, we can speak freely. Tansy went and checked on the baboons on your security detail. They've already fallen asleep on the job. Fortunately, this isn't a real prison. Just temporary holding cells. Otherwise, it would be a much more complicated situation."

"So you have a plan?" I asked eagerly. "Did Scott send you?"

She scowled. "I'm through doing his bidding. I spent years working on his stupid project and received nothing in return. I'm done with him."

I swallowed hard, staring at her in shock. Her eyes seemed vacant, like a part of her was elsewhere or missing. "What project? You're not making any sense."

"He gave me some sob story about how I was meant to save the world. And he needed my help to find all the Elite."

I frowned at her, puzzled. "They're only nine of us. And he

knows exactly where we all are. What's there to find? Do you mean he wanted you to keep tabs on us?"

Luna piped up from behind. "You helped him spy on us? What the hell?"

Madeline sneered at Luna. "Stop talking. You're making yourself look like an idiot. We're all aware you're the only spy here."

Luna clenched her fists to her sides. Her mouth set in a firm line.

"She wants to get under your skin, Luna." I interjected. "Ignore her. Madeline, didn't you come to talk to me? Leave Luna out of it."

Her eyes lit up with pleasure as she stared back at me. "That's true, angel, I did come down to have a little chat with you," she purred. "Now, where were we?" She traced a finger over my neck and pushed her fingers down into my skin a little too hard.

"You were about to tell me what you did for Scott."

She grimaced. "Right. Look, Zander. Scott's been lying. Hell, he's been lying to all of us."

I pushed a hand through my hair. "This doesn't add up," I said. "Why do you think he's deceiving us?"

She crossed her arms smugly. "Oh, I don't just think, I know."

I sighed. "Really Madeline? Are you going to keep beating around the bush or are you going to spill it?"

She put her hands on her hips and glared at me. "I'm taking a real risk coming down here to warn you. And so are Tansy and Arliss."

"Why are they here, anyway?" I demanded.

"They're my friends," she said through gritted teeth. "And I expect you to give them respect."

I put my hands up. "Fine. Sorry."

She smiled again, doing a quick one-eighty. Madeline was clearly losing her mind.

"I love this new stubble, Zander," she crooned, cupping my face. I pushed back away from the jail door.

"Come on. That's not fair. Luna is standing right there. Stop trying to upset her."

She shrugged. "That would just be a bonus."

Arliss finally interrupted. He looked tired, his blue streaked hair in complete disarray as if Madeline had pulled him from his bed to be here. He'd clearly reached the end of his rope with her. "Come on, Madeline. Tell him about Scott already so we can jet. There's no way to gauge how long the security goons will sleep."

She rolled her eyes. "I get the message. You don't have to act like such a dweeb."

I tried not to scoff. She sounded like a valley girl now. What kind of game was she playing?

She studied her perfectly manicured nails, then looked up at me with fluttering eyelashes. "Here's the deal. Scott believed there were more than nine of us."

"How many more?" I pressed.

"Try thirty."

"Thirty?" I said incredulously. "How is that possible? There was barely enough mineral for nine of us."

"He didn't fill me in on the details, but he seemed pretty certain. And he thought it safer for everyone involved if they believed only nine Elite existed."

"My guess is, he asked you to go into the games to search for them," I said.

Madeline nodded. "Smart lad."

"Did you find any more Elite?"

The air hung heavy with silence as I waited for a reply. She paused, cocking her head at me and said, "I think you can figure out the answer on your own. You seem bright enough."

I shook the jail door in exasperation. "How in the hell am I supposed to do that?"

Madeline crossed her arms and stared me down. "Don't over-react, you're being childish. Let's just say I know about your little secret. You're special, aren't you? I saw you inside the game. You can't fool me."

My mouth went dry. Had she realized I was psychic?

"It's not hard to figure out how to exit the game," Luna said, trying to cover for me. "It hardly makes him special."

Madeline waved her hand, indicating she was tired of our conversation. "Look, I don't have time for this. All you need to understand is that Scott is a liar and can't be trusted. He withheld information. And now look what a pickle you're in. You're lucky you're Elite, or the government would have fried your asses by now."

"I have to talk to him, Madeline," I said. "I'm sure Scott has his reasons."

Madeline's eyes flashed, turning them from gray to deadly steel. She placed her hands over mine in a tight grip over the bars. "You're a fool for going against the cause, Zander. You'll end up dead like Sepha. I'm warning you, don't mess up the program."

"Sepha's dead?" I choked, my stomach turning to acid.

She smiled triumphantly. "Yes, she is."

"What happened? How did they kill her?"

"Come on, Zander, even an idiot knows that. Remember how she always carried around that gadget she made? I don't even think it had a name."

"She gave herself a lethal injection?" I whispered barely able to say the words, emotion choking me.

"You got it."

"Why would she do that?" Luna insisted.

"Because she was a fool," Madeline scoffed.

"Yeah, talk about being brainwashed by the resistors," Arliss sneered.

"She wasn't brainwashed," I said through clenched teeth. "She helped us. She would rather die than give up the resistor's secrets. As one of our top hackers, she would have a lot of damaging information to provide the government, so she always carried around a deadly dose of poison. She said it was her insurance against them." My voice cracked. "She sacrificed herself for us."

Tansy snorted. "You give her too much credit, Zander. She only looked out for herself."

My hackles rose, but I didn't respond to her barb. Tansy had never been part of the resistors movement.

I stared at Madeline, trying to work out her angle. In the shadows, the strong planes of her cheeks were accentuated. But I could still make out the scorn written plainly across her features.

"Zander, you've obviously been brainwashed. Fighting for the resistors has brought you nothing but heartache. Why not let go of this animosity and start fighting for the winning team."

I shook my head. I couldn't believe what I was hearing. "Madeline, you can't be serious. They treated us like lab rats, pawns for their own experiments. Only a few days ago, you saved my life. Don't you remember? What's changed?"

She stepped back. "Oh, I remember. Just don't make me regret it." She lifted her chin higher. "Are you in or not? I can bust you out of here, Zander. Just say the word."

I pushed my hands into my jeans to keep them from balling into fists. "Please think about this. The government is using you. If you get us out of here, we can help."

Madeline scoffed. "Like I would trust my life to you two. Final offer, Zander. If you come over to the government side, I can get you released—simple as that."

"You know I can't," I whispered. "Besides, I would never desert Luna. We're a package deal."

Madeline slammed her hands against the bars in fury. "You're a fool, Zander Barringer. Don't say I didn't warn you. Both of you are no better than the scum that roams the streets of New Earth."

"The feeling is mutual," Luna muttered.

Madeline must have heard, but ignored her, having eyes only

for me. "You will live to regret this. You just made your life very difficult." She turned and sauntered away.

"Wait! Don't do this," I yelped.

She glanced back at me. A flash of pity crossing her face. "Oh, you poor delusional creature. I can do whatever I want. Now that I'm on the government's side, they will soon find out how many Elite there really are. And..." she tilted her head as if thinking for a moment. "I guess that means you won't be irre-placeable after all."

She smiled a sickly-sweet smile that didn't quite reach her eyes. Something drastic must have happened to her. But what?

"I can help you. Let me figure out what's going on...we can—"

"Save it, lover boy," she snapped. "You just signed your death warrant. And Crane's."

"You know where Crane is?" I asked, hope filling me.

"Of course I do. I'm not an imbecile. He's alive, but not for long."

"Madeline, please try to help him."

"Why should I? He's a walking moron. And he's not even Elite. He's replaceable. Learn to discern the difference."

"You're a real piece of work," Luna spat.

She turned surprised, lifting a hand to her heart. "You scared me, Luna, I forgot you were there. So easy to do, you under-stand. Now I must be going. I'm not even supposed to be here. And Zander apparently doesn't want my help."

I watched her leave, mouth agape. *What the hell just happened?*

"Well, she's a regular ray of sunshine," Luna said sarcastically. "Are you sure she's your friend?"

"Yeah. At least I think so. They've done something to her Luna, they must have somehow convinced her to switch sides. We've got to escape and find Crane."

Luna looked around as if she possessed laser vision to spot the hidden cameras. I could guess her thoughts.

"Don't worry, Madeline isn't stupid," I said. "She wouldn't

talk that readily unless she'd disengaged the surveillance feed. They said the security guys were asleep. But she's probably on her way now to restore it. There's not much time. Let's not waste it on her."

"Okay. What's the plan?"

I leaned in closer to the bars, my voice barely a whisper. "Do you still have the clock key?"

"Yes."

"We need to repair it. We can use it to free ourselves from this hellhole."

"But without tools—"

"We'll think of something. But we'll have to do it while it's still dark, so we're not seen. Go over to the toilet, hopefully the camera's range doesn't reach that far into the corner. You have a little bit of moonlight coming into your cell. Will that be enough?"

"It's going to have to be. Don't worry, I'll make it work." Her eyes took on a determined look. "We'll find a way out of this." She pulled a couple of items from her sleeve and held them up for me to look at. I strained to see them in the wan light. As if sensing my struggle, she said, "It's a hair pin and cufflink, stolen from dear old Mom and Dad. I take it you have a plan for these?"

I nodded. "Yeah. I'd say toss them over, but even if you threw them, I'm afraid they wouldn't make it all the way over. Hold onto them for now."

She tucked them away again and smiled at me. I wish I had her confidence about getting out of dodge.

But the burning acid in my stomach told me otherwise. I couldn't foresee the future, but I had a sinking suspicion things were about to take a turn. And it wasn't in our favor.

To add to my woes, I needed to somehow explain to Luna what I'd learned when my hands brushed Dara's foot earlier tonight. If something happened to me, or we got separated for any reason I would always regret not saying anything.

"Luna, I have to tell you something."

She came closer, squeezing her face between the bars, her eyes shadowed in worry. "What? Did you get a vision? Has something horrible been done to Crane?"

I grimaced. "No. I didn't. But I got one from Dara."

"Dara?" Her eyebrows shot up in surprise.

"Yes. When I touched her, I saw something. She knows exactly who I am. And she's been conscious of my identity since my birth."

Luna bit her lip, something she often did when trying to piece things together. She looked so pretty, even with all the dirt smudges on her face. How had I got so lucky with her? Well, lucky if you didn't count being locked up in a cell and scared for your life. Still, if I had to be stuck in a cage, I would rather be with her than anyone else.

"I don't understand. Did she meet you before you were in the game with me? She never mentioned you. Not that I would have recognized your name," she said apologetically.

"No, I'm not sure if she was aware of the connection between you and I. But there is one thing she did know."

"What?"

"I'm her grandson."

CHAPTER 29

LUNA

The silence between us was palpable as I let the words sink in. "Are you sure about this?" I finally managed to squeak out.

"Positive. I felt a very strong connection to her. Almost like we were plugged in to each other. Perhaps both of us being psychic cemented our bond."

"Maybe," I said. "It could also be because you're a blood relative."

Zander nodded.

I wondered if she realized that back in the real world Zander and I were close. Did she seek me out on purpose? Or was it some cruel trick of the gamers to make us neighbors? Something else still niggled at me though.

"Zander, if she's your grandmother, she can identify your parents. You can find out the truth. Tell me exactly what you saw."

Zander shrugged. "Maybe. I saw my mother with Dara. I realized they had a look of one another. But it was more than that. It was an instinctual gut feeling that I was looking at my grandmother and mom. There was some tension between them, I felt it had something to do with me. I just haven't been able to discern what they fought about. And in my other vision when I was a baby, my Mom was wearing that pin. What does that mean?"

I hesitated, then blurted out the first thing that came to mind. "I don't know about the pin. But your Mom and Dad might have been like mine and wanted to sell you down the river to the government. Dara probably tried to stop it."

Zander pushed a hand through his considerably tangled locks. "That may be true, but that doesn't explain why I don't have any memories of them. Why give me up as a baby? At least your parents were decent enough to wait until you were a teenager to dump you into the program."

"Yeah, those two are a real bowl full of love," I said sarcastically. My stomach churned, thinking of our earlier encounter.

Suddenly, Zander froze and placed a finger to his lips, indicating I should be quiet. His eyes darted around the cell, as if looking for something.

I didn't dare speak. My heart thundered in my chest.

"Did you hear the click?" he whispered, barely audible. "I think they turned the video back on."

"No. But I've been expecting it," I said in a low tone.

Madeline had probably set the equipment back to rights when she returned upstairs. Unfortunately, even if the security detail remained asleep on the job, it would be easy for them to rewind the footage later and find out exactly what went down. We'd best be careful from now on.

Zander stretched out his arms and yawned for the cameras benefit, a little over dramatically if you asked me. "Let's get some sleep. Things will make more sense in the morning."

"Sure, sounds like a good plan," I said. Like him, I didn't want to give the feds anymore intel.

Zander went to lie down, but I stood there for a moment thinking of Dara. I wanted to talk to her again, but she could be miles from here by now, at any one of the many energy outposts. If I wanted to locate her, I'd have to find some way to escape and then acquire outside help. I sighed. It all seemed so complicated.

I went over to my rudimentary cot and sat down, thinking of the other big bombshell of the night. The unexpected visit from Madeline. Why did she seem so desperate to have Zander join her and be on the government's side? Whatever her agenda, he had infuriated her and that was bound to backfire on us. Times a million.

I shivered, huddling up into a ball. The chill bit into my flesh —sleep would be almost impossible tonight. Plus, I had so many unanswered questions swirling around in my mind. Zander was right. I had to figure out how to repair the clock key. And fast. If that thing could bust us out of our glass cages, then it just might help us break out of these cells.

I unraveled myself from my tight cocoon and got up. Still shivering, I tiptoed over to the back corner of my holding area. Anyone watching would assume that I needed to use the bathroom. But hopefully, like Zander said, the feed didn't stretch that far. I sat on the toilet seat, reached down and carefully pulled the small box containing the clock key from my boot. The wan moonlight filtering through the porthole illuminated the small mechanism I held in my hand. I scrutinized it intently. How did I seal these two pieces back together? It would require sealant, which of course I didn't have. I regretted putting all my stuff into that bag under the tree outside the dome. But I guess we would never have made it across the border if we'd taken anything with us.

I gently ran my fingers over the piece, then stopped when I thought I detected a minuscule groove. I sat up straighter, trying not to get my hopes up. It was probably just a part of the design. I rubbed my thumb over the depression again. No, it was definitely a groove. Had something been in there before? I held the unit up to the silvery light, squinting my eyes to get a better look.

That's when I noticed a tiny microscopic opening, no bigger than a pinhole. Maybe a screw had come loose. Surely someone would've noticed that before now though.

I glanced around, searching for something tiny that would fit in the hole. My shoulders sagged in disappointment. The place was bare save for the cot. I sighed in frustration.

Think. Luna. Think.

I rested my head in my hands, racking my brain for an idea. And then something slipped from my sleeve, making a tiny ping as it hit the ground.

My mother's stolen hair pin.

I swallowed the large lump in my throat, hands shaking as I hastily picked it up. This was the first good look I'd had of the clip, a petite piece with a diminutive diamond decorating the tip. It didn't appear to be very functional for gripping hair.

Hurriedly, I snapped the delicate spindle at the back into two pieces, all the while praying that Zander would still able to read something from it. Taking a deep breath, I stood up and stretched my arms high toward the small square window, holding the device above my head for more light. I gently pushed one half of my clip into the hole, wiggling it back and forth to gain some purchase until eventually it caught on something. With the hair fastener firmly in place, I tried to open the clock key, and to my relief the contraption stayed closed—not only that, it started to glow. I hastily placed the gadget back in the box. The last thing I needed was to attract the attention of the goons upstairs. They would be down here like a rocket if they saw the light. I didn't want them to discover I was in possession of their most valuable instrument.

I smiled to myself, pleased I managed to cobble together a workable arrangement with the key. I wanted to use it to break out of the cell immediately. We could figure out a plan—the end was in sight. I would bet my life that these cells linked to a security system, which meant we must be ready to run as soon as we broke out. What kept bugging me was the fact that the longer we waited, the less likely we were to get free.

Madeline said she would tell the officers there were more than nine of us. But that didn't make sense. Weren't the Black

Mark the ones who injected us with the Elite 9 in the first place? How could they not be aware of the statistics? I always assumed the Black Mark were in the government's pocket.

I shook my head and left the comparative safety of the corner. Based on the even breathing coming from across the room, I assumed Zander was asleep. "Zander," I hissed between the bars. "Wake up!"

I heard a clanging metal sound close by. Maybe Zander was stirring.

"Zander?" I breathed.

I startled when I realized a figure loomed over me, casting a shadow on the floor. It wasn't Zander.

The government agent came closer and scanned his wrist over the door latch to unlock it, his smile sickeningly fake. I found myself wishing for the guard from yesterday instead.

"Time for you and your little friend to come with me. There's something you need to see."

I eased away from him as he stepped into my cell blocking my view. "Where are you taking us?"

The fake smile faded as he eyed me with a cold, calculating stare—his face a harsh rectangle of strong bones under taut, ashen skin. "The answers to all your questions can be found upstairs. Shall we go?"

He dangled a set of handcuffs from his fingertips, and I gritted my teeth. "I don't want to go anywhere with you."

His jaw clenched, red rage rising up past the tips of his ears as he made a vain attempt to remain calm. In two quick strides he was upon me, clipping restraints on my wrist and hauling me toward the door.

"Luna!" Zander yelled.

Great. Now he was awake.

I struggled against the brute, but he was built like iron man.

I turned to look for Zander, but his cell lay empty—then I saw him, already cuffed and being dragged towards the stairs by another agent.

Our eyes met and my heart sank.

He gave me a warning glance. He knew something bad was about to happen.

At that moment, I wondered if everything I'd fought so hard for would now come crashing down.

CHAPTER 30

ZANDER

Death, Death, Death.

The words flashed again and again across my mind as I awoke from a restless sleep—right before an agent came and pulled me from my cot with no warning.

In that moment, I knew as clearly as the air I breathed someone was about to die.

Now, standing beside Luna, in this downright bizarre glass room, I wondered if I had foreseen my own demise. Or God forbid, Luna's. Would there be a way for me to prevent it?

I stared at my reflection in the glass wall before me, my expression stiff and unyielding. My hair stuck out in every direction, not having been washed in days, and deep shadows hung beneath my eyes. The clothes we wore were covered with grime from the filthy jail cells and our haggard faces gleamed a ghastly grey under the blazing artificial light. Our images flickered like horrific wallpaper all around the room, a cursed reminder of our plight.

Luna stood stoic and unmoving next to me, but her fear was palpable. Her eyes remained transfixed on the mirrored wall in front of us and I understood she'd come to the same realization as me—people were watching us, hidden behind this spine-chilling glass.

They'd left us alone for what seemed an eternity, and I waited with bated breath to see what would happen next.

A crackled voice from somewhere overhead blasted through the small space, jolting me back to attention. "Good morning, my cheerful love birds. Welcome to our little showcase. We have something exciting we want to show you today. But a few rules before we begin. Some light admin if you will." A small, tight laugh filtered through the speakers, and I shivered. "Rule number one: don't try to get too close or involve yourself in any way. This enclosure gives off the illusion of being bigger than it really is. What you are about to see is actually happening in a connecting room, and they cannot hear you. Rule two: please save your screams, they aren't welcome here. We do have sensitive ears, you know."

Luna and I exchanged horrified glances. Her gaze lingered on mine, as if trying to glean information from me. I clenched my hands, still tied behind my back, and shook my head. I had no clue.

"Let the fun begin. Happy viewing!" she chirped before cutting out.

An agent came into view, dragging a boy with him. He was cuffed with a burlap sack over his head, to hide his face. He had a tall lanky build and my heart hammered in my chest as I began to fear the worst. When my eyes landed on his shoes—red high-top sneakers with glitter laces—my most wretched fears were confirmed.

"God, Luna, it's Crane," I whispered.

"What?" She hissed. She stepped forward to get a better look, then inhaled sharply as she realized the truth. She glanced around the room, not sure who to address. Finally, she just yelled into the empty expanse, her words echoing off the glass walls. "Leave him alone. He hasn't done anything wrong. We're the ones you want, aren't we? Why can't you be woman enough to show your face to us?"

"Luna, stop it," I warned, stepping up beside her. "You're making things worse. Whatever you say won't change their minds."

"You would be wise to listen to Zander, Luna. We don't like messy cleanups."

Luna pressed her pale lips into a firm line. It took everything in her not to yell back. But to her credit, she kept it together. Her eyes returned to Crane. He now stood alone in the room.

I'd observed Crane while Luna was busy yelling at the loud-speakers. He never reacted to it.

The government hadn't lied about that. Crane couldn't detect sound. Tears pricked my eyes. He must feel so abandoned.

A shudder torpedoed through my body. Something horrible was about to happen. Still, my heart didn't want to believe it. I might still be asleep, having a bad dream. Heck, this could be another one of those simulations that the feds loved to conjure up. A fake-out, so to speak.

I closed my eyes and willed myself to wake up from this nightmare.

Unfortunately, when I opened them again everything turned out to be frighteningly real. An agent had stepped back into the room. He wore the standard black and gray military uniform, with hair cropped short in a buzz cut. He circled Crane, surveying him as if were some sort of cockroach, and I saw my friend visibly stiffen under the snakelike scrutiny. The henchman paused for a moment, then suddenly kicked his boot into the back of Crane's knees, causing him to collapse on the floor. With his hands tied behind him, there was nothing to stop the fall, and his face smashed hard against the tiles.

Luna and I let out a simultaneous cry and moved closer to the clear pane, checking to see if he was okay. The agent hauled him to his knees, even as blood seeped through the sac where he injured his face. Small red droplets dripped down onto his t-shirt. And for the first time I noticed the bruises that peppered his arms. It looked like they'd already tortured him.

"What the hell did you do to him?" I demanded. "He doesn't deserve this."

It appeared as though I was talking to myself, but they were there. Watching. Always observing.

"Crane Sky failed us on every conceivable level," the cold female voice said. "He was provided with multiple chances to redeem himself, but refused. His loyalty to the resistors is almost laughable," she scoffed. "Apparently, the movement has a bunch of Peter Pan boys who like to play dress-up."

"What are you going to do to him?" I asked, my voice filled with dread. Luna leaned against me and our arms brushed.

"Zander—" she whispered, but before she could continue the mystery woman gave a warning.

"I don't like to be interrupted. Don't cross me."

Luna's eyes grew wide with concern. Satisfied she had the floor, the woman pressed on. "Crane has served his purpose."

Then without warning, another figure, lithe and toned, clad in tight, full-body leather entered Crane's room. Judging by the way she moved and the nutmeg hair pinned back neatly at the nape of her neck with a silver bow, I'd guess this person to be female. As if in slow motion, she turned to face us, her black-gloved hand revealing an old-fashioned pistol that had been outlawed two decades ago.

As our eyes met, my heart froze.

Madeline.

She never wavered, hand steady as a rock, as she pointed the gun at Crane.

Somewhere in the recesses of my brain I heard Luna shriek, "No!" as she lunged forward.

My reflexes must have been on automatic because we both managed to smash into the glass barrier at the same time. My face pressed against the clear façade, watching helplessly as Madeline's thumb clicked back the safety catch and pulled the trigger. Crane's torso spasmed, as the bullet hit him in the chest the bag slipping off his head as he zigzagged and collapsed in a crumbled heap to the floor. Our gaze met and he mouthed, "Bye friend." With a blood choking gurgle, his head slumped sideways and he was gone. I stared in horrified shock at Crane's crumpled form.

Madeline gave me a little wave and blew on the tip of her gun. She smiled, turned and sauntered out of the room, leaving Crane dead in a pool of blood.

I stayed there pounding against the barrier again and again with my foot, yelling, wanting to get to him, before finally collapsing to my knees.

Everything seemed so far away. I crawled backward, trying to comprehend what I'd witnessed, not willing to believe it actually happened.

Luna screamed Crane's name, again and again, but it didn't compute.

Madeline had killed Crane.

There was no going back from this.

We were on a clear descent into hell with no way out.

CHAPTER 31

LUNA

When I came to, the smell of formaldehyde and acid burned my nostrils. I didn't move, every inch of my body ached. My wrists burned, rubbed raw by the rope tying me to a chair. I kicked my feet to gain purchase, but they were bound with plastic ties that bit into my ankles. My mouth had a metallic taste, my tongue thick and fuzzy, and my head swam like I was in some under-water dream. I endeavored to open my eyelids, but they seemed glued shut. I cursed inwardly. I'd been drugged.

I tried to recall my last memory. Where had I been? I searched my mind until a sudden flash of the events of the last hours lined up before me like a nightmare.

Madeline had killed Crane, then everything turned to chaos.

Four agents had burst into the room, faces drawn in marked determination. Zander and I tried to fight them off, but we were outnumbered. One of them stuck a needle in my neck. I didn't remember anything after that.

I gritted my teeth, remembering the feeling. I ventured once more to pry open my eyes, but to no avail. I wanted to call out to Zander, but nothing came out when I tried to speak. Was he even here?

The sound of footsteps approaching caught my attention—

they were getting closer. Then voices. They were in the room with me.

"Well it looks like the drugs haven't warn off yet. How much sedative did you give her?"

"A syringe full. She should be coming around in under an hour."

"Very well, I can be patient. How's the boy?"

"He's much the same, sir."

"Right. I would say we can safely commence the experiment within a few days. I want to make sure this other drug is completely out of her system first. I'm just sorry I ever agreed to it. Ruining a perfectly good hypothesis right from the beginning is a horrible way to start."

"Yes, Doctor."

"Be sure you let me know the minute she wakes up. I want to be kept informed of her progress. Better yet, send Madeline in to keep an eye on things. I think she's proved herself well today."

He had a British accent, deep and authoritative. The head of the research department maybe? No, he had to be bigger than that.

"What about Zander, sir?"

"You can watch him. I don't trust Madeline with him. He appears to be her weak spot. I'd like to observe their initial inter-action before I allow her any jurisdiction over him."

"Of course, Doctor."

"When Luna wakes, tell Madeline to contact a security detail to return her to basement level. You can do the same with Zander when he returns to consciousness. Make sure they both receive good quality food. I don't want poor nutrition to mar the science. With a little luck, we might improve Luna's flawed personality. Otherwise, it's going to be such a waste of Elite 9 mineral."

"I agree sir."

"I shall leave everything in your capable hands, Marcus. Don't let me down."

"No, sir."

One set of footsteps moved away followed by Marcus' heavy breathing as he furiously tapped his com.

"Hey, Brevard. I need Madeline up here stat for babysitting detail. Lab room seven. Tell her to report A.S.A.P."

He laughed a little at whatever was said on the other end. "Yeah, Dr. Harrison's orders, so be smart about it. I'll be waiting outside the door. I have instructions to cover the boy until he wakes up."

My heart pounded. Why the hell did Madeline have to be the one to stand guard? She'd literally just shot Crane in the chest. I hated her for what she'd done and I didn't want to be anywhere near her. And Dr. Harrison, leader of the Black Mark, the scumbag that injected Elite 9 into embryos, was giving the orders? The guy my so-called parents were best buddies with? Yeah, I was really screwed.

I kept my ears alert, but all remained quiet, save for the sound of a buzzing light somewhere overhead. I decided to take a risk and make another attempt to peel apart my crusted eyelids. I longed to rub them, but my hands, which were now numb, were still tied behind my back.

I concentrated hard. I must have moved every muscle in my face a dozen times, before finally succeeding in opening my eyes, the light gradually filtering through. I glanced around, glad to see no one in the lab yet. A black bench took up most of the space, its surface covered with glass beakers filled with liquid of different purple hues, ranging from pale lavender to ultraviolet. A small circular gadget with a gold metallic finish stood on a small table near the door. It had a hole in the middle, almost as if it were made to have something fit snugly inside. Small crystal stones were embedded on the surface. Stranger still, it had been enclosed in a glass box, as if it were something valuable. I strained to see if there were any distinguishing characteristics and gasped.

The symbol was engraved on the side of the protective glass.

The one I'd first noticed in P8, then again on the pin in the duffel bag. The tree with the keyhole.

Before I could wrap my head around it, voices sounded in the hallway, and Dr. Harrison's deep timbre filled the room as the door swung open. I quickly feigned sleep.

"Here she is, Dr. Fennel, I just wanted you to get a good look at what we'd be working with."

"Yes, she appears to be in pretty good health. Though she could use a bath. Have you done the blood work?" A voice I assumed belonged to Dr. Fennel asked.

"No. We've got to wait until the drug they gave her this morning is out of her system. She was quite hysterical. I think we might be getting to her just in time."

"What's the plan?" Fennel inquired.

"I've brought the disk which contains the prototype of the original brain altering experiment, but I've included some adjustments for phase II. You may want to look these over at your earliest convenience. We'll want to get started on this in a few days."

The words whirled in my mind like a familiar echo, and a familiar pain erupted in my head. I bit my tongue to bite back a scream.

I crouched in the nook under the stairwell barely daring to breathe, as I watched my parents come back into the living room. My Dad held a small silver disk in his palm. They both looked at it in wonder.

"It's so exciting! Tyrone was so kind to let us see the plans," Mom cooed.

"Well, we do happen to have one of his first participants under our roof," Dad said proudly as if he owned some kind of prized cow.

Confusion and panic rose in my throat. But I clamped it down as I inched just a hair closer.

"Where's Luna?" Dad asked.

"She isn't home yet. I sent her out—I didn't want her here when Tyrone arrived."

I swallowed hard. They hadn't heard me come in— now I was grateful I had snuck in to eavesdrop.

Dad tapped the disk with his phone to read the contents. "Brain augmentation. Phase I— placing the chip in the frontal lobe of the brain to see if the patient displays necessary removal of the current flawed personality. Traits beneficial to the human race will be inputted. Reference footnote one for list of traits. Following the procedure, the patient should show complete compliance. See section two for initial brain prototype NMBE..."

His voice trailed off as I was pulled away from the scene and found myself suddenly back in this cold room tied to a chair.

Of course, how could I have been so stupid? I thought. It was clear now I had seen the contents of this disk before. Damn it all to hell. But why wouldn't I have told Zander? Perhaps I'd been worried about his safety as I was now. Or perhaps I didn't want him to do anything stupid to try to save me.

One thing was for sure. I'd been right.

The contents of this disk changed everything.

A physical ache welled up in my chest when I realized I might never escape this hellhole. And that meant I'd never find Trinity. I squeezed my eyes tight, trying to push past the ache. I couldn't give up, not yet. I had to concentrate.

"I appreciate your discretion," Dr. Harrison said bringing me back to my senses.

"Of course," Dr. Fennel replied. "I commend you on the important research you've been working on for your government. We've made great strides in this field thanks to your efforts. Trust me, it won't go unnoticed. If this is successful, you will be well compensated."

"Thank you. I want this particular case to be perfect. There can be no mistakes. I won't go into details. But I have my reasons."

"Fair enough. Who am I to question brilliance? I look forward to reading the details of the new and improved prototype and seeing your preliminary results. Please keep me abreast of any interesting developments."

"Certainly, Dr. Fennel. Shall I walk you out?"

"Yes, thank you. I have a meeting with the President in an hour. Best not be late."

"Of course. Send him my regards, and thank him again for the funding of this groundbreaking experiment."

"Will do, Dr. Harrison."

The conversation faded away as they exited the room.

My mind reeled, still processing it all.

They planned on putting a chip in my brain? Like hell. How dare they say I had a flawed personality. I prayed that the clock key got me out of here in time, before I became their test subject.

If I didn't, in less than forty-eight hours the real me would cease to exist.

⚜

Not long after Dr. Harrison left, Madeline showed up. Her hair hung loose down her back in a gleaming chestnut sheet. She had changed into fresh clothing and her countenance bore more resemblance to someone who'd just attended a high tea rather than a person who'd committed cold-blooded murder.

I didn't even bother to feign sleep now. I got the feeling Madeline would know I was faking. Besides, the sooner I got this over with the better. Especially if it meant I wouldn't have to look upon Madeline's traitorous face for longer than necessary.

She scowled as she walked into the lab. "Oh, you're awake, too bad. I hoped to have a little fun with you before you woke up," she tittered as if she'd made a joke. "Well, that doesn't mean we still can't amuse ourselves, does it?"

She came close, puffing sweet, hot cherry breath onto my face, no doubt the smell originating from the shiny pink lip gloss she'd applied to her pouty lips. I flinched as she traced a finger down my cheek.

I glared at her, not giving her the satisfaction of turning my head away. And for the first time I noticed how odd her eyes looked. The irises were extremely dilated, and they flickered in and out as if they were a television channel not coming in properly.

I frowned. "What's up with your eyes? They look creepy."

I realized my mistake as soon as I said it. Her cheeks flushed crimson, and I swear that her heavily dilated pupils encroached into the whites of her eyes, transmuting them into inky black pools—making her appear like she'd been possessed by a demon.

"How dare you!" she hissed, slapping me across my cheek, the hard stone of her ruby ring catching my jaw, drawing blood.

"What do you think you're doing Madeline? Are you insane?" I spat.

"You think I'm insane?" she trilled, her voice seemingly five octaves higher than normal. "I'm not the one tied to a chair, and put under lock and key. Everyone here thinks you're a nut job."

I shrugged, causing a pain to shoot through my shoulder blades. If only I had a hair pin to bust out of these damn hand cuffs. Even the half of one I hid under my cot would do. "I've been called worse."

My indifference seemed to fuel her anger. But she somehow got herself together enough to step away and take a deep breath. Then, with a sneer, she swiftly smoothed her hands down her blue dress like she was removing radioactive waste— as if coming in contact with me had been the vilest thing imaginable.

The girl clearly had a few screws loose...I paused mid thought, my mouth dry, calculating...

Madeline crossed her arms. "What? Why are you ogling me like that, freak?"

Dr. Harrison said I would be the second prototype. Could Madeline be the first? Had he planted a chip in her brain? She'd been acting strangely since last night, when she'd turned up at our jail cells. And her eyes definitely weren't normal.

"Why did you decide to leave the resistors, Madeline? And why is it so important to you that Zander switches to the government's side?"

Madeline edged closer again, leaning her hands on both sides of the chair, so she loomed over me. "The government's plan is the best thing for all of us, Luna. Don't you understand that? They're the only ones that can save us from ourselves and rescue this planet."

"But Madeline, they asked you to kill Crane. They made you a murderer. How is that improving your life?"

"I had to demonstrate my loyalty to the cause. Crane wasn't important," her words shot out of her mouth like bullets, spattering my face with spit.

"He used to be your friend," I hissed.

Madeline's face contorted into a cruel grimace as she grabbed my chin and twisted the skin under her fingertips. I struggled to free myself from her grasp. "Until you begin to see the governments side of things, Luna Redwood, things are going to get really bad for you. The government wants to help you achieve your dreams. You should be grateful."

"Is that a threat?" I yelled, not backing down.

"Oh no, Luna, that's a promise. I would have no problem doing an encore performance. In fact, I believe I might rather enjoy it."

"What's that supposed to mean?"

Madeline pulled something out of her jacket pocket. The gleam of a revolver sparkled under the lab light.

My eyes opened wide in surprise, and I licked my dry lips.

"You wouldn't dare. Zander would never forgive you," I whispered.

She laughed pressing the cold tip of the gun to my head. "Zander has always wanted you. It's always been you. And I'm tired of playing his pathetic games. He couldn't see how wonderful I am, so he can rot in hell for all I care. Maybe I will give you both a one-way ticket. Won't that be fun?"

"Don't try it, Madeline. I can kill you before you even pull that trigger," I bluffed.

She snickered, then smashed the barrel against my head. The room began to spin and dots filled my vision. "Shut up. I hate liars. All any of you have ever done is lie to me."

The click of the pistol startled me, and I jumped. Crap, she really was going to do it. I tried to focus, my mind scrambling trying to come up with something, anything that might stop her.

But before I could react two men burst into the room. One of them knocked the weapon out of Madeline's hand, I breathed a sigh of relief.

"Madeline, what are you doing? You had strict orders to guard her, not kill her. Jerry, bring her straight to Dr. Harrison. He needs to know what happened. Adjust her meds."

"Will do."

"Tell Dr. Harrison patient B is returning to her cell, and she'll need a medic to seal the open wound on her face."

"Patient B?" My voice sounded slurred, even to my ears, and I was having trouble concentrating.

The security guard cut the ties holding me to the chair and dragged me to my feet. Something wet and sticky ran down my face and splatted to the floor. I didn't have time to analyze what it could be because the world went dark.

CHAPTER 32
LUNA

"Luna? What happened? Luna!" Zander's frantic voice pierced through the haze as I returned to consciousness. The chilling cold of the concrete floor penetrated right through my clothes, numbing my skin.

I groaned and rolled over. A dull ache throbbed at my temple. I slowly opened my eyes and lifted a finger to the bruise, touching the medical glue still tacky from where someone had sealed up my wound. I fought against my thick, dry tongue, struggling to speak. Finally, I managed to mumble, "I'm fine, Zander."

"Thank God," Zander breathed. "I've been sitting here freaking out for hours. They checked my vitals and brought me back down here, but you were missing. And they wouldn't tell me anything."

"Yeah, well, I had a visitor," I said, pushing myself up to a seated position.

I turned to face his cell, and eyed him as his expression changed from concern to puzzlement. A frown creased his forehead. "Did your parents come back?"

I gave a harsh laugh. "Not even close. They barely tolerated me the first time. No. It was Madeline. The government cronies

268

sent her to stand guard over me until I came to." I left out the part about how I'd overheard the doctor's conversation, knowing security was listening in.

Zander stared at me, mouth agape. "But Luna...she—"

I shook my head and raised my hands up in protest. "Don't say it. I don't want to hear it. Let's just say she is officially off her rocker and leave it at that. Fortunately for me, the henchman arrived and took her away before things got really dicey."

"Did she hurt you?" The horror on Zander's face was apparent. And I didn't want to freak him out, but I didn't want to lie to him either.

"Not much. They closed up the cut on my head. Now all I have is a little headache. Nothing I can't handle."

Zander didn't look convinced but said nothing. Instead, he searched my face for the truth. Damn him and his psychic powers. I hoped he couldn't see through my façade. Our eyes locked, and for a long minute, no space existed between us—we were somehow linked. I gasped at the power of it, breaking my gaze from his.

Unsure how to react, I stood shakily, my knees wobbling like jelly. A rush of emotions cascaded over me like crashing waves. I shook myself off to regain my equilibrium. Time to refocus and get a grip. I took a deep breath. The most important thing now was to get us both out of here. Since I had the clock key, it was my responsibility.

I bit my lip. How could I communicate with Zander without the security detail overhearing?

I looked across to Zander. He hadn't moved. His green eyes bored into me, as if he were trying to infiltrate the deepest recesses of my mind.

This time, I wished he could.

"Zander, do you know what time it is?" I had no idea how much time we had left to escape.

"We were out for quite a long time," he replied. "Based on the long shadows coming through the window, we're only about thirty minutes from sunset. Which means the lights will go out soon."

"Crap."

"Why?"

"Um... I'm afraid of the dark?"

"Good effort, Lun. But I've known you way too long to fall for that one."

"Oh yeah? If you know me that well, then where did these boots come from?"

"Seriously? I saw you take them out of the donation bin." He grinned at me. "They look very sexy on you, though."

I rolled my eyes. The boy just wasn't getting it. My attempts to remind him of the clock key in my boot were going completely off course. And why now, of all moments, was he choosing to focusing on my sexiness? I snorted. Like I had any. Maybe Zander received a bash on the head, too. I tried again, leaning over, pretending to admire my boots.

"I think you look great in whatever you wear. Once we break free of here, I'm going to show you how much you mean to me, Luna. I'll prove that I'm worthy of you."

I looked up, surprised. "You, be worthy of me? No Zander, you have it all wrong. You're a great guy, way too good for me. You wouldn't even be in this mess if it weren't for me."

Zander pressed his face to the guardrails. "Luna, you're the best person I know. You're fierce, loyal and brave. And you'll do anything for those that you love. You have a big heart that's been broken too many times. And I hope that one day you'll trust me enough to help you heal."

Tears pricked my eyes as I stretched my hands through the slats. "Maybe we're here to heal each other."

He let out a wistful sigh. "I wish I could hug you," he breathed.

"Me too."

Zander leaned his arms out as far as he dared, at this angle the tips of our fingers managed to brush against each other. His eyes grew wide. "Oh." He smiled coyly. "Boots, huh?"

I stared at him, surprised, but then considered a moment. He'd received a telepathic link to Dara, why not me? Besides, what did I know about this woo woo stuff anyway?

"Yeah," I stammered. "Boots."

"Do you leave them on when you're sleeping?"

"I plan to tonight. I think if I keep them on, they might bring me some luck."

Zander withdrew his hand. "Not a bad idea, but aren't they damaged? Second hand items are hard to repair."

Maybe this would be one of those moments we would laugh about later, but not now, the stakes were too high. "Yeah, but I managed to cobble them back together, good as new."

Zander raised an eyebrow at me. "Really?"

I nodded. "Yes."

"Okay, well I guess it's a good idea to give things a second chance, even when they appear damaged."

I grinned. "I'm glad you agree."

And as if on cue, the lights went out. Whoever watched over us must be bored. If I had to hazard a guess, I would bet they were about fifteen minutes early. Probably sick of our completely idiotic conversation. My smile grew even wider. The fools just helped me escape sooner.

I crouched down, and moved away from where I thought the cameras might be hidden. Zander regarded me, his eyes glittering in the darkness. Casually, and without fuss I pulled the box containing the clock key from my boot, grasping it in my palm.

"Are you ready?" I murmured.

"Yes," he whispered. "Luna? Whatever happens, I love you." The words were faint, scarcely audible, but they still pierced my heart like a knife, making my throat constrict with emotion, rendering me speechless. All I could do as I looked into those emerald pools of green was nod.

Then I quickly turned away, concentrating on the task at hand. I tried to remember how Zander had used the clock key all that time ago when we first escaped our coffins. Hadn't he pressed it against the glass? With shaking fingers, I held the key in my hand, it glowed in the shadows as it connected with my skin and I allowed it to envelop me, giving all my energy to its pull. Once more I felt like I could fly, lit up so powerfully from within that I realized that I was illuminated from the inside out —the radiant light leaping from my body in iridescent rainbows. Somewhere in the background, Zander yelled something. I couldn't make out the words. All I could focus on was the wonderment that filled my veins.

My nerves disappeared and with a calm hand I pressed the clock key to the digital lock of my cell. A wind appeared out of nowhere, blowing my hair into my eyes, but I didn't dare move my hand. White spots dotted my vision, but I didn't let go, knowing how close we were to our freedom. Off in the distance, a security siren wailed, and dizziness overtook me as white sparkling light exploded into thousands of tiny stars.

CHAPTER 33

LUNA

Grass tickled my fingertips, and I opened my eyes. Above me, the glassy fake sky of the dome rose up in brilliant blue hues, enhanced by the artificial setting sun. It bled like yellow highlighter into the white clouds, reflecting on the glass prism like delicate butterfly wings. I blinked rapidly in an effort to gain my bearings.

Then it all came crashing back.

I sat up abruptly. "Zander?" I glanced around, searching desperately for him. Then realized I was alone on a grassy knoll at the back of the science center. Panicked, I tried to stand, and instantly felt like I was on a roller coaster ride. I stumbled forward and pushed my feet hard into the ground to stop my momentum. I paused to take a couple of deep breaths to steady myself—then turned to search the landscape.

The sun's glare momentarily blinded me as I squinted anxiously through the swirling clouds now gathering on the horizon, trying to make out any movement. But there was nothing.

A metallic tang rose up in my throat, and I clutched my sweatshirt in panic. Zander hadn't made it out.

The sound of recorded birdsong reverberated around me like a reverent prayer, but it didn't make my agony any easier to bear.

I swept a hand across my forehead to wipe the sweat from my face and tried not to freak out. What the hell happened? The clock key was supposed to open my cell door, but I'd ended up here instead. I vaguely remembered a siren going off, and I assumed the alarm system was warning of a security breach after the clock key opened the jail. But had it? Or had I simply left?

Oh, my God. The clock key. I did a body search and came up empty. My knees buckled as I fell back into the grass. I began searching frantically, my hands combing the lawn. I breathed a sigh of relief when my eyes caught a glint of copper about a foot away. I scrambled over and snatched up the key. The device, ice-cold, failed to react to my touch. I bit my lip.

My mind raced. Had too much power flowed through the apparatus? I mean, the thing catapulted me completely out of the science center, rather than simply unlocking my jail cell. This had all gone wrong. My head pounded and I wondered if this was what a hangover felt like.

I needed to calm down and figure out a plan.

The clock key had moved me from the cell to outside the complex in a matter of seconds. But how?

A horrifying thought occurred to me. Had I accidentally time traveled and left Zander behind? No. That was ridiculous.

I gritted my teeth and pushed all the farfetched scenarios from my head before I went insane. I needed to focus on getting Zander out of that building.

Did I go for help? Did I attempt to get back inside? I doubted my heart could take leaving him behind.

Before I could come up with any kind of strategy, a wall of uniformed men appeared over the hillside. I counted them as they kept coming, too stunned to do anything else.

"Ten...twenty...thirty...thirty-one, thirty-two..."

I stopped. There were too many soldiers forming a barrier between me and Zander, still trapped inside. But I couldn't leave him. That wasn't an option.

The man in front of the brigade spotted me first and let out a cry of triumph urging the others forward.

With no other choice now, I turned on my heel and ran fast as lightning in the opposite direction—not knowing if I would make it out alive.

The clock key bit into my palm, and I clutched it tightly not daring to let go. I could think of nothing except one thing as I fled.

I may never see Zander again.

As the men drew closer, I pumped my legs to their maximum.

And at that moment, I realized with sudden clarity I never told Zander I loved him.

Choking back tears, I pushed harder.

I had to win this war.

For the both of us.

ABOUT THE AUTHOR

Genevieve Crownson graduated from the College of Charleston with a Bachelors of Science degree. A love of writing led her to pen her debut novel, *The Soul of the Sun*, book one in her highly anticipated trilogy, The Argos Dynasty. She currently lives in beautiful Charleston, SC with her family and beloved four legged friends. You can find her at www.genevievecrownson.com or any of her social media sites @gcrownson.

ALSO BY GENEVIEVE CROWNSON

In the Cage of Glass Series:

Cage of Glass

In the Argos Dynasty Series:

The Soul of the Sun

The Power of Alchemy

Ring of Fire

For free books, behind the scenes sneak peaks, special offers, plus other fun goodies join Genevieve Crownson's mailing list here:

www.genevievecrownson.com